PRAISE FOR
SUE HUBBARD'S NOVELS

'A triumph… Masterly, moving and beautifully written'

FAY WELDON

'I recommend this haunting book'

JOHN BERGER

'Beautifully-written and evocative'

AMANDA CRAIG

'A writer of genuine talent'

ELAINE FEINSTEIN

'Lyrical, highly visual and beautifully observed'

JOHN BURNSIDE

'A beautifully-written meditation on love, loss and grief'

IRISH INDEPENDENT

'Hubbard deserves a place in the literary pantheon near Colm Tóibín, Anne Enright, and William Trevor'

AMERICAN LIBRARY ASSOCIATION

'Gently absorbing… Wistful but never morose'

DAILY MAIL

SUE HUBBARD is an award-winning poet, novelist and freelance art critic. She has published three acclaimed novels and numerous collections of poetry, and was commissioned to create London's largest public art poem at Waterloo. *Flatlands* was loosely inspired by Paul Gallico's classic wartime novella *The Snow Goose*.

SUE HUBBARD

FLATLANDS

PUSHKIN PRESS

Pushkin Press
Somerset House, Strand
London WC2R 1LA

Copyright © Sue Hubbard, 2023

First published by Pushkin Press in 2023

1 3 5 7 9 8 6 4 2

ISBN 13: 978-1-91159-084-2

Designed and typeset by Tetragon, London
Printed and bound in the United States of America

www.pushkinpress.com

I cannot picture what the life of the spirit would have been without him. He found me when my mind and soul were hungry and thirsty, and he fed them till our last hour together.

A Backward Glance, EDITH WHARTON

Do you think, because I am poor, obscure, plain and little, I am soulless and heartless?

Jane Eyre, CHARLOTTE BRONTË

Acknowledgements

My special thanks are due to Stephen Duncan for his cajoling, prodding and persistent support to get this book written. To Marianne Lewin and the late Linda Rose Parkes for reading the manuscript, and Annie Wilson for her eagle-eyed corrections. To Doug Hilton and his wife for making me welcome at the lighthouse and pointing me in the right directions. To Peter Scott's daughter Dafila for having me to stay and talking about birds, and to those at Slimbridge who educated me about geese, and to the Tyrone Guthrie Centre at Annaghmakerrig where much of this was written.

I would also like to thank Captain Patrick Jary, Harbour Master of King's Lynn, for 'talking' me out of the River Nene into the Wash, and my son, Ben Hubbard, for walking the fifteen lonely miles from Peter Scott's lighthouse to King's Lynn.

A Note from the Author

In 1933 the ornithologist and wildlife artist, Peter Scott, took possession of a deserted lighthouse situated on the mouth of the River Nene on the Wash. It was in this isolated spot that he created his first bird sanctuary. In 1941, his friend the American journalist and short-story writer, Paul Gallico, published a children's novella, a parable on the regenerative power of friendship and love, *The Snow Goose*, inspired by Scott's lighthouse, which he relocated to Essex for his book.

In this novel, I have developed the bare bones of Gallico's tale into a story for adults, and returned the narrative to the remote corner of Lincolnshire where Peter Scott's lighthouse stands.

I have kept the original names, Fritha and Philip Rhayader, from *The Snow Goose*, but I have changed the species of the bird they care for. Pink-footed geese breed in eastern Greenland, Iceland and Svalbard. They are migratory, wintering in north-west Europe, especially Ireland, the Netherlands, western Denmark and Great Britain. The snow goose in Paul Gallico's novel is native to North America, and is rarely found in these islands.

PART 1

1939

I WAS TWELVE WHEN I WAS SENT to that cold place. I could never have dreamt that anywhere so lonely existed. In my mind's eye it was always cold, though I arrived in September. A hot day, the sort of day for a picnic not a war. From the stuffy train we could see gangs of women in the fields dressed in old sun bonnets and aprons, weeding rows of potatoes and stacking bundles of hay. Land Girls in khaki drill. And above, the tiny dot of a skylark hovering, soaring up-up-and-up until it finally disappeared into the high wide blue. But still, what stays with me are the winter flurries of sleet over the tidal estuaries. The whalebone-coloured skies and frozen tidal creeks. The eerie honking of wintering geese as they lifted their strong-muscled necks and angel wings in the mist above the reed beds and frosted fields. Hands and toes chapped raw with chilblains. No, after Bethnal Green with its crabbed back-to-backs, its soot-blackened tenements, bustling markets and noisy pubs, I could never have dreamt that such a place existed.

Very few people lived there. A clutch of tenant farmers and poachers. Local oyster catchers plying their ancient trade. It was known as Black Fen. Black for the peaty soil and melancholy of the place. For its dark, hidden histories. A flat, flat land extending as far as the eye could see, with nothing to help a stranger distinguish one stretch of sugar beet from another monotonous field of swede or celery. With few hedges and even fewer trees, the bitter wind swept in from the Wash gathering up topsoil, depositing it in cottages, blocking dykes and ditches. Chilling the bones. The Fen blows they called it. Murky as London smog, it filled lungs, clogged eyelashes and turned mucus black.

Hardly a day goes by when I don't think of that place. I knew only that it was far from home. Far from my beloved nan and the small world I'd grown to know during my twelve years living above that cramped hardware shop in the East End. Once, when wool was in demand, the Fens had been one of the richest areas in England. In medieval times exports from the Lincolnshire town of Boston were booming and the town paid more tax than any other except London, but by the time I was sent there, the area was down-at-heel, neglected and forgotten. Ancient villages and flint churches sat lonely as widows among the sad, flat fields of potatoes and sugar beet. When the local landowners first drained the marsh, the fen dwellers were bitterly opposed. Worried the drainage systems would destroy their fisheries, stop them catching the eels that teemed in their thousands in the waterways. Concerned that the reclaimed land would be given to the men who'd carried out the work, not back to those who rightfully owned it. Dykes were breached. Ditches filled, the peat shrank and water levels rose, so gradually the canals became higher than the land. Windmills were built to scoop up the water.

Now the dykes are several feet above ground.

With few roads it became a refuge for the lawless and the feral. Even the Romans thought the place ungovernable. Found themselves outwitted by the cunning Fen folk who strode across the marshes on tall wooden stilts. A skill they failed to master.

The Great Marsh. A place between somewhere and nowhere. Created by the gradual build-up of mud from the rivers that flow into the Wash. Neither land nor water, constantly flooded by salt tides. One of the last wildernesses in England. Grass and reeds, half-submerged meadowlands, mudflats and saltings appear stitched to the huge skies and wide expanse of open sea. And everywhere there are birds. At first, I couldn't tell them apart. But slowly you taught me their names. Teal and wigeon. Redshanks and curlews. Terns and gulls. Greylag and brent geese. The black-tailed godwits and dunlin that swirled in their hundreds of thousands between their high-tide roosts and food-rich mudflats.

When I arrived, a shingle and shell embankment, covered in yellow horned poppies, formed a bulwark against the ever-encroaching sea. It's still there but breached by many tides. The shape of the land has changed over the years. Bits have fallen away, become silted over. Where pink-foot and little tern used to fish, cows now graze. And, at low tide, the deserted light-house appears like a lost thought. Once a beacon shining out across the North Sea, warning ships from Jutland or coal vessels making their way down south from Newcastle of dangerous tidal currents and sandbanks, its rafters, now, are inhabited by bats and nesting owls. Its lantern dark.

*

I don't live in that lonely place now. A lot of water has flowed under a lot of bridges. Now I'm old. My life mostly behind me. I don't expect anything else much to happen. I live each day as best I can. Try to be positive, despite the sciatica. Inside, I'm the same person I've always been. That's the thing. The heart remains unchanged. It's just the body that ages. But the longing remains. The longing for those moments all those years ago in that place where sea and sky met. Now the old woman others see bears no relation to the young girl I once was and still, inside, often feel myself to be. Mostly I'm invisible. Voices change when people speak to me. I call it their 'wallpaper voice'. Flat and even, it papers over the cracks. No one really wants to know how I am, even if they bother to ask. Wrinkles have a way of making you disappear one line at a time. I'm just the lady in the green cardigan and sensible shoes. But life has its blessings if you choose to count them. And I have my story to tell. Each of us does. All of us are simply trying to make sense of a world we don't quite understand. Dipping our toes into that black box of memories to answer those nagging questions: the whats, the hows and whys.

But I'm lucky. I have my health—apart from the pain in my leg—and mostly my mind. Though what happened seventy-five years ago is easier to recall than where I left my glasses. When it's fine I go to Victoria Park, where I used to play all those years ago as a child, and sit on the bench. Watch the toddlers eating ice creams, the young boys doing tricks on their skateboards, the swans on the lake floating past in flotillas. Swans are the romantics of the bird world. They mate for life. I've always liked birds. There's a robin that comes to the ledge outside my bedroom window. I save him my breakfast crusts. Robins are very territorial. He thinks he owns the place.

I like to watch the spray from the fountains make rainbows on the artificial lake. Sometimes I take my battered copy of *Palgrave's Golden Treasury* with me in my handbag and sit there with a cup of tea. The book's very worn now. The spine coming apart. I like Keats and Edward Thomas. I'm not so keen on more modern stuff. I enjoy rereading the poems I learnt as a girl, and know many of them by heart. As a child, Victoria Park was the only green space I knew. I'd never been to the country, except on a coach trip with Mum to Southend where I sat on a miniature clockwork train that ran round and round the edge of the municipal garden with its flower clock planted with golden marigolds, where fat-bottomed ladies in white skirts played bowls. I remember I had a strawberry cornet that dripped all down my blue cotton dress, and a donkey ride. By the time I got home, my bare shoulders were so red and raw that Mum had to smother them in pink calamine. Though that was the seaside, not the country. But still.

In summer, while Mum was minding the shop, Iris and I'd go to the park. Tuck our dresses in our knickers and paddle in the ponds, daring each other to go up to our knees without getting our clothes wet. We knew we'd cop it if we did. Sundays we'd hang around the men on their soapboxes. We hadn't a clue what they were on about as they waved their arms, spat and barked about socialism and fascism. But we thought they were funny. There was a man in a torn mac with a sandwich board that said, 'The End Is Nigh'. Another who claimed he was a prophet inspired by the Holy Ghost. But they locked him up in the loony bin.

During the war, the park was closed to the public. Used as an ack-ack site to target the Luftwaffe's bombers looping back north after an attack on the docks, and a holding camp for foreign internees was set up just beyond the tennis courts. Even Signor Giuseppe, who ran the ice cream parlour in Bethnal Green Road, where he made his own ice cream with real lemons, got put in there before being sent to the Isle of Man. Another corner was used to launch barrage balloons, and another turned into an allotment. The railings were melted down for guns, and an air-raid shelter was built near St Mark's Gate. But Mum would never go there.

You won't catch me doing my business in a bucket in front of the neighbours. I'll take me chances with the Hun, thanks very much, and keep me knickers to meself.

I was born into a family of shopkeepers. My grandfather's name, D.W. Cooper, was written over the door in gold letters. The D.W. for Donald Walter. Though towards the end of his life everyone just called him Duck. I still have an old photograph of him with his big moustache, standing outside on the pavement in his white apron among the besoms and brooms, the shovels and galvanized baths. The buckets hanging above the doorway in the cobbled street. Coopers of Bethnal Green sold balls of string, packets of starch and Reckitt's Blue for whitening the weekly wash. Laundry dollies, fuse wire and nails by the ounce, which were weighed out on the brass scales and poured into brown paper bags like boiled sweets. Duck died when I was four. So the shop was run by my nan and mum. A family of women. Our lives were lived in the tiny dark room behind the shop we called the scullery. When I was small there was a black range with two ovens on either side, surrounded by a fender with a padded seat. But when Duck died, Nan got two men from Mile End to rip it out and put in a modern one with beige tiles. The new gas cooker—at least new to us—stood behind the door opposite the old Belfast sink with its hairline crack and dripping cold-water tap. Pushed against the wall was the table covered in a checked oilskin that you had to squeeze past to get to Nan's armchair squashed between the fireplace and window. And on the high shelf, beside the print of Sir John Everett Millais's *Bubbles* that Mum got free with Pears soap and hung in the gilt frame she found in Brick Lane, was our mahogany radio. The one with a mesh grill that Nan bought with the insurance money after Duck had gone. Mum had to ask Mr Baker from next door to fix up the wire aerial or it just crackled and faded in the middle of a programme. We always listened to the six o'clock news and Mum loved the Glenn Miller Orchestra. She liked to sing 'Doin' the Jive' as she sashayed round the kitchen getting the tea. Outside the back door, a flight of stone steps led down to a concrete yard, not much bigger than the scullery, surrounded by a high wall. At the far end was the lavatory. It was dark and cold, and you had to stand holding the chain until it finished flushing or the water just stopped.

*

Since my dad, Sid, had upped and left with Vera from the bookie's, it had just been the three of us. I couldn't really remember living with Dad. Though I dimly recollect him coming home smelling of the Black Horse, singing 'It's De-Lovely' in an American accent, pretending to be Eddy Duchin. He'd be in the Horse till closing time, wisecracking with his mates. Small-time crooks and East End stallholders. Peeling a ten-bob note from the wad in his back pocket, placing illegal bets on the gee-gees and the dogs.

Scottie had two winners today, missus, he'd announce, rolling into the kitchen with his mates, the worse for wear. Mum was always missus. Or, if he was in a lovey-dovey mood, Doll.

Don't bleedin' tell you nothing about all his losers, though, does he? she'd answer tight-lipped, slamming the bedroom door and telling him to sleep on the sofa. After that, he'd settle at the kitchen table with his cronies for a game of whist and a couple of bottles of Burton Old. But he always managed to charm Nan. Kissing her on the cheek and asking: How's my gal? when he came in the door.

He and Mum met in a dance hall in Clacton-on-Sea. A smooth talker, my dad, he soon had Mum pregnant. A commission agent's clerk—which was just a posh way of saying he worked in the bookie's—he always looked sharp. Brilliantined hair and a double-breasted from Harry Cohen's in Petticoat Lane. After he went with Vera, he always sent me birthday cards with my age embossed on the front in golden numbers. Once he took me to London zoo. I remember the tigers and throwing fish to the penguins who walked like Charlie Chaplin. Riding on a little wooden seat with some other kids, high up on a swaying elephant, terrified at being so far off the ground. My first toffee apple.

I thought Dad was wonderful because he did tricks. Fished out coins from behind my ear or from underneath an empty handkerchief. Made an ace of spades vanish into thin air. He was a born showman, a raconteur, a wide boy, but he loved me. How do I know? Because when he shaved, he'd stand in his string vest, a towel thrown over his shoulder like a prize fighter and pull funny faces at me in the small, fogged-up mirror. Push up a piggy-nose to reach that bit above his top lip, sticking out his tongue from the foam beard lathered over his cheeks with the big bristle brush, to make me laugh. And when he got back from the pub, he'd tiptoe across the creaking landing and climb onto my narrow bed. Shove me up against the wall with his sharp elbow and, in a beery whisper, tell me about *The Little Mermaid* or *Sleeping Beauty*. Stories where he always gave the heroine my name. Freda.

But after he went with Vera, Mum wouldn't have him back in the house.

Not long after I was sent away, he was called up. At the time I didn't know where. He was drafted into the Royal Army Pay Corps, the unit responsible for administering all the army's financial affairs. Stationed in Foots Cray, near Sidcup, there was always the chance for the odd scam. Many years later, going through his things after he'd passed away, I found a photograph of him in uniform. It seems he toyed with the idea of deserting. Happier to face prison, with the guarantee of three hot meals a day and a warm bed, than the Jerries. Though that was never a real possibility in the Pay Corps. The most dangerous thing he was likely to encounter was an angry sergeant major.

It's bad enough being your fancy woman, Sid, Vera protested. But I'm buggered if I'm going to be a deserter's fancy woman. You bloody well go and do your duty.

In many ways the Pay Corps suited him. Got him away from women. He liked a kiss and a cuddle, but women were always wanting things. A bob for this. A tanner for that. Always wanting to know if you loved them. Foots Cray became his fiefdom. When rationing started, he could get his hands on whatever you fancied for a few readies. Extra tea. A pat of butter. A jerrycan of petrol. With a bit of wheeling and dealing, he could conjure up ciggies and nylons, a bottle of Johnnie Walker, a tin or two of corned beef. Even French perfume. Spivs, runners and ticket touts. They were his friends. But looking back, I realize, he was already slipping from my life.

I never appreciated that we were poor. But we must have struggled. Mum was still a pretty woman; though her looks were beginning to fade, she still had thick auburn hair that fell in natural curls. But like most East End women over thirty, her face was beginning to line and the first grey hairs appear. She was always trying 'something new'. Egg-white face masks. Pond's Cold Cream slathered across her cheeks and forehead at bedtime, her hair set in tight pin curls under a rayon scarf.

You don't look a bit like your mum, people would say if we stopped and chatted when out shopping in the market. By which they meant that with her thick wavy hair and small waist, she was pretty. While I, with my lank pudding basin, my scrawny arms and legs, was not.

I often wondered if it was my fault that Dad left. If I got in the way. Stopped Mum from spending nights out with him at the Black Horse. Prevented her from having a new dress or that coveted compact of Rimmel face powder she so wanted because she had to clothe and feed me. She was a romantic and liked nothing better than an afternoon at the Gaumont with a box of Milk Tray, watching Bette Davis play Jezebel. That headstrong young Southern belle who wore a scandalous red dress to the local ball. Mum cried at the bit where Jezebel's sweetheart left to marry a respectable northerner. Mum always wanted a Prince Charming to come and save her after Dad left. But he never turned up.

She longed to be fashionable but didn't have the means. Up each morning before I left for school, she'd slip her pinny over her cotton dress and go through to open up the shop, hanging up the mops and dusters in the street outside the front door. The galvanized buckets and bristle brooms. The rubber sink plungers. It would be Nan scrubbing the egg-stained plates or knitting by the gas fire when I got home from school. Her big girdle and lisle stockings airing on the wooden kitchen maid. Her shins mottling in the heat.

If I close my eyes, I can still hear the clack of her needles. Feel the cold windowpane against my cheek. It's winter and I'm staring out into a brown pea-souper, watching the rain condense into greasy drops on the glass, placing bets with myself to see which will reach the bottom first. I've been arranging the cigarette cards Dad saves for me into sets, hoping he might turn up. Not the footballers. I didn't like those. I swap those at school for Cottage Garden Flowers: blue hollyhocks, pink roses and dahlias. Or Film Favourites: Clark Gable, Jean Harlow and Errol Flynn. Though I never could find Bette Davis.

The day before I was sent away to that cold place, Iris and I went to look at the burst water main in Roman Road. Iris was my friend. My only friend. Her mum worked in the fish shop, so her clothes always smelt of coley.

Ooh it's like a fountain, she squealed, her frizzy red curls bouncing up and down as the water gushed from the pipes.

When we peered into the hole the workmen had dug, I noticed a single sandal dropped in the mud. It upset me, that lost shoe. Made me think of Nan alone in the dark back bedroom. Until recently she'd be waiting for me every Friday after school at the scullery table with the big yellow mixing bowl and a jar of plain flour to make pies and jam tarts for the weekend. We'd sift the flour through the wire sieve, rub in cubes of margarine, add water and salt, then knead the dough with our cold hands. She taught me how to roll the pastry on a floury board with the wooden rolling pin. Cut out circles for jam tarts with the rim of a teacup. Make gooseberry and apple pies, crimping the edges between thumb and forefinger, then cutting little pastry leaves to decorate the top, before brushing them in egg white with the special pastry brush so the crusts turned golden brown. I'd practise peeling the apples so the skin came off in one go and I could make a wish. And while the pies were in the oven, Nan would sit in her special chair, her veined legs propped on the wooden stool, her red hands resting in the floury lap of her apron, the thin gold wedding band cutting into her swollen fourth finger. When the pies were ready, we'd cut a slit in the top to let out the steam.

That day, after visiting the broken water main, Iris and I went to the sweetshop, sauntering home past the kosher butcher, the coal merchant and the barber's red-and-white-striped pole, sherbet lemons exploding on our tongues. When I got in Mum was in the scullery talking with the doctor.

There's nothing more to be done, I'm afraid, he was saying in a voice like the vicar's, rocking backwards and forwards on the worn lino in his shoes with the polished toecaps.

I couldn't listen and ran upstairs to the back bedroom where Nan was propped up against the bolster in the iron bedstead like a small grey-haired child. The room was dark and damp, filled with a fug of coal dust and Wright's coal tar soap. A cup of half-drunk beef tea was sitting on the bedside table and, even though it was summer, a fire was burning in the grate. Above, on the mantelpiece, beside the row of ivory elephants that got smaller and smaller right down to the baby, was a photograph of Duck before he left for the Somme. And, at either end, two plaster horses reared up on their hind legs, their wire reins held by a pair of naked ladies with roses in their hair that Duck had won in a Test Your Strength booth on Clacton pier when he and Nan were courting. I climbed onto the bed beside her, but she felt so shrunken and small under her winceyette nightie that I started to cry.

Now lovey, no fuss, she said, kissing the top of my head. You're a big girl now.

I shake the rain off my umbrella, put it in the stand by the door and settle at a table that looks over the fountain. If the weather clears, I'll walk round the lake. I try to do it twice a week. But I'm slow now. I always start at the main entrance on Sewardstone Road. Near the wrought-iron gates with their stone Dogs of Alcibiades. I like watching the seasons change. The crab-apple blossom coming into bloom and the lilac. The ripening conkers. Small details that keep me anchored in the present. Often, I doubt my memories that belong to another century. There's no one left to corroborate them now.

Number five?

A pot of tea and a scone. A dish of strawberry jam. One of my small indulgences is to come to the park café. I like to sit here and write in my journal. My memory isn't what it once was, so it helps me to remember. Enjoy, says the girl, as she puts down the tray. I've not seen her before. She has a blond ponytail, heavily made-up eyes and is wearing a boy's checked shirt and jeans. There's a small swallow tattooed on the inside of her wrist. I can't get used to these young girls having tattoos. In my day it was only sailors and criminals. You never saw them on a woman. She's pretty and I wonder if she has a sweetheart. Where she's from. Poland? Lithuania? A migrating bird blown off course. This part of London has always been a melting pot. Jews, Bengalis, Turks. Now Romanians and Albanians. There are few left, like me, who were actually born around here. Houses that once held three families sharing an outside toilet have been done up with expensive bathrooms and IKEA kitchens by couples whose children have names like Noah and Mia. I wonder, where have all the Dorises gone?

The room I live in now looks out onto a small garden. Sparrows, so common in my childhood, are rare. Though there's the occasional tit or blackbird. The other day one flew in through my open window and crashed against the glass in a panic before I could help it back outside. On warm days, the carers bring the less mobile residents out in their wheelchairs to sit in the sun. A tartan rug tucked around their knees, their liver-spotted hands fluttering like butterflies in the spring warmth.

I don't mind the place. You hear stories about homes like this, but the staff are very kind. There's not an English girl among them. Gloria's from the Philippines. Beverly from Guyana. Svetlana from Tbilisi. Oh, and there's an Irish girl from Leitrim, Bernadette, who's going home soon to marry her childhood sweetheart, Declan, and run a B & B. Bernadette likes to chat. I know her parents own a farm, mostly dairy cattle, and that she has three brothers, and a sister who is a district midwife. Bernadette's the second youngest and wanted to be a nurse too, but there weren't the funds to send her to college.

Why are you here? they ask, as they plump pillows and fill water jugs. Why aren't you with your family?

But I've a comfy single bed and the curtains are covered with yellow primroses. There's a matching bedspread and a blue crocheted cushion on the chair where I sit and read and watch the birds. I still enjoy reading, though my eyes aren't as good as they once were. Mostly I like the classics. Rereading *The Mill on the Floss* or *The Mayor of Casterbridge*. Books I discovered as a young woman when training to be a librarian. Outside my window there's a laburnum. It seems something of a trick of nature that such a pretty tree, with its cascade of golden clusters, should be so poisonous. I also have my own dressing table. We could bring one small piece of furniture with us to make it feel more like home. It's where I keep my trinket box with my mother's wedding ring. Her marcasite swan brooch. The amber beads I never wear because they need restringing. I don't have much to remember her by. There are other odds and ends, too, that I can't bring myself to throw away. A spool of negatives. Old tickets. A single white feather. Life soon becomes reduced to a pile of ephemera.

Why do I keep these things? These bits and bobs, meaningless to anyone other than me. Because they take me straight back, provide tangible evidence of what really happened. Proof that everything isn't just a figment of my overblown imagination.

When I'm gone there'll barely be anyone to remember me. I don't have children. Books have been my life. I enjoyed being a librarian. There's something comforting about the Dewey decimal system: 100 for philosophy and psychology, 200 for religion and mythology, through to social science and folklore, dictionaries and encyclopaedias. I liked the fact that each book has its own position. Its own shelf. I prided myself on my card index system. Blue for fiction. Yellow for history. Pink for romance. Each card housed neatly in its small wooden drawer with a brass handle. Typed with its category number, author and title. That, of course, was long before computers. It's all different now. And there are far fewer libraries. They all seem to be closing. I don't think people read so much any more, what with all these new-fangled electronic games. There are too many other distractions.

In my day, all sorts came to the library. Men looking for jobs in the small ads. Down-and-outs wanting shelter from the rain for a few hours. Children in search of the new Enid Blyton. I lived on my own, so liked the company. Helping people find a book on the Tudors or instructions on how to make a rabbit hutch. You'd get to know the regulars. The lady from the wool shop who came in every week for the new Mills & Boon. Her favourite, I seem to remember, was *In the Name of Love* by Guy Trent. She took that one out many times. The lonely old gentleman who liked Greek myths. I particularly enjoyed the quiet after closing time when everyone had gone, when I was there alone, making sure all the books had been put back on the right shelves. The magazines and newspapers folded and placed in the correct racks. It gave me a sense of satisfaction when I turned the lights out and locked up, that everything was shipshape. Ready for the next day. In truth, I suppose, I'm quite solitary. Happiest with my own company. It's always felt easier that way. But working with books gave me a window onto other worlds, other experiences I'd never otherwise have had.

On the mantlepiece, above the gas fire, are my photographs. A faded black-and-white snap of my parents on their wedding day. My mother in a little cloche hat with a veil, holding a bunch of forget-me-nots tied with a white ribbon. Dad raising a toast.

They are in the Black Horse. Mum smiling and looking happy. And then there's one of me as a five-year-old, sitting cross-legged in the front row on the playground tarmac. I remember how the photographer ducked behind a little curtain before the flash of his big tripod camera went off. Sitting just behind me, her hands on her knees and her hair braided in two plaits and twisted over her ears like earphones, is Miss Wilson. I liked Miss Wilson. She had sticky-out teeth but was kind and smelt of lily of the valley. Her fiancé died in the Great War and, like many of her generation, she never married but made some sense of her life teaching and singing in the local choir. She must be long gone by now. Next to me is Iris, one eye of her glasses covered with thick Elastoplast to correct her squint. I wish I knew what had happened to her. She married a Scot at the end of the war and went to live in Glasgow. Had three children. But then we lost touch.

I do so wish I had a photograph of you. Though I still have the little Bakelite-and-glass snow globe. A child's toy, more than seventy years old. You gave it to me that Christmas, wrapped in blue paper covered with little gold stars and I kept it under my mattress. A secret. It was the most precious thing I'd ever owned. When I shook it, a blizzard swirled over the thatched cottage, turning everything white. I imagined a happy family huddled by a crackling fire. A shimmering Christmas tree and, underneath, presents tied with coloured string. A plum pudding boiling in muslin on the stove. Outside, the iron-hard fields of the Fens. Kale and cabbage dusted with rime. Frosted sea holly.

So much is considered beautiful because it's valuable, but my little snow globe is quite worthless, except for the memories it conjures.

Snow shrouds the dirty and broken. The things we'd rather forget.

I also have your notebook and the painting of the young girl with watchful eyes. It hangs above my bed. Her skin's so white you can almost see the blue veins beneath it, and her fringe is frayed and ratty, as though she's taken the scissors to it herself.

I hope you'd be pleased I have them, that they've been preserved.

It's something of a cliché to say that grief is the price we pay for love. I've always assumed this was said by somebody literary. Emily Brontë, say, or Thomas Hardy. But when I looked it up, it was the Queen. Our Queen, on the death of Princess Diana. The People's Princess. I don't suppose the Queen actually wrote it. Presumably, it was a speech writer. I like the Queen. We're pretty much the same age. I think if we were ever to sit down to tea together, we'd get on. Have things to talk about. The Blitz. Rationing. The countryside. She likes animals. Horses as well as corgis. She may be rich, but she's never struck me as extravagant. During the war she collected coupons for her wedding dress. Keeps her cornflakes and rich tea biscuits in a Tupperware box. Heats her private rooms with a gas fire. I think we'd understand one another.

*

All that summer there was talk of the Crisis. After weeks of grey skies and rain there was a heatwave. It was so hot we had to have the back door open to let in some air. I was playing patience at the kitchen table and could see into next door where Mrs Baker was scrubbing her husband's pyjamas on the wooden washboard, when the wireless began to broadcast instructions for Operation Pied Piper. Next morning the Prime Minister interrupted the regular programmes to announce that we were at war with Germany. Air raid sirens began to wail. In the park, steam shovels started to dig up the turf so the parks could be used for growing food, while men in flat caps stood in rows filling sandbags. Overhead barrage balloons floated against the blue sky like big silvery fish, while AA scouts, who'd joined forces with the military police, rode around on freshly painted khaki motorbikes, taking down signposts and street names, replacing them with notices that told motorists the main routes out of town would be one-way traffic for the next three days. Cars packed with suitcases, children's perambulators, dogs, cats and bird cages, took to the road. Above, the skies droned with squadrons of bombers making their way towards France and Poland.

Young squaddies packed into army lorries waved and shouted 'Give us a smile!' to any passing shop girl, then bawled out 'Tipperary', not knowing what else to sing. All the girls loved a bit of khaki, and these lads were off to be soldiers, unlike those poor sods who had to go down the pits or cycle to work in their bicycle clips and second-hand suits to spend the day as junior clerks in the post office.

*

Evacuation. It was a new word.

What does it mean, Mum?

Going away somewhere in the country, she sighed, as I stood in my baggy knickers waiting for the saucepans to boil on the gas stove, staggering with pans of hot water to the tin bath, then back again for the next one.

Recently Bert, the eldest in my class, had been to the Roxy to see H.G. Wells's *Things to Come*. Mum didn't think it suitable for children, so I wasn't allowed to go. Afterwards, he terrified us with lurid descriptions of massed bombers, poison gas and heaps of smoking rubble. At night I lay in bed in abject fear.

We were issued with a list of things to pack. Gas mask. Vest and combinations. One pair of knickers. One liberty bodice and petticoat. Socks or stockings. Plimsolls. A comb. A toothbrush and a bar of soap. Before I went to bed Mum ran me up a rucksack from an old pillowcase on the treadle Singer that sat in the corner of the scullery where she made most of our clothes.

Up early, I put on the lilac cardigan Nan had knitted for my birthday over my summer dress. And, despite the heat, the coat with the rabbit-fur collar Mum had bought at the vicarage jumble. Then I brushed my hair. It was thin and cut in a ragged bob. Kept out of my eyes with a kirby grip. When I was ready, I ran in to say goodbye to Nan. But she was asleep. Her mouth flopped open like the flap of an envelope so I could see her pink gums. Her teeth in a glass beside the bed. She was breathing so heavily I was scared to kiss her, so picked up the clean hankie on her bedside table that smelt of Parma Violets and put it in my pocket. I wondered if I'd ever see her again.

Mum was wearing her best astrakhan coat, even though it was so hot. Her hair was tied in a maroon turban with one of Sid's silk scarves.

Come on now, Freda. Get your skates on. We'll be late, she said, dragging me along the pavement, her heels clicking against the hot cobbles.

Groups of children were already gathered in the school playground. Girls by the girls' toilets. Boys by the boys'. I looked for Iris but couldn't see her. A man with half-moon spectacles came and pinned a label on my coat with my name typed on it.

Find someone to pair up with, he said. We don't want anyone to get lost now, do we? And there's to be no drinking from now on. I don't want any accidents.

It was an exquisite day, the sky high and clear. London looked beautiful. It was the weekend and, with the roads and railways cleared of ordinary travellers, it felt as if we were going on holiday. As though we should be carrying buckets and spades, not gas masks. Outside Liverpool Street station I was still searching for Iris when we were told to form a crocodile behind Miss Wilson who was holding a banner with our school's name on it. We lined up behind her clutching our home-made rucksacks and gas masks. Our packets of sandwiches that were beginning to curl at the edges in the heat.

Then a policeman strode into the middle of the road, his helmet barely visible among the buses and military lorries, thrust a white-gloved hand into the air, blew his whistle and waved us across to the station. A double-decker ground to a halt at the lights and the bus driver tooted his horn, leant out of his cab and shouted cheerio as we hurried across the tramlines. When we got to the ticket hall, the name of the station had been obliterated with black paint.

So the Jerries won't know where they are when they get here, Bert whispered conspiratorially.

Where we going?

Dunno, he shrugged. A long way out into the country, me dad says.

The place was chock-a-block with troops shovelling coal and munitions into wagons. Shouting officials and sobbing mothers. Clouds of steam belched from the iron engines as pistons slowly ground into action.

D'you mind, miss, if it's all the same to you, a nursing mother in the front of a long queue was saying to a carnation-faced member of the Women's Voluntary Service, built like a sentry box, I don't think I'll send me Alfie after all. Y'see, I never left him before. How's he going to manage? she asked, nodding at a small, whey-faced boy, torn knee socks collapsing round his scuffed boots. You see, she whispered under her breath, he still has a little problem at night, if you know what I mean.

Come on. Get in, get in. Chop-chop. You can't go back now, the flustered volunteer with a London County Council armband barked, clapping her hands. Others are waiting.

How long? How long would it be before the first air raid? Hours? Minutes? Hitler had promised to darken the sky with his aeroplanes. Two small girls, faces striped with dirt and anxiety, were lugging around a grizzling, bare-bottomed baby. The older one was jigging him up and down, the younger clutching a cardboard box holding a bottle of grey milk and a ragged shawl.

By the WVS tea urn, we bumped into Mrs Brown and her daughter Betty. They lived in the same terrace as Iris and her brother Fred. Mrs Brown was also wearing her best coat and seemed to think she was the bee's knees.

They're not coming, she said to Mum, pulling a face as if sucking on a lemon. Mr Taylor's got an Anderson shelter in his back garden, dug a hole and covered those blessed metal sheets with a ton of earth. Said it took him ages. Mark my words, it'll be cold and damp and stink of pee in there but he says he's not letting the kiddies go. That he didn't fight the last war to ship his children off to god-knows-where with god-knows-who. They've been married twelve years, though he's been unemployed for seven, she tutted lowering her voice, and straightening the bow in Betty's hair. Mrs Taylor says her sister's offered to take her and Iris countless times, if only she'd put Fred in a home. But Mr Taylor, he says he's having none of it. We'll stick together, thank you very much. He reckons if it's bombs, they'll be safe enough in the shelter. He says he doesn't know why the government's so bothered about them all of a sudden. Never shown any bloody interest before.

So, Iris isn't coming, Mrs Brown continued, looking directly at me and shifting her mock-crocodile handbag from one arm to another. Downright wicked, I call it, making the kiddies stick around to be murdered. Mrs Taylor thinks there'll be time enough to send them to her sister in Wales if the Jerries do turn up. But how could anyone, even the Krauts, murder people in cold blood? Some people just don't have no sense, do they? The government's told us to send the kiddies off. So off they must go. But what can you expect from the likes of the Taylors? she continued, turning on her heels and dragging Betty towards the waiting train. Common as muck.

It was a Sunday. In the distance the church bells were ringing for the last time. For the rest of the war, if they rang again it would be to warn of invasion.

Be a good girl now, Mum said, wiping my mouth with a gob of spit balanced on the corner of her handkerchief as if I were five. I'd better be off, she said, kissing me roughly on the cheek. The shop won't open itself. You got your sandwiches, now. There's ham ones and sugar ones in the greaseproof. And I put two extra pairs of knickers in the bottom of your rucksack. And mind your manners. It's ever so kind of those nice people to take you in. I don't want no complaints.

It was chaos. A lady health visitor and special constable lined us up on the platform to inspect our kit. Some of the children were little more than toddlers. Small girls dressed in hats and coats as if it was winter, clutching their bald dolls. Undernourished boys with runny noses, no socks and broken shoes. Their hair cut well above the ears.

The sun was high, and teachers came around with big white jugs of lemonade, handing us each a cardboard cup and telling us to unpack our sandwiches.

Bert put his in his gas mask case.

What will you do if there's a gas attack? the man with the half-moon spectacles asked.

Piss on me 'andkerchief and put it over me face, sir! That's what me uncle said he done in the last war, sir!

The man with the half-moon spectacles blushed, then ushered us into the third carriage along. I wished that Iris had come. I had to sit next to Bert whose breath stank because he didn't clean his teeth. I pressed my face to the window, hoping to see Mum, but she'd already headed back to the shop. A row of ticket collectors and policemen were linking arms to hold back the forest of waving hands and fluttering handkerchiefs. Everywhere puffy, tear-stained faces were pushed up against the iron gates.

Ta-ta. Goodbye. God bless. Write home as soon as you can…

Then the engine whistled, sending up a puff of steam into the high station roof, and the guard, a short bald man in blue serge, shouted, Keep clear! as he strode down the platform, flicking the heavy varnished doors shut with his wrist. Stand back! Stand back! he boomed as the carriages jerked forward and those of us not sitting fell in a heap.

I'd never been on a train before. How long would the journey take? The material on the seats felt scratchy against the back of my legs. The string luggage racks overhead were stacked with cardboard suitcases and canvas haversacks. A poster with big red letters announced: 'FOOD, SHELLS AND FUEL MUST COME FIRST. If your train is late or crowded—DO YOU MIND?' and showed a long line of railway wagons piled high with artillery shells. On the other side of the carriage was a poster of a lady in a checked summer dress and sunglasses, next to a man in a blazer. The man had a neat moustache and was wearing white cricket trousers. They seemed to be having a day out because they were sitting above the bay at Scarborough with their sandwiches and binoculars, looking out to sea. The sea was very blue. In the distance was a little sailing boat with white sails. I'd never been to Scarborough and had no idea where it was. The man with half-moon spectacles, who'd given us our labels, told us not to stick our heads out of the window. But, when he wasn't looking, Bert dragged down the leather strap fixed to a brass hook and stuck his head out to have a butcher's, so when we went through a tunnel, the skin on his face went all crinkly, and black cinders blew back from the train's chimney, covering him in smuts.

When we emerged, we could see typists and office girls making their way to work in insurance firms and solicitors' offices. Some were only a few years older than us. On one side of an invisible line you were still considered a child. On the other a young lady with a handbag, peep-toe sandals and a gas mask who had to go to the office, as long as there was an office still to go to. Two paunchy businessmen carrying gas masks in canvas boxes and neatly rolled copies of *The Times* under their arms, strolled past a City church where the steps to the crypt had been stuffed with sandbags. In a narrow side street, a grocer's boy was unloading flitches of bacon and bags of sugar from a Co-op wagon.

I pressed my face to the window and London flashed past, giving way to a patchwork of small towns and villages. Rows of squalid, soot-blackened houses, often accommodating two families, sat squashed beside the railway lines, their dingy yards draped with lines of drab washing. At the weekends the streets were usually full of children pushing one another around in old prams. Playing hopscotch on the chalked pavements or cantering behind each other waving a pair of string reins, pretending to be a horse and cart. But now the streets were empty, as if some Pied Piper had called all the children away. A few women, taking advantage of the sun, were scrubbing their doorsteps. Others, an elbow resting on the garden fence, were having a chinwag with their neighbour. Down by the reservoir a row of new red-brick council houses fringed the empty recreation ground, where the freshly painted swings sat in wait for the vanished children.

Of course, we don't have a child to send, the young teacher in the corner of our carriage, her blond hair twisted into a victory roll, was telling Miss Wilson. We only got married last month. It was Ron's holiday week. Shoreditch church, she said, pouring two cups of strong tea from her thermos into a couple of Bakelite cups. You know the 'Oranges and Lemons' one. It's very grand, but Mum's friends with the curate and had a little word. Have you ever been inside, Miss Wilson? Oh, I had such a lovely costume. Mum made it from a roll of moiré satin she'd been saving specially. And I had a little hat with a polka-dot veil from Derry & Toms. We had to save for two years to furnish our place. It's only small, mind, but ever so nice. I made the curtains myself. Bought the fabric in Petticoat Lane. It's got a lovely pattern. Sort of zigzags. Abstract I think they call it. Very modern. I said to Ron, I don't want any of those washed-out-looking patterns. Just bright, gay colours. And the furniture, well that's all modern too. I like new things. My sister Hazel said, rent a flat somewhere, Doreen. But I said, no, I want a garden. You must have a garden, I said, if you want children. Now I'm thanking God we didn't start one. Ron'll be called up. He's twenty-four, like me, and we'll have to give up the house. We shan't have the money for rent. And my things—I don't know what I'll do with my things. I thought of trying to let furnished, but other people don't take care like you do, do they? I can't understand this war, can you, Miss Wilson? Tell me why it had to come, spoiling everything. Maybe we'll never have a child now, she said, starting to cry. Oh, excuse me, but when I look at all my nice stuff—over two pounds we paid for that carpet—and there's Ron's shelf for his books. He likes those ones with little Penguins on the spine. They only cost sixpence. There's orange for fiction. Blue for biography and green for crime. He especially likes those Agatha Christies: *Death on the Nile, Murder on the Orient Express*. Oh Miss Wilson, we were going— she sobbed, taking in a great gulp of air.

Hush, not now, Doreen. Not in front of the children. Here, Miss Wilson said, fishing up the sleeve of her cardigan for a hankie. It's quite clean.

I spy with my little eye something beginning with G.

A goat, said Bert. And everyone laughed.

There aren't any goats, stupid. A gasometer, I said, looking out of the window at the iron giants disappearing along the track.

Then Frank Higgs wrote on his gas mask in big black letters, pulling it on over his head and rolling his eyes behind the dirty mica lens, nodding to make the rubbery snout move up and down like an elephant's trunk. Everyone started to laugh until he began to choke and had to be helped, sobbing and spluttering, to take it off.

See, you've spoilt your mask now, his sister said, primly.

What do you think the families will be like? Bert asked. Will they be rich? Maybe I'll get one that lives in a sweetshop. If the Nazis invade, perhaps we'll be kidnapped.

We played ludo and snakes and ladders, and read our *Beano* comics as suburban sprawl gave way to cows and fields. But, with the windows up, the carriage grew hotter and hotter and, with no conveniences, the little ones started to wet themselves and cry.

When the train pulled into the station two red-faced men were heaving sacks of coal onto the back of a cart, their broad leather belts pulled tight under their bulging bellies. A dray, with big, feathered feet, was chomping hay from a nosebag, trying to swat a swarm of flies circling its head in the heat with its long swishing tail. No one had the least idea where we were.

Now listen carefully, Miss Wilson said. Take all your luggage and make sure you don't leave anything behind. We followed her up the steps and over the bridge. My pillowcase rucksack chafing my shoulders, my gas mask box digging into my ribs. By the time we reached the other side, my cotton dress was rucked up under my coat and I was sweating. There were children everywhere. Some in blazers with purple and white stripes. Boy Scouts in green and gold caps. Joining the crush in our second-hand raincoats and hand-me-down shoes, we looked like the dog's dinner.

Outside the Lamb and Flag a handful of men in grey suits, armed with Manila files, was rushing up and down the lines of children, herding us onto two waiting buses. I hardly knew anyone on mine except Bert. Suddenly I was glad he was there. In the past he'd have made a fuss about having to sit next to a girl. Now he was uncharacteristically quiet. Where the road divided on the edge of town, we took the right-hand fork, winding between flat fields that stretched away as far as the eye could see. The harvest had just been cut and rows of corn stooks sat huddled like small yellow tents on the stubble.

I'd never seen so much sky.

Could there really be a war on? Had the raids on London started yet? Everything was so peaceful. I glanced up to see if I could see any German planes. But there was nothing. Still, I worried about Mum and Nan. What would they do? Nan was bedridden and couldn't walk. How would Mum get her from her bed in the back bedroom to the shelter?

Do you think it's started yet? I whispered, leaning over to Bert so the two bigger boys behind us wouldn't hear.

Dunno. They said they'd blow sirens or somefink. Don't 'spect we'd hear 'em 'ere.

But there were no aeroplanes. Not even a distant drone in the wide, high blue. I prayed that Hitler wouldn't drop a bomb on Nan.

Eventually the bus stopped. A blackboard leaning against the wooden gatepost announced: 'St Peter's Church Hall. Evacuee Centre.' The building was like something out of a picture book with white walls and black beams. Trestle tables had been arranged under the arched ceiling, piled with supplies for us to take to our billets. A tin each of corned beef and condensed milk. A quarter pound of tea and a pound of biscuits. Half a pound of chocolate in a large brown paper bag. Two women in dark-green uniforms were sitting knitting behind a pile of files, chatting to a bald man in a black jacket and white dog collar. After a glass of orange squash and a currant bun, the billeting officer told us to line up so the nurse could inspect our heads. I was clean. Though I'd had nits before and had to go to school with my hair cropped to the skull. Still, I felt dirty and thought of Mum spending her hard-earned money on Derbac soap and that special steel comb, searching out the little beggars every Friday bath night so I wouldn't be shown up by Nitty Nora.

Then it was the turn of the locals who strolled up and down checking us over like prize cows, making sure we didn't have impetigo. When they were done, the doctor's wife, in a blue coat and string of pearls, stepped forward.

I'll take that one, she said, pointing to a blonde girl with yellow ribbons in her plaits. You'd like to come and help me, wouldn't you? she said, ushering the bewildered child outside into a waiting Humber.

Gradually most of the children were chosen. The big girls to help around the house. The larger boys like Bert to give a hand on local farms. Those of us who weren't picked bedded down for the night on straw sacks. Only a few of the smaller boys were left. No one seemed to want them. Or me. I felt a rush of shame. Maybe if I'd had long plaits, instead of lank mousy hair, someone would have chosen me. I cried myself to sleep. In the morning, the last two little brothers were taken off in opposite directions. The big one by the vicar. The smaller boy by the butcher. I can still hear him snivelling: Tommy, Tommy. I don't want to go without me brother Tommy.

It's stopped raining and the sun's come out. A group of young mothers trail in from the playground and park their buggies in the corner of the café. Shake off their wet anoraks, strip raincoats and wellingtons from their little ones, propping them in wooden highchairs before taking out carrot sticks and rice cakes from Tupperware boxes. The café's been renovated from the old greasy spoon with its thick white mugs of strong tea and beans on toast. Now it's all blond wood, baskets of carrot cake and home-made brownies. Twenty years ago, I rarely came to this park. The place was full of down-and-outs and kids from the nearby estate playing football amid the dog mess. Then the council dredged the lakes. A new playground with wooden climbing frames and rubber safety mats replaced the rusty swings and roundabouts. The tennis courts were resurfaced. The lakes stocked with Chinese ducks and Egyptian geese. The young mothers sip their lattes and chat among themselves, ignoring their toddlers throwing carrot sticks on the floor.

I finish my tea and scone. I need to get back. This afternoon we have our weekly art class with Jade. We've been making collages. Doing a bit of potato printing and tie-and-dye. I expect Jade will bring her poster paints and tubes of glitter as if we were in kindergarten. But she's a lovely girl, and painting passes the time. Today we're making bunting to decorate the TV room. Next week we're going to watch the seventy-fifth anniversary celebrations of Dunkirk. The staff are planning a small tea party. Some of the original little ships are going over to France from Ramsgate and Dover. I imagine there'll be lots of French schoolchildren waving tricolours and Union Jacks in the town square. The last few veterans wrapped up against the wind, huddled in their wheelchairs. A brass band playing the Marseillaise and 'God Save the Queen'. The BBC is doing a special commemorative broadcast with David Dimbleby. Who knows if this will be the last one? There are fewer and fewer left who actually took part. Soon it will pass from living memory and be no more relevant than the Battle of Waterloo or 1066.

I pay and pick up my umbrella from the stand behind the door, then make my way slowly round the lake. The cygnets born earlier in the year are shedding their grey feathers and turning into swans. A moorhen with yellow feet is bobbing for snails. It gives me solace, the natural world. Makes me feel that life's still worth living. As I've got older, I've come to realize that memory isn't a question of simply recalling the things that happened day after day, year after year, but a patchwork of events etched across our hearts.

A LOW SUN LIT UP the distant college spires, turning the grazing cattle spectral in the early morning mist. Port Meadow was dissolving. It was a reflection of his state of mind, of course. The result of those long evenings sitting alone in the college chapel. The night sweats brought on by anxiety and doubt. His lack of concentration and inability to study or read. He had sat for hours staring at Holman Hunt's *The Light of the World*. At Jesus with his lantern, his flowing hair and crown of thorns, preparing to knock on the overgrown, long-unopened door. Philip knew the text from his biblical studies. Revelations 3: 20: 'Behold, I stand at the door and knock: if any man hear my voice and open the door, I will come in to him and will sup with him, and he with me.' But the more he stared, the more he realized that the door didn't have a handle and could only be opened from the inside. And he knew then, that however hard he tried, his mind would remain shut to any sort of divine revelation. That he didn't have a vocation.

When he'd been at school he'd convinced himself, during the long grey hours of evensong, that he could hear God speaking to him. Amid the crepuscular shadows, the wooden pews and stained glass, surrounded by the stale smells of other eleven-year-old boys, the words filled his head, telling him that belief was a matter of faith, of concentration and listening. He remembered the Christmas carol service. The cold stone chapel decorated with holly and ivy. The flickering flames of the beeswax candles and vases of Christmas roses. He'd had a sweet voice then and sung in the choir. Worn a white surplice over a scarlet robe. Even now he could still hear those soaring trebles: 'In the bleak mid-winter, long ago…' The purity of those young voices had touched something deep inside.

But now there was only silence. Of course there was. Those feelings had been little more than the susceptibility of a vulnerable young boy. Now only the natural world brought him solace. That and painting. The intricate patterns and rhythms of nature. The smell of pigment and turps. The black crush of charcoal and Indian ink. The teeming pictures that pressed against the inside of his head. Pictures he could get lost in.

He'd walked out of college as the city slept and stood in the dawn light among the herd of lowing cows that gathered round, curiously jostling him with their soft pink noses, their steaming coats giving off a dusty, fetid smell. Then had broken down. He felt utterly dejected, utterly alone. He had no idea who he was or what he believed. Surrounded by a herd of curious cattle, his face streaked with snot, he was found by a Brasenose scout cycling to work across the meadows and returned to Keble.

He was twenty-two and a total failure. He would never sit finals. Never be ordained. Never be a curate or a rector, let alone a bishop. That's what his mother had been banking on, wasn't it? Coming to stay with him in some charming Dorset rectory. A summer fete on the lawn. A young wife by his side serving home-made scones and strawberry jam on the loggia. A coconut shy and a guess-the-weight-of-the-fruitcake competition. A flower tent full of sweet peas. He'd only agreed to read theology to avoid the army. His father had been a hero, hadn't he? Both his mother and housemaster had told him so constantly. Didn't his posthumous Victoria Cross sit in pride of place in its glass case on the black marble mantlepiece in the drawing room of the villa in Buckingham Palace Road? Both a rebuke and a reliquary.

He was four when his mother told him that his father wasn't coming home. Gerald Rhayader had been a talented young major with the 1st Battalion, Lincolnshire Regiment. The son of a gentleman farmer, Lincolnshire had been his boyhood home. Originally from Wales, from the town of Rhayader, his relatives had for centuries been sheep breeders on the banks of the River Wye at the edge of the Cambrian Mountains. The family crest consisted of two rams, their curled horns locked together in combat. But Philip's grandfather had married a Lincolnshire girl he'd met at a country-house dance and moved east to help her father farm. When her father died without an heir, they'd inherited the estate. Philip's own father, Gerald, had grown up there, among the flat black fens. The only connection to his Welsh heritage being the family name.

Now Gerald Rhayader was just another of the fallen. A statistic of the Great War. One of the quarter of a million casualties suffered for a pointless five-mile advance gained stumbling through no man's land, feet rotting with trench foot, nerves giving way under fire. Philip would never forgive General Haig's stubborn hubris for depriving him of his parent. A father to tousle his hair and cheer him on during school sports day. Those lost boyhood games of cricket on the beach.

His father's battalion had been forced to attack in the early hours during a torrential downpour. The heaviest rain for thirty years. British and Canadian troops found themselves fighting not only the Germans, but a quagmire of stinking mud that swallowed up men, horses and tanks. Shell holes became swamps. Privates and officers, pack mules and ponies drowned in the noxious bogs. As a small boy Philip had lain awake in his nursery, the shadows from the street lamps outside making elfin faces on the ceiling, and clearly seen those poor men and beasts sinking into the sludge. The gas shells exploding overhead.

Later, he spent a good deal of time trying to remember what his father had been like. But there wasn't much to remember, not really. A vague smell of tweed and tobacco. The scratchy sensation of a moss-green jacket brushing against his cheek as he was lifted high onto his father's shoulders and they'd galloped across the dining room in a noisy cavalry charge. He no longer knew what was real memory and what wasn't. At prep school, when the other boys talked of their fathers, he'd close his eyes and see his walking towards him in a beam of sunlight dressed in khaki, his peaked officer's cap decorated with its regimental badge. His webbed belt, jodhpurs and puttees. A leather binocular case slung over his shoulder. But in truth, he wasn't sure whether this was an accurate memory or just wishful thinking. A way of keeping his father close.

An extract in the *London Gazette* spoke of his father's bravery. His devotion to duty and fearless dedication to his men. Noted the quiet respect in which he was held. Early one morning an infantry patrol had gone out to attack an enemy post in a ruined village. When Gerald Rhayader heard the firing back at company headquarters, he'd followed the patrol out onto the battlefield to give assistance. Four hundred yards beyond the front line, amid the stench of sulphur and smoke, the strewn limbs and body parts, he'd come across a wounded Tommy and stayed with him while the bullets and shrapnel zinged overhead. Crouched in a foxhole waiting for help, an enemy patrol had manoeuvred between their hideout and the front line, detonating a shell that had blown both men to smithereens.

It was expected that Philip would join his father's regiment. But he wanted none of it. He wouldn't kill. Not after all the bloody, pointless slaughter of Ypres and Passchendaele. He didn't believe the Great War—he refused to call it that, there had been nothing *great* about it except the amount of slaughter—had been the war to end all wars. As a boy he'd been puzzled by the number of people all over town with missing limbs, hobbling around on crutches. He knew that we'd won the war. Yet these men were sick wrecks, ignored by those hurrying down the street on their way to work or to the dentist. He would never forget them. The ten million who'd died on the battlefields. The twenty million wounded. The six million civilians killed. Those who'd lost fathers, husbands and brothers. A whole generation.

At Oundle, he registered as a conscientious objector and was made to scrub lavatories while the other boys attended drill.

While bent over a shit-encrusted bog one dreary autumn afternoon with a bottle of bleach and a toilet brush, Stephen Bartley-Jones, his dorm prefect, and his friend Humphrey Woodham, had come into the empty cloakroom. Both were older and larger than Philip. Bartley-Jones was built like a pit prop, a blond, tousled-haired boy with an air of entitlement who everyone expected to be prime minister one day. Pressing into the cubicle behind him, the pair grabbed him by the shoulders and shoved his head into the bleach-filled pan until he thought he would either drown or be asphyxiated.

Bit of a pansy, are you, Rhayader? Bat for the other team? Is that why you wear a white poppy instead of a red? A secret sign to all the other little bum boys. Think you're too good for the corps, do you? Better than all those brave officers who gave their lives for our country to give little shits like you the freedom to grow up and be even bigger shits?

He told no one. Though the headmaster wrote to his mother informing her of his growing pacifist tendencies, suggesting a meeting to discuss her oversensitive son. When she arrived at the school in her little dove-grey hat, the headmaster held out his hand and blushed, ushering the pretty young widow into his study where a brass plaque displayed the names of all the boys who'd given their lives for king and country. Including his father.

If he wasn't going to try for Sandhurst, Philip could perhaps, the headmaster suggested, read greats. Though theology might suit him better. Ordination and a quiet country living might be just the thing. Philip was keen on drawing, wasn't he? No career to be had in that, of course. A bit too bohemian, he chuckled, but a suitable pastime for a country vicar with, what he liked to call, alternative views. Keble would be the place. Second league, of course. But he'd have a word.

It had been at Oundle that Philip had become friends with Isaac Aaronovitch, a studious boy with owlish glasses and yellow teeth. It was Aaronovitch who'd introduced him to the local second-hand bookshop where, for a few pence, they'd picked up art books and battered copies of Sassoon and Wilfred Owen. They'd slip into town and go to Dolly's tea shop next to the Rose & Crown, the seventeenth-century inn reputedly haunted by a White Cavalier, and order jam and toasted teacakes. Aaronovitch was considered a swot and a weirdo. But Philip liked him and was pleased to have a friend. At breakfast, the other boys thought it fun to dangle slices of bacon in his face and make oinking noises. Philip was always impressed that Isaac simply shrugged and went on eating his toast and marmalade.

It was at the Downs, his prep school, that Philip developed an interest in natural history. He'd dreaded leaving home. His nanny packed the black tin trunk, taken down from the loft, that had belonged to his father. The patch on the lid, where his father's initials had been, had been painted over with grate blacking and replaced with his own. He was discouraged from taking his fur rabbit but allowed his wildlife books, including his favourite, T.A. Coward's *The Birds of the British Isles* from the Wayside and Woodland series.

At the Downs he nursed a jay with a broken wing. Went bug-hunting for lime hawk-moths in the lime trees above the cricket field. His first puss moths slept like a pair of black and green kittens on a bed of willow leaves he made in an old shoe box. He was more at ease with bugs, blackbirds and thrushes than with other children. Such idiosyncrasies were indulged at the Downs in ways they wouldn't be later at Oundle.

Owls were a favourite. Giles Beale, his housemaster, was an amateur ornithologist who reared tawny, barn and little owls in nest boxes up by the cricket pitch. One day he lent Philip a special glove and let him hold a tawny. It sat on his hand staring at him with its big round eyes as though it knew something he didn't. Tawnies were the friendliest, barn owls the shyest and little owls the fiercest. He fed them rabbits caught by the ferret he was allowed to keep in a pen at the back of Beale's garden, and sparrows from the sparrow trap set up on the school farm. Not all the masters were so understanding. Stephen Dilke hauled him over the coals when a fit of giggling broke out at the back of the class one morning while they were supposed to be translating Ovid. Philip had brought his pet ferret into the lesson hidden in a poacher's pocket sewn into the lining of his blazer and she'd poked her head out, much to the amusement of his classmates, while they were supposed to be working on an elegiac couplet from the *Tristia*.

Supposing, said Dilke, brushing chalk from his gown and drawing back his skinny shoulders after order was restored, supposing twenty-five small boys all kept ferrets in their pockets and brought them into Latin. Chaos would ensue, would it not? Though, I suppose it is possible, he continued sarcastically, that we might have a more classically minded population of mustelids. Then he sent Philip to the headmaster.

*

54

But Philip missed home. A Victorian villa on Buckingham Palace Road with its black-and-white tiled path fringed with low privet hedges that led across the small front garden to a blue front door. He was homesick for the smell of lavender polish on the heavy mahogany furniture. The dark portraits of relatives he'd never met. The Persian rugs, and the small gong mounted on a real elephant's foot at the bottom of the stairs that summoned him to lunch. The conservatory, with its aroma of compost and damp earth. Its rattan chairs, large aspidistra and ferns, where his mother took tea and read. When small, he'd stood at the nursery window at the back of the house watching the engines in Victoria station shunt backwards and forwards to the turntable in front of the engine shed, their sides painted in green and gold letters. LB & SCR for London Brighton and South Coast Railway. LCDR in blue and red for London Chatham and Dover. He'd stand for hours watching people coming and going or waiting at the taxi rank in front of the red-brick wall for a cab. And each morning, he and his nanny walked to Pimlico, past the guards in their red tunics and bearskins marching out from Chelsea Barracks towards the palace, the brass instruments of the bandsmen gleaming in the morning sun.

And he missed playing the pianola that performed Chopin's 'Polonaise militaire' and one of Liszt's 'Hungarian Rhapsodies'. From the time his feet could reach the pedals he was allowed to operate its pneumatic mechanism. The little levers that controlled the speed and volume of the perforated paper rolls. He'd pedal, while his mother sang arias from Rossini's *Boutique Fantasque*. She had a lovely voice.

Even so, he never saw enough of her. Often, she seemed little more than a beautiful mirage. The closer he tried to get, the more she seemed to disappear. Nanny would have given him his bath, made him clean his teeth and say his prayers and he'd be lying in the dark, watching the shadows from the street lamp flickering on the ceiling, willing his mother to come and kiss him goodnight. He knew she'd be changing out of her day dress into her black Chantilly lace with the ruffled cap sleeves. It was the dress she always wore to the theatre or if invited to sing at a little soirée at the Army and Navy Club in Pall Mall. His father's friends liked to keep an eye on her. To see that the pretty young widow was not left too much alone. As he lay clutching his fur rabbit, Philip worried that she'd forget. That she'd leave without saying goodbye. Then, just as his anxiety peaked, the bedroom door would open, a sliver of light pour in from the landing, and in would come his mother in a rustle of lace to sit on the edge of his bed, tousle his hair and kiss him on the nose.

Nighty-night, Philly darling, don't let the bugs bite, she'd say, smoothing down his eiderdown.

Engulfed in a cloud of Elizabeth Arden Blue Grass, he'd wonder, when she brought her face close to his to kiss him, how the tiny pearl and diamond studs she wore in the evenings went right through the lobes of her ears. When she left, he'd feel desolate and reach for the small glass snow globe he kept by his bed, found at the bottom of his Christmas stocking the previous year, and shake it, watching the white flakes float over the miniature streets and cottages, till he drifted off to sleep.

*

After the incident in Port Meadow, he left Keble with a minimum of fuss. It was agreed it would be for the best if he didn't sit finals. Arrangements were made for him go to the Warneford on Headington Hill. By then, no one called it a lunatic asylum. Rather a care home for distressed mental patients of the educated classes. Diagnosed with neurasthenia brought on by anxiety, he was treated with hydrotherapy. Placed in a canvas hammock slung from a metal frame in a bath and covered in a sheet with a hole cut for his head to rest on a rubber pillow, while water was poured in around him. Sometime these dousings lasted for hours. Afterwards he'd be wrapped in a wet sheet to keep his mood stable.

As he improved, he began to keep a diary and was given permission to work in the kitchen garden producing food for the patients. He grew marrows and soft fruit. Tended the hens and guinea fowl with their white, mask-like faces. Turned the manure heap and pricked out seedlings in the greenhouse— tomatoes and thyme, cabbage and carrots—savouring the feel of the gritty dirt under his nails. And he was encouraged to use the art room at the top of the building with its northern skylight. Occasionally Maud would be up there, weaving willow baskets by the window. A feeble-minded young woman, she'd been put in the Warneford by her family and conveniently forgotten. One morning he was given a pencil and a sheaf of paper and sat in a shaft of sunlight filling sheet after sheet with intricate, obsessive patterns. And, every day, he hoped that his mother, her ivory bangles jangling to announce her arrival, would come and collect him. But she never did.

*

Not long after he'd started at the Downs, she moved to Paris to teach music to the British ambassador's children. Despite the chore of having to teach the petulant Hermione arpeggios and put up with seven-year-old Harry's total indifference to the whole process, she was in her element. Reading in the rose garden. Singing at the evening soirées in the *salon jaune* dominated by the painting of the 1st Duke of Wellington. Teaching spoilt children was, she calculated, a small price to pay for meeting the many and varied embassy guests. The writer, Axel Munthe, who came to Paris from his Villa San Michele on the Isle of Capri to see his heart specialist. Sir Eric Phipps, the one-time private secretary to the British ambassador. The Master of Christ's College, Cambridge. Evelyne Rhayader soon became both an asset and a fixture, a particular favourite with Somerset Maugham who'd been born in the embassy and whose father had been its lawyer. A short man with a stutter, Maugham liked to park himself on the double piano stool beside Evelyne while she played 'Polly Wolly Doodle', until fits of laughter could be heard coming from the music room.

It wasn't long before she started to spend her summers in France rather than return to England for Philip's school holidays. He'd be farmed out to spend them in a series of strange houses with classmates, boys who, at school, weren't really his friends. He would never feel at home, never quite master the different breakfast routines or whether he should wear his blazer or mufti. His mother became a regular guest at the chateau in Noirmoutier on the mouth of the Loire. The British historian

Edward Pemberton, a frequent embassy guest, had inherited the property from his French mother and now lived there most of the year as it provided a better climate for his invalid wife than London. Set in a spinney of pine trees that led down to a sheltered little inlet on the river bank, Noirmoutier was reached from the mainland at low tide across a narrow causeway. During his last school holiday from the Downs, Philip was invited to join his mother there for a month. He was twelve and had never travelled alone. He took a wagon-lit from Victoria station, spending an anxious night in a compartment with a businessman from Singapore dressed in a pinstriped suit who smoked endless cigarillos and played solo whist. He had—the gentleman insisted on telling Philip, who'd rather have been reading his *Treasure Island*—been educated at a Christian mission school but now was an importer and exporter.

Tobacco, indigo, tea. And coffee. Coffee's the thing, he said, puffing smoke rings into the already stuffy carriage.

France is my main customer, of course, for coffee. The French do love their breakfast *café au lait* and croissants. I supply all the best Parisian restaurants but I'm trying to break into the English market. That's why I was in London. For a meeting at the Savoy. But the Brits seem wedded to their 'cuppas', he chuckled, and with this tricky political climate, you can never be sure which way things are going to go.

At Montparnasse Philip was relieved to disembark and catch another train on to Nantes, where he was picked up by Pemberton's chauffeur. But although that summer he learnt to sail with the local fisherman on the Loire in a dory with red lug sails, and his legs and back turned a healthy nut brown, the trip wasn't a success. Edward Pemberton didn't much like children and there was no one of his own age for him to play with.

And he hardly saw his mother. He'd missed her very much at school and hoped he'd be spending time with her in France. Going on picnics, visiting the sandy river-beach. He wanted to show off his improved piano skills. Play for her while she sang. He'd been practising all term. But Pemberton demanded most of her attention. So Philip was left to explore the chateau's many rooms, wandering down empty corridors into the unused salons where ormolu clocks and ornate Louis XV chairs sat covered in dust sheets. The blinds drawn to prevent the wall tapestries, with their scenes of wild-boar hunts in the forests of Fontainebleau, from fading.

He played chess against himself on the small rosewood table while the August sun streamed in through the half-closed shutters from the parterre outside with its symmetrical flower beds and clipped privet hedges. When he couldn't bear to be in the house any longer, he went and found his cotton sun hat and sat at the iron table on the gravel terrace to draw under the lilac tree. In the heavy heat, he'd listen to the water from the verdigris-coated faun splash into the stone basin in the middle of the green pond, where koi carp slipped between the lily pads. Then rolling the remains of his breakfast baguette into pellets, he'd scatter them on the water, watching the fish break the surface with their O-shaped mouths. Most were a golden bronze. But there were two fat ones with black-and-white markings that he particularly liked. And, if she remembered, Chantal might bring him out a glass of her home-made blackcurrant and elderflower *sirop*.

Every lunchtime he'd join his mother and Pemberton in the dining room with its carved rosewood furniture. Pemberton's wife always ate alone in her room. The table was laid with cut glass, and napkins trimmed, Pemberton informed him, with Brussels lace. Chantal would bring in the *pot-au-feu*, pearl onions nestling among the potatoes and meat, which Pemberton would serve into big porcelain soup dishes with a silver ladle. Philip soon learnt to eat with a fork and broken hunk of bread, rather than using a knife, and was encouraged to taste wine for the first time and pour a few drops of Beaujolais into his glass of water.

Philly, darling, do tell Edward about your ferret, his mother suggested eagerly.

But Philip knew that Pemberton wouldn't want to know about his pets.

It was very hot and after lunch everybody retired for a siesta, leaving him to his own devices. When he passed his mother's room, he could hear her calling out in a strange voice. He worried she might be ill and lingered by the closed door not knowing what to do, afraid someone would catch him and tell him off. Then, just as he was slipping back into the garden, he saw Pemberton come out, adjust his cufflinks, and head for his study. When he met his mother later for afternoon tea, she was unusually skittish.

His main consolation during that lonely summer was to go down to the river in search of newts and butterflies. There were species he'd never seen in England. He made a collection of beetles and woodlice, which he kept in glass Kilner jars begged from Chantal. Caught a grass snake and set up a wormery. Animals didn't let you down.

The letter arrived while he was still in the Warneford. His mother was getting married again. Edward Pemberton's wife had sadly passed away after her long illness and Evelyne was honoured that he'd asked her to be his wife. They'd waited, she wrote, before telling anyone, out of respect. When in Paris, Edward made his home in the Hôtel Alexandre III on the Rond-Point-des-Champs-Élysées and, though he kept a small flat in Kensington and they'd be spending much of their time there, it wasn't really large enough to accommodate Philip as well.

I know you'll understand, darling, that Edward needs the peace and quiet to write. But he's very generously agreed to provide you with a small allowance. Isn't that marvellous? It's such a weight off my mind. Now it's simply a question of deciding what you'd like to do. Go travelling, perhaps? Vienna, to visit the church organs? Florence, Granada or Lisbon? The wedding's in a couple of weeks. Just a few close friends. The ambassador has kindly agreed to hold a little party. I do so wish you could join us, my darling. But, of course, that's not possible.

WOOHOO? Anyone there? She had Coty-red lips, high heels and was holding a clipboard.

Freda? I wondered where you were hiding. You're the last.

I was waiting on a bench outside the ladies flipping through my *School Friend Annual,* trying not to cry. I didn't want to be there. Didn't want to go to a stupid family. I wanted to go home. To be sitting on the end of Nan's bed wrapped in her paisley eiderdown, playing with her paste pearls. I'd take my chance on the bombs.

Come along now, Freda. Mr Willock's waiting. You can have a cream cracker if you're a good girl. Cat got your tongue?

I didn't answer. Just picked up my pillowcase rucksack and followed her outside where a man in mud-spattered wellingtons and a tweed coat tied at the waist with baler twine was sitting on a battered tractor. The red-lipped lady went over and spoke to him and the man on the tractor nodded, indicating that I should climb up beside him. Then the lady with the red lipstick left.

The metal seat was cold against my bare legs and I could see the road through a hole in the floor where the rusty metal had corroded. The man didn't speak to me. Just scratched his greasy hair, started the engine, and then off we juddered, leaving the black-and-white church hall behind us. At the crossroads we cut down a narrow lane between two flat fields where, in the distance, I could see a horse-drawn plough trailed by a spinnaker of gulls, turning stubble back into the black earth. I'd no idea where we were and, as I bumped in the seat next to Mr Willock, I tried not to look at his left hand. It didn't have a thumb or forefinger. Only two shiny stumps where his lost digits should have been.

A grass-covered sea wall ran along the side of the road. It must have been twenty feet high. The inland side was bare enough but, between road and wall, there was an eerie emptiness. Apart from the occasional belt of trees and the spike of a distant church spire etched like a thin pencil line against the low sky, everything was drawn in horizontals. The field boundaries. The dykes and rivers that ran in man-made channels out to the Wash. The Ouse, the Nene and the Welland. Names that would soon come to signify a special kind of loneliness.

In the distance I could see the sea. A shimmering strip beyond the sands. In time, I'd get to know their names too. Breast Sand, Bulldog Sand, Thief Sand, Old South, Mare Tail, Blue Back and Black Buoy. These were the great Wash mudflats. I'd learn, too, that although you could walk out across the marsh towards them, unless you knew them well, you'd be unwise to do so. The sea wall formed the frontier to a world of sea asters and crab grass that grew in the iodine-smelling sand, and the line of driftwood and netting that marked the tide's highest reaches. As we bounced down the narrow track, emerald vegetation gave way to the dark-green grass that marshmen called 'the stalk edges' and to a network of webbed waterways that ran out towards the open sea. These hidden creeks, deep enough to hide a man, were fringed with clumps of coarse grass so thick they could swallow a wounded goose that even a well-trained Labrador couldn't find. And further out, in the far distance, were the true sands, where great flocks of grey geese and migrating birds roosted in winter. Apart from the chug of the tractor engine everything was silent, the quiet broken only by the occasional cry of a sea bird. It was so desolate I could have been on the moon.

I remember it as if it were yesterday, arriving at that broken-down cottage hunkered on the edge of the marsh. There wasn't another building in sight. Newly enclosed, the land was thick with thistles. Mr Willock stopped the tractor and told me to get down. I jumped, grazing my knee on the bumper, so a trickle of blood ran down into my white sock. A woman, dressed in a man's frayed coat over her flowered apron, was busy feeding a flock of hissing geese.

This here be Aunty, Mr Willock said of the sallow-faced figure. And I be your uncle now.

It was the first time he'd spoken since we'd left the church hall.

I just did whatever I was told. What else could I do but follow the woman inside, up a flight of dark stairs, into a small attic room? There was a narrow iron bedstead and washstand, a faded rag rug on the bare boards. Tendrils of ivy poked through the chalky clunch walls, so the cracks and crevices seemed to form themselves into ever-changing patterns. The woman didn't say anything, didn't ask about my journey or if I was hungry or wanted a drink. She just left me alone in the middle of the room and shut the door without speaking. I sat down on the narrow bed and unpacked my bag, putting my hairbrush on the washstand next to my toothbrush and Kirby grips. My precious *School Friend Annual* on the upturned vegetable box that served as a bedside table. My nightdress under the lumpy bolster, and my vest and knickers in the drawer, along with the spare cardigan that Nan had knitted. Then I lined up my plimsolls exactly parallel to the floorboards at the foot of the bed. I kept my coat on.

I had no idea what to expect. What I was supposed to do. So I just waited. Then I waited some more. The light began to fade, and the room fill with shadows as the cracks in the walls slowly turned into strange beasts and birds. In the growing dark I lay tracing the crevices with my finger until the shapes seemed to come alive. At home I always slept with my door open, afraid of the dark, reassured by the sliver of light bleeding across the landing from under Nan's door. But here it seemed safer to keep it shut. I thought someone would come upstairs to get me. Ask if I wanted something to eat. But no one did. Eventually I managed to drag the wooden vegetable box to the high window and stand on tiptoes to peer out. Outside was nothing except mile upon mile of flat dark peat fields beneath an endless grey sky. When I'd left London there'd been a heat-wave. Now louring storm clouds threatened rain. I sat on the bed, uncertain what to do, biting my lip until it bled. I wanted to cry but wouldn't; wouldn't let these people see I was upset, wouldn't blub. And I wouldn't, I absolutely wouldn't, call them Aunty and Uncle. I curled up in my coat under the thin eider-down and tried to sleep but the mattress smelt of mildew. And, as the room grew dark, a pixie-faced moon leered through the curtainless window.

You get up from that bed now, girl. I ain't be here to wait on you. The woman was standing at the side of my bed in her tweed coat, shaking my shoulder. There be a cup of tea and some bread and dripping on the kitchen table. You can mind the babby while I see to the hens. I hope you're not going to be bothersome, now. I don't have the time.

I washed my face in the cold water from the jug on the washstand and went downstairs in the thin dawn light without changing my clothes. The flagstone floor felt cold through my flimsy plimsolls. The woman was standing at the stone sink scrubbing potatoes, a row of muddy overalls hanging on a wooden pulley above the unlit range, where a pair of wolfish dogs sat waiting for some heat. On the deal table the innards of a shotgun lay spread out on a filthy sheet of newspaper beside a black frying pan caked with bacon grease. In the corner a snot-encrusted toddler sat grizzling in a battered high chair.

That be Billy, the woman said. You can mind him.

Mrs Willock directed me to a pair of wellingtons in the porch, telling me to take the child to fetch some eggs. I slipped my bare legs inside, afraid of spiders. They were cold and damp.

The coop's down the far end of the field, she indicated with a nod.

The wellingtons were too big and I kept getting stuck in the mud, while Billy trailed after me, snivelling, weighed down by his shitty nappy, his scruffy pyjamas stuffed into his boots. It was barely light.

Is this the right way, Billy? Can you show me what to do?

I thought of the eggs from Robinson's dairy on the corner of Roman Road that Mum bought in a cardboard box. But these were warm and streaked with limey shit. Billy stuck his arm into one of the nesting boxes and pulled a brown egg out of the straw, putting it in the white enamel basin, careful not to crack it. We needed six before we could go back to the house. I was frightened of the hens scratching around my feet in the dirt. They seemed so big. There were also a couple of bantams, one of which, Joey, was Billy's special pet. He picked it up, holding it close to feed it tufts of groundsel, chatting to it all the while, then, although I was a bit scared, I did the same with a big brown hen, hugging her against my grubby cardigan. She sat in my arms staring at me with her beady, red-rimmed eyes from under her fleshy crown, her bones hollow as straws under her fluffed-out feathers.

Before being evacuated the only chickens I'd ever seen were the scrawny white bundles, their featherless necks dangling over the side of a table, dripping blood onto the cobblestones from Mrs Feinstein's stall in Wentworth Street Market. Wentworth Street was where the Jews shopped. From time to time a man in a skull cap with a long white beard and bloodstained apron came out, a pair of hens hanging by their legs in one hand, a sharp knife in the other. If flush, Mum would buy one of these birds for our Sunday dinner as a special treat. Mrs

Feinstein was friendly and didn't seem to mind *goyim* or non-Jews like us. And Mum said it was worth it because you always knew the meat was fresh, and afterwards could make soup, so spending the extra made sense. I remember her clutching her old leather purse, haggling over the price of the giblets. When we took the chicken home, its skinny neck swinging loosely above the pavement, it would be me who had to pull out the stray feathers from the pimply flesh that Mrs Feinstein had missed.

Still it wasn't light, the sky heavy with rain. Overhead a cloud of wild geese honked eerily in the early autumn mist. I released the struggling brown hen and began to cry.

What the matter? Billy asked.

I hate these chickens. I hate the mud and this place. I want to go home. I want to be with my mum and nan, I wept, wiping my nose on the sleeve of my cardigan. Then, grabbing Billy by the hand, I picked up the bowl of eggs and squelched back to the cottage. It was my job to give him breakfast.

Was it the right thing to do? Evacuation was aimed at working-class families like mine. 'Cheerful little cockneys' from densely populated inner cities. Most of us hadn't a clue what was happening as we were labelled like pieces of luggage and separated from our parents, from all we knew. We thought we were going on an adventure but things would never be the same again.

You'll be back in a week. Have a nice holiday. The weather's glorious.

But it was an eternity. By the time I returned I was no longer Freda but Frith. The secret name you'd given me.

But it must have been hard for the Willocks. I realize that now. I was an inconvenience they could ill afford in war time. The new Milk Marketing Board had promised small milk producers like Mr Willock a better deal, but, he railed, all they did was help the middleman. I didn't know it then, but they didn't even own their smallholding. It was rented from the Land Settlement Association.

And it was remote, even by the standards of that remote corner of England. Cabbage, beet and kale. A few cows and hens. Mr Willock also helped with odd jobs on other farms to make ends meet. Mending fences. Lambing in spring. Work was always uncertain. Dropping and treading potatoes into the narrow trenches he could put in 1,000 a day. But five shillings was all he got for his troubles. Part of a formidable Romany clan from up north, his father mended pots and pans, while his mother, Leviathan, had been known to spot a pheasant on its nest and trap both bird and eggs under her wide skirts. When Stan Willock was a child, she'd caught sparrows in a clap-net, painting them yellow and selling them as canaries in King's Lynn market, while a team of uncles with exotic names—Dolphus, Esau and Bendigo—scraped a living on the land with the help of a catapult and a bit of snare wire, netting small birds for food.

But it was poaching that kept food on Stan Willock's table. It was even more risky in the spring. If he were caught carrying a gun in the closed season, he'd be in for it. Early morning he'd set snares by the marsh wall, then later wander down to see if he'd caught anything for dinner. With luck, there might be a hare. Rabbits were rarer along the bank. And he gathered samphire out on the far mud with his mate Charlie, selling it in bundles for pickle making. It wasn't easy to reach. The creeks filled quickly, cutting you off. And though he hated having to do so, he did odd jobs for other farmers like Mackman down by the East Lighthouse, clearing out dykes on the farm boundary. It was a dirty work. The black slime was full of clots of frogspawn, wriggling eels and bulbous red roots that stank when he tossed them up onto the bank, smothering the early violets. At noon, he'd sit on the old bridge and have a smoke, eat the bread and slices of cold bacon fat he'd brought wrapped in a dirty cloth.

School had barely left its mark. The attendance officer had been a regular at his mother's door but was usually sent away with a flea in his ear. She would beat the living daylights out of her own but was buggered if any outsider was going to tell her what to do with her children. Willock was nabbed countless times for pelting telegraph wires while stoning sparrows or stealing pears from a neighbour's orchard.

The marsh villages were full of flight-netters and punt-gunners scratching a living in winter from shooting and snaring wildfowl. Willock's career began aged twelve when he and Ernie Burton went to work on Fred Morris's farm. Old Morris gave him the job of scaring rooks off the corn with an ancient muzzle-loader, but the rusty gun was too slow for Willock. Next day Ernie mentioned that he'd spied a single-barrel shotgun in one of Fred's sheds.

Why don't you snitch the darn thing, then? Willock suggested.

The following morning Ernie showed up with the gun wrapped in an old sack. Plus a box of cartridges, a red hand holding a lightning bolt painted on the lid. They took the gun to the field on the far side of Fred's land to try her out and she went better than they could have hoped. Afterwards, they wrapped it back in the sacking, and hid it in a tunnel in the dyke.

Then Ernie spotted another shotgun in Arthur Porter's shed. It's as full of rust as hell's full of davils, but there for the taking.

That night Willock squeezed through the narrow window and fished out the gun, emerging in a veil of cobwebs, before secreting it in his father's pigsty.

It was pitch black and blowing half a gale when the boys made their way across Morris's stubbles, blundering every now and again into a roosting pheasant or a jugging covey of partridges. In the middle of the field they stopped to fire three barrels but when they crept over to collect their kill there wasn't a single feather. After another three rounds they packed it in, nervous the noise would bring PC Watson pedalling down the sea wall from Sutton Bridge with a column of reinforcements following behind and sneaked the stolen gun back to the shed. But when PC Watson didn't show up, Willock suggested another outing.

This time we'll do things different, he said. This time I'll be in charge.

As dusk fell, they crept down to the Nene outfall where, hidden by a belt of trees, he called a halt.

Pheasants, he hissed, letting rip the old single barrel. Then out of the night, something landed with a thud.

After that he was never at home. During the nesting season his mother made endless jugs of pigeon's-egg custard, and he and Ernie would go hotching for hedgehogs, turning them over and rubbing them on their backs till they stuck out their noses. Then they'd knock them out, bleed them and burn off the spines, before splitting them down the middle to roast on a pile of glowing twigs.

But his real love was guns.

How do I know all this? Well though Mr Willock never spoke to me much he liked to brag about his exploits, and I was a captive audience. He'd sit at the kitchen table while I scrubbed the grease-blackened frying pan in the stone sink, oiling the mechanism of his gun that lay broken open on a sheet of newspaper. Often, I'd be alone with him and Billy, Mrs Willock having gone to her charring job or, on Saturdays, to Gostling the butcher's, where she scrubbed the bloody counters for a shilling's worth of meat. Of course, I didn't actually witness his escapades. But, often, it felt as though I had.

We didn't mix much with the locals. The Willocks' cottage sat someway outside the village, which wasn't a friendly place. The school was too small for all the extra children. The local kids attended lessons in the morning, while we evacuees went for a few hours in the afternoon. Anyway, their accents were so thick that half the time we hadn't a clue what they were on about, so there was no love lost between us.

A little gang of us used to meet by the sluice on the big dyke after our morning jobs, a heel of bread or an apple stuffed in our pockets. Bert from his farm, and the Tucker twins, in their short trousers and gumboots, from theirs; Molly White, whose dad worked in the coal merchant's in Dalston but who was younger than me and in a different class. It was a long walk. The teachers kept the afternoon register open to give us time to get there but in bad weather we often arrived soaked, and by the time we went home again, it would be dark.

The school wasn't anything like ours in Bethnal Green where Miss Wilson read us stories before we put on our coats to go home. I was naturally left-handed and Mrs Bint bent my arm up behind my back, ordering me to write with my right hand. And I was set upon by the other girls, called Rails because of my skinny arms and legs. I'd hide in the cloakroom, but they'd find me. Lift up my dress and laugh at my puny thighs poking out of my baggy knickers, pulling them down to see if I had hair 'down there'. There were three, in particular, who frightened the life out of me.

You dirty cockneys think you're better than anybody else. But you're not. You stink and have nits. Why don't you go back where you came from? We don't want you here taking our food.

Bert, who'd never have given me the time of day at home, was the person I stayed closest to. I walked with him whenever I could. He seemed to relish the role of guardian and liked to put the wind up the younger kids.

Y'know there's a ghost down on the fens? Down where the beginning of the water is, by that broken boat house. They say an old man killed 'is missus there. Drowned her dead or somefink and there was a little white dog looking for her all the time, but the missus never come back. And Mr Williams, where I'm billeted, he says that in the old coal yard some men came to nick some anthracite but somefink come along the top of the wall and there were some dogs and they were scared and barked, and the men legged it and everyone reckoned it were the devil.

One afternoon after the going-home bell sounded, we trailed out of the school playground, dragging our coats and satchels behind us, to find a group of boys waiting in ambush behind the cattle shed. Pelting us with dried cow pats filled with stones, they swore and shouted at us to go back where we'd come from. Then they tried to catch us and shove dung down our collars. I got away. Billy fought back and got a bloody nose, but they caught Milly, the littlest of our group, by the sleeve of her cardigan.

Cry-baby, cry-baby, 'ankerchief for the cry-baby, they jeered, until she became hysterical.

None of us knew what was happening at home. Bert had a letter from his dad who said that within a few nights of war being declared the London skies lit up with searchlights sweeping the city, looking for German aircraft. So far there hadn't been any, but our planes were constantly practising overhead for what was expected any day now. And the government had demanded that all street lights be switched off or dimmed. Traffic lights and vehicle headlights had to be fitted with special slotted covers. Bert's dad said he'd stood on the bank of the Thames by Tower

Bridge watching the lights being snuffed out across the city until there was just one left, twinkling over on the South Bank, down Bermondsey way. Then that went out too.

It were bleeding dark, he said. They'd painted white stripes on the pavements to stop people from going arse over tit. But everyone kept bumping into each other trying to find the door to the bloody pub. And the phone box? Well, he'd walked straight into that, hadn't he? Had got a right ocean liner. And the bobbies' capes had been dipped in luminous paint, so they looked like bloody Dracula. It was, he said, a bloomin' tea leaf's paradise out there.

And his mum, Bert said, had been making blackout curtains. Everyone had to or you'd cop it from one of the air-raid wardens if light leaked out. His mum had received a leaflet. Leaflet No. 2, giving due warning, he explained. You had to stick brown tape on the windows to prevent being cut to shreds by the flying glass. The splinters could kill you with one strike, he warned gravely, like King Harold getting an arrow in his eye at the Battle of Hastings.

I was missing more and more school. Mrs Willock kept me back, saying she needed help to mind Billy. There were always jobs. Fetching logs, collecting eggs, pegging out washing in the orchard while the morning mist rose over the black fields. No one seemed to care whether I went to school or not. No one said anything. Even though the local children made fun of me, I missed sitting huddled by the stove while they played in the yard. I hated chasing games, could never run fast enough to find a door or fence to 'touch wood', but I liked the quiet of the empty classroom, reading about how the Romans came to Britain and built straight roads.

It was three miles to the post office. Mrs Willock got 10s 6d from the government for having me. It must have been a fortune for them. No wonder they wanted me. I dragged Billy's pushchair across the fields, the wheels churning in the muddy furrows, the air thick with mizzle, scared I'd meet the man-woman. The one with whiskers growing out of her chin. She frightened the life out of me, mumbling nonsense under her breath as she carried a bucket of pigswill up to her sow.

The postmistress looked suspicious when I gave her Mrs Willock's note asking for the money. I had to wrap it in a strip of material, stick it in my knickers so as not to lose the ten bob note and tanner, then hand it straight over when I got in. It was only later I learnt that Mum had sent me a package with a warm vest and an extra pair of socks, and that Mrs Willock had sold them.

On the way back, I took a short cut through the spinney. I wasn't sure of the way, but where the path split I took the left fork and bumped into it stretched across the track: a gamekeeper's line of hanging pigeons, stoats and magpies, their decomposing bodies stiff with rigor mortis, their paws and claws curled like little arthritic hands. Pinioned to the trunk of a nearby elm was a dead crow, its wings nailed open like two shiny black fans. All night I lay in bed wondering who'd do such a horrible thing, thinking about those sooty feathers, those mummified silhouettes. Later, I learnt it was a gamekeeper's gibbet. Proof to landowners that their employees were doing their job. Though Stan Willock might have said it were no more than a warning to those other darned vermin to 'mind their noses'.

I'd just come out of the spinney and was pushing Billy across the corrugated furrows when, suddenly, they came out of nowhere like a pair of great black birds. Two planes, swooping so low I could see the swastikas painted on the underside of their wings. I stood stock still in the middle of that turnip field, terrified, while Billy sat in his pushchair sucking on his bottle of cold tea. Then, just as quickly as they'd appeared, they turned and flew off into the distance.

Was this it? Was this the war? Had anyone else seen them? Would they hit Bethnal Green, Mum and Nan? Next day, in school, there were rumours that they hadn't made it through to London.

This morning there aren't any birds on my bird table, though I've put out the crusts from my breakfast toast as usual. The carers have just brought round our elevenses. Tea or coffee. Garibaldis and chocolate Bourbons. At teatime we're spoilt with home-made cake. Coffee and walnut is my favourite. Though I do like a nice Victoria sponge. I'm lucky I've always been thin. Can eat what I want. Just as well as I have a sweet tooth and usually have a packet of mint Polos in my cardigan pocket. But as sins go, it's better than many.

The staff are getting ready for our little celebration. There'll be cucumber sandwiches. Red, white and blue cupcakes. They're good like that. Make an effort. Most afternoons there are activities of one sort or another. Jade's art class. Flower arranging and singing. Singing is supposed to be good for those whose memories are going. It seems to perk them up. They all seem to remember the words of 'Tea for Two' even when they don't know what day of the week it is. I join in for the company but am really happiest in my room, writing in my little journal. Reading and remembering. Still, it's hard to believe that Dunkirk was really seventy-five years ago. The carers say, you must have such wonderful memories. They mean it kindly, of course, as if memories are a source of solace. A badge of honour. How could they possibly know that I've been haunted by what-ifs and might-have-beens all these long years? That longing has been my constant companion? Stories are created from silence and absence, though the space between words can be so wide you feel you might drown.

A T OXFORD Philip joined numerous clubs and societies, made a concerted effort to get to know people, but the Liberal Debating Society was just talk-talk-talk. As for the Conservative Club, well, all those old Etonians with their Bullingdon Club manners, vandalizing pubs and college rooms, had no idea how most people lived, and the Labour Party was too full of communists. He did, though, rather like the Fabians with their reformist tendencies and notions of improvement through public service. A democracy based on liberty and human rights. One afternoon in London he attended a meeting in Essex Hall just off the Strand and heard the Indian politician, Jawaharlal Nehru, give a lecture. He was impressed.

He rowed with his college eight. Went nude bathing in the Cherwell's Parson's Pleasure and attended sherry parties with his tutor. Joined the Inklings that met each Monday evening in the Eagle and Child, known locally as the Bird and Baby. There he got to know Clive Staples Lewis and John Tolkien, arguing with them about faith over a pint of best bitter. Clive, known as Jack to his friends, claimed that when he became an atheist at the age of fifteen, he was furious with God for not existing, realizing that from then on he'd have to be responsible for everything that happened to him, that there'd be no one else to blame, no one to intercede on his behalf or make things better. But the meetings weren't all serious. They took it in turns to read the latest stories in *Woman's Weekly* out loud, seeing who'd corpse first at the purple prose of 'All Loveliness is Hers' or 'Home at Last'. He signed up for the radical Student Christian Movement. Every other Sunday they met to discuss social justice and spirituality. There were those of secure faith and those of none. He liked its ecumenical approach; the tea and Battenberg weren't bad either. There was much discussion as to the merits of Methodism and other Low Church denominations, compared with the smells and bells of High Anglicanism which, some argued, were integral to the religious experience.

It was at one of those meetings that he met Peter and Jess McKenna. Jess was the one interested in the SCM and had dragged her reluctant, handsome brother along to keep her company. Peter was tall, slender and blond, with narrow shoulders and hips; Jess, a compact redhead with translucent, freckled skin. With only eighteen months between them, brother and sister were inseparable. Peter was reading philosophy at Christ Church. Jess studying English at Lady Margaret Hall.

Their mother was a friend of the social reformers and Fabians, Beatrice and Sydney Webb, as well as Nehru, with whom Philip had been so impressed during that talk in Essex Hall. Apparently Nehru was a frequent guest at their rambling Holland Park home when in London. At the end of his first term Philip was invited down to stay for Peter's birthday. The house was a shambles. A clutter of Clarice Cliff teapots, Omega Workshop rugs and smelly Siamese cats. A Vanessa Bell hung in the hall next to a small Samuel Palmer etching. There seemed to be no domestic regime that he could discern. Breakfast might be at lunchtime. Tea when you felt like it. Peter's mother wafting around most of the day in a Japanese silk kimono embroidered with dragons. His father lying in a frayed sweater with leather elbow patches on the chaise longue among the potted geraniums in the conservatory, reading Freud.

Peter and Jess became regulars for tea in Philip's Keble rooms. They had buttered crumpets toasted on a long brass fork in front of the gas fire. Raspberry jam. Peter liked to flaunt his wit and intellect, self-consciously crossing and uncrossing his long rumpled trouser legs as he leant forward to crush out his cigarette butt in the saucer of the Limoges teacup Philip had inherited from his grandmother. Jess was the more naturally talkative of the two, speaking enthusiastically about women's education and healthcare, the need for contraception and the end to backstreet abortions. She complained that women were outnumbered by men at the university, yet had to be twice as good. Pacifism and Christianity, she insisted, were, for her, inseparable.

If I weren't a pacifist I wouldn't have any time for Christianity, she said, licking at the melting butter dripping down her chin. War's been tried over and over and always fails miserably, she said, leaning back in her chair and raising her arms above her head, so Philip could see her small breasts pressing against her thin muslin blouse. That it brings out the best in a man is simply a lie, she continued. It just harnesses the best to the vilest and most immoral of ends.

Philip, you goose, look, you've dribbled jam all down your tie.

*

May. The sun was high, the sky blue the afternoon they rode their bikes down to the Vicky Arms to go punting. Philip tied the punt to a branch in the dappled shade of a weeping willow, then lay back on the green cushions, trailing his hand in the serrated leaf patterns stencilled on the dark water. They discussed atheism and free love, and Peter announced that he fancied becoming a don.

I wouldn't mind being paid to read Plato and dine at high table, followed by a good bottle of port, in return for teaching a few jejune first years a couple of hours a week. Better than going down the pits!

Jess, on the other hand, said she might stand for Parliament after finals in order to legislate for equal pay for women. Of course, she probably wouldn't get in, but it might be worth a try. The House needed a few women to buck it up. Bring it kicking and screaming into the twentieth century. How else were things going to change? Her red hair was tied up in an untidy bun and Philip imagined how she'd look when she took out the pins. The wave of copper falling round her pale freckled shoulders, like Rossetti's Lizzie Siddal. Jess was the sort of girl he should marry.

After she left to cycle back to college for a tutorial, Peter came back to his room and they lay on the floor smoking a packet of Sobranie Black Russians that he'd acquired from some exotic friend, blowing smoke rings into the warm evening air to mingle with the smell of lilac drifting in through the window from the quad below. There was an élan about Peter that Philip knew he could never emulate. Lying side by side on the rug, deep in discussion about Plato's *Symposium*, he suddenly leant over and kissed Philip hard on the mouth. Philip was stunned and said nothing, not knowing what to say. It was his first kiss. That night he lay in bed, his heart racing, imagining Peter's legs wrapped around his own. His stubbled cheek and wet mouth moving slowly down his naked stomach. They began to meet up without Jess. Peter would cycle over, smoke, and lie on the battered sofa drinking mugs of cocoa, while Philip sat at his desk finishing his essay. Then, one evening he sauntered over and undid Philip's shirt, slipping his hand inside, before unbuttoning his own. Peter's skin was milky white and hairless, and his small hard nipples took Philip's breath away. It was Philip's first time and he was terribly shy. It wasn't Peter's and he was not.

They spent the rest of the term together until it all began to feel too complicated. Philip was worried he was coming between brother and sister. Peter was so demanding, and Philip over-whelmed with guilt, terrified someone would find out what was going on between them. When he told Peter, he just laughed. Philip had thought he was falling for Jess; then this. He didn't know what he wanted, was afraid Peter would swamp him. He couldn't struggle with this emotional maelstrom while struggling with a fading vocation.

No, he was happiest alone. Down on Port Meadow on a misty morning watching the ruddy shelducks and shovelers gathering on the flooded mudflats. Where, if he was lucky, he might see a peregrine.

Home from prep school one half-term, he'd watched the Women's Peacemakers' Pilgrimage converge on London. Women from towns and villages all across England had marched to Speakers' Corner to declare their pacifism from the top of soapboxes. It was the first time he'd heard anyone speak out against war. More recently he'd slipped into a couple of lectures given by the charismatic Dick Sheppard, vicar of St Martin-in-the Fields, where he'd signed the Peace Pledge. His mother never knew.

During his last term at Oundle there'd been a debate at the Oxford Union. The motion that 'This House Will Under No Circumstances Fight for Its King and Country' was carried by 275 votes to 153. His housemaster had sided with Churchill who denounced the result as spineless. At assembly the following morning, the head read out an article from the *Daily Telegraph*, no doubt as a deterrent to any wavering pacifists in their midst, calling those who'd given the motion their support, 'woozy-minded Communists' and 'sexual indeterminates'. White feathers were sent to those who had supported the motion, which the head considered little more than the cowards deserved. But Philip was heartened to be going to a university where such views were freely expressed.

In the Warneford he kept a diary, sat on the wrought-iron loggia in the pale morning sun trying to make sense of his confusion. He wouldn't fight. He'd decided that as a boy and wouldn't go back on it now. He may have lost his faith but not his belief in pacifism. Weeks before, the vicar in Headington, where he was still half-heartedly attending Sunday services, had been preaching peace. Now he was preaching war. Had God really changed his mind so quickly? His mother had always tried to pretend that his father's death had been heroic. But it hadn't been. It had been pointless. Nothing made sense. Not God. Not this coming war. He wanted no part in any of it. He knew he wasn't alone, that many felt the same, that there were solid economic and political arguments for the pursuit of international peace. The British Empire had reached its peak by 1918. Surely there was no real desire for further territorial gains? The fragile economy had everything to lose from another conflict and there seemed little appetite for reliving the horrors of the Great War. There'd be no winners. Only losers. Nothing but suffering and ruin. Even the King had slammed his fist on his desk, declaring that he wouldn't tolerate another war, that the last one had been none of his doing and, if there were to be another and we were threatened with being brought into it, he'd put on his coat and personally go down to Trafalgar Square to wave a red flag in protest.

All Philip wanted now was to paint. To be far away from Oxford. And maybe it would never happen. Maybe Hitler would be satisfied with the *Anschluss* of Austria and the Sudetenland. After all, he was a veteran of the Great War. Why would he want more carnage? Hadn't he promised that he had no ambitions for Germany? Philip's Oxford friend Piers Wainwright had spent the previous summer in Germany and been impressed by its cleanliness, order and modernity. By the scantily dressed German students he'd met out hiking in the mountains or sunbathing unselfconsciously naked beside lakes and pools. He hadn't described a country planning for war. But even if we were to fight, how could we possibly stop Germany from taking Poland when we had so few resources? We had been hit by a sharp global economic downturn after the Great War and that had led to high unemployment and widespread poverty. We didn't have either the funds or the hardware to counter the Luftwaffe's Me109s and Stukas. It would be another bloodbath. Chamberlain was right. We had to preserve what we believed in without recourse to war. Negotiation. That was the only decent thing to do. It could all be over by Christmas.

He knew that after his breakdown he wouldn't be conscripted, would be declared unfit. There was a greater tolerance now towards conscientious objectors. Most wouldn't face the long prison sentences handed out in the Great War. But he didn't want to be exempt just because they thought him a loony. He wanted to appear before a tribunal. Make his case and register his disapproval at yet more armed combat. Still, lying in bed at night, he was assailed by misgivings. He'd read that for Jews and gypsies, Germany was becoming an increasingly horrific place. He knew he was being inconsistent in his support for the struggle against fascism in Spain while demanding pacifism at home. A group of Oxford friends had gone to fight with the Republicans or to be stretcher-bearers and ambulance drivers. But was armed force always the best solution? An endless chain of military murder, countered by yet more murder? By taking a stand he would, he knew, be cutting himself off even further from his mother and Pemberton. But his conscience was all he had.

*

He'd heard of a pacifist community at Frating Hall Farm in Essex that had been set up by the writers John Middleton Murry and Vera Brittain. Unmarked on any map, they were farming an impressive 370 acres of potatoes and cabbages. For a while he thought of joining them, but a friend of Jess and Peter's who'd spent the previous summer there had reported on a volatile mix of Quakers, Plymouth Brethren, Catholics and anarchists. With a handful of vegetarians, bicycle-club enthusiasts, Esperantists and nudists thrown in for good measure. They even had, according to the McKennas' friend, their own self-professed satanist.

No, he couldn't cope with all those people. All that drama. He was better off on his own.

He wasn't sure why he chose Lincolnshire, but he had to go somewhere. He decided on a whim. It was clear his mother was never going to collect him from the Warneford. He had a recollection, after his father's death, of visiting his grandparents in a large house near King's Lynn. Of a grandfather clock ticking into a silent hall and a mosaic tile floor like something out of a Roman villa. There'd been a large wooden stand full of umbrellas and shooting sticks and his grandmother, dressed in black like a character from a nineteenth-century novel, had wandered around the house rearranging her Staffordshire porcelain dogs. And there'd been Rufus. The sandy Labrador who'd kept him company. They'd taken long walks together across the Fens to watch the Snettisham Spectacular. It had been quite a sight. The incoming tide washing in over the vast mudflats, forcing tens of thousands of wading birds to take flight until there was no more mud left for them to land on and they came to rest on the sand on the other side of the lagoon.

In London he was called before a tribunal. The judge registered him as a conscientious objector. This meant he was put on a military register for duties with the Non-Combatant Labour Corps and had to undertake foot drill (without arms) and physical training, as well as anti-gas and decontamination procedures. It wasn't the prospect of the work he would be assigned that bothered him but the whole ersatz military set-up. He just couldn't bear it. So, taking his cue from a couple of the other men up before the judge the same morning as him, he decided to leg it.

The promised allowance from Pemberton hadn't yet come through but he had just enough money to pay for a train ticket from King's Cross to King's Lynn. The London train was packed with troops. Young soldiers with acne and a Woodbine stuck behind each ear. Lads who'd never been further than five miles from home. Wreathed in cheap cigarette smoke, they took little notice of him as they joked and joshed, belting out 'Run Rabbit Run', whooping each time the word 'rabbit' was replaced by Hitler. He found a space by the lavatory and sat on the floor huddled on his rucksack, hoping that no one would ask him where he was going and why.

From King's Lynn he walked, for no particular reason, towards Sutton Bridge. Down small roads and along empty lanes, with no clear idea which direction to take. He couldn't remember exactly where his grandparents had lived. Anyway, they were dead and the place long since sold. With the last of his money he paid for a cheap room at the back of the Anchor

Inn that looked over a yard where a Suffolk Punch was stamping its big, feathered hooves, while the publican unloaded kegs of ale for the public bar.

He hoped to find some farm work, clearing ditches, draining the land. He knew that the local farmers needed labour with so many of the able-bodied drafted, and out here few would bother to ask any questions. He sought employment on small holdings among local labourers and Land Girls. Sometimes there'd be forty people working a single potato field. While pulling beets one wet morning, the gang master had lifted his horsewhip to him, cursing him for being a toff and a conchie shirker. It was a German internee who intervened, standing between him and the turkey-necked man till he calmed down. A teacher at the grammar school in Norwich until a few weeks earlier, he was, Fritz Müller told Philip, married to an English girl.

They're frightened I might be a spy, but I've never done anything more dangerous than teach Goethe. I'm worried, though. My wife Annie's pregnant. I don't know if she's all right. She's gone back to her parents' in Birmingham. There've been complications. High blood pressure. Swollen ankles. That sort of thing.

After hearing of the disturbance, the landlord at the Anchor threw Philip out, though he'd paid for another week. With no more money and nowhere to go, he slept in ditches and barns. Ate windfalls. Stole biscuits from a farm dog's dish, apologizing to the dog for taking its food. After an uncomfortable night under a hedge, he woke to find a face, framed by a mat of grey hair, peering at him. It belonged to Tom. A man of the road. A tramp. Tom sat on the bank and offered him a mouthful of cold sweet tea from his jerrycan. It tasted vile but, Philip realized, he'd come closer to being a beggar than a chooser. A one-time docker, Tom's arm had been crushed in an accident and he'd never worked again. Had been on the road ever since.

Here boy, take another swig. You don't look the type for this. Me? The road's home now. Beats the fleas and other men's fucking farts in a doss house, he said, standing up and brushing the twigs off his tattered coat before heading north.

Philip was standing on the embankment watching a marsh harrier flying silent and owl-like over the saltings when a red-faced man came past on a rusty bicycle. He might have been from any of the marshland villages. From Gedney Drove End, Lutton or Holbeach St Marks. These marshland people were tough. Descendants of those who'd once lived on islands in an inland sea that stretched nearly to Cambridge. The Dutch, who'd drained the fens three hundred years earlier, had barely convinced them that they were connected by dry land or had any allegiance to the rest of England. They'd lived by fishing and snaring. Shooting the clouds of wildfowl that flocked to the inland sea in winter. Much as many still did.

Willock slowed, dismounted his bicycle and offered Philip a wary 'good day'. His heavy tweed coat was tied with baler twine and rough ginger bristles sprouted from his upper lip and chin. He obviously wanted to find out what this stranger was doing walking alone along the sea wall with a bag slung over his shoulder. He asked a few pointed questions but already seemed to know that Philip had been kicked out of the pub. A fact he appeared to find amusing.

Did he, Philip asked, know of any work going? Preferably where there might be a bed thrown in. Willock thought there might be a couple of days to be had down at Sutton Bridge unloading timber from one of the deal boats tied up along the pier. The schooners carried coals and pig iron. Almost anything, in fact, that needed transporting around the British Isles. Or he could try Mackman down by the East Lighthouse. He was about to start drilling peas and might need some help.

Philip didn't bother with the timber yard but went straight to Mackman, who offered him work there and then. What's more, he said, there were two lighthouses down on the mouth of the Nene. The East one was on his land and had been empty for a long time. It was damp and cold, but Philip could lodge there if he had a mind, in lieu of wages. He'd throw in dinner, too, on the days he worked. Nothing fancy, mind. But it'd keep the wolf from the door. And no one would bother him there. He had an old Valor stove he could lend him to keep warm as it could get pretty nippy. The lighthouses had been built, he explained, to commemorate the draining of the Great Fens. The entrance to the Nene provided an important navigation route. Although there were no rocks, the lamps were lit after dark to guide the ships through the sandbanks into the river, which rose and fell thirty feet at low tide, exposing the soft mud. An officer stationed at Sutton Bridge, three miles upriver, would arrive on his bicycle with a megaphone half an hour before high water to hail the ships entering or leaving. Each lighthouse had a half-moon window, north facing on the west bank, and south on the East Lighthouse, so that any ship picking up either of the side lights knew it was not in the channel. The place needed a good clear out, Mackman added, but it was quite spacious.

Terrington Marsh. Philip checked the map. He could see the East Lighthouse at the end of the small promontory jutting out into the saltings. He followed the river from the swing bridge along the road and railway, past a handful of smallholdings and cottages. At first the road was metalled, then it gave way to little more than a grassy sea wall. Where wall and riverbank met, there was a broken gate and a path that led to the East Lighthouse. It had been constructed in the most desolate of places, three miles out into the tidal marshes, built from rendered brick with a rounded lead roof and central hexagonal stack topped by a lantern. A hundred yards across the water was its double, the West Lighthouse.

He pushed against the heavy door. It wasn't locked and gave way on its corroded hinges. The place was a litter of fishing nets, buoys and broken storm lanterns. Rusted winches and bits of boat engine. There were four storeys, the round rooms all connected by a spiral staircase, the highest reached by a steep ladder. He dropped his canvas bag and scrambled to the top. The uppermost was little more than six feet across, strewn with cobwebs and bat droppings. Just big enough, he estimated, for a bed. He wiped the grimy porthole with his sleeve, peering out through the guano-covered glass onto a patchwork of streams and tidal creeks meandering across the empty lagoon, towards the sea. The winter sky was huge. In the gathering dusk he could see wigeon and redshanks, sandpipers and curlews picking their way through the salt pools in search of molluscs.

He found a pile of old sacking. It smelt rank but he bedded down for the night using his bag as a pillow, falling into an exhausted sleep. He had to be up early. There was a pile of dung and ash to shovel onto Mackman's field before the wheat stubble could be ploughed in to plant peas. And Mackman had asked him to clear a small patch, overgrown with tufts of couch grass, brambles and weeds that he wanted to put down to turnips. It would be tough work. He hoped he'd be up to it.

He woke to a finger of sun creeping across the sill and, stiff from a night on the floor, climbed out of his makeshift bed. From the small window he could see the saltings shimmering a gun-metal grey in the early mist. The lonely silence was broken only by the cry of wildfowl. He went to his bag and broke off a lump of stale bread. Then climbed down the ladder. The water in the pump outside was icy. Too cold to wash more than his neck and ears. Later, after a day's work and some food, he'd begin to sort the place out. Boil some water for a shave, start to think about painting.

Mrs Willock hardly spoke to me. There was a coldness about her I didn't understand, as though I'd done something wrong. She was bad tempered with Billy too. Scolding him for hanging round her legs and whining for her to lift up her woolly jumper to give him the breast while she was doing the washing or wringing the wet laundry through the heavy iron mangle. She didn't speak much to Mr Willock either. Or he to her. And, as he barely spoke to me except to tell me of his hunting exploits, my days passed largely in silence if I wasn't at school or minding Billy. She'd bang down her husband's tripe and mash on the kitchen table. Moan at him to take off his muddy boots when he came in for his tea. Mostly he just ignored her, though she worked just as hard as he did. If she wasn't charring or doing Saturdays at the butcher's, she was pulling beets or pegging rugs. The draper in the village let her have his old sample books for a few pence and she'd be sitting there till two in the morning pulling off the sticky labels from the back to use the strips for pegging. Her fingers were worn to the bone from the imprint of the scissors.

Looking back, I realize that she was only young, but she seemed like an old woman to me then.

Nothing was easy. Even to go to the shops was a long trek out over the fen bank, carting all the shopping back on foot. And in winter, it was terrible. There were no hard roads. I remember slipping and getting a clip round the ear for dropping a bag of sugar that split open in the mud, and Mr Willock cycling up to the village and carrying back all our paraffin for the lamps on the handlebars of his bike. Often the pump didn't work. So we had to collect water from the rain butt or, if that was dry, from the River Nene that ran into the Wash.

The last shrivelled blackberries were dangling on the briars, and the grass along the banks was turning yellow. In the low fields, the broad bean pods had become black with the first frost. And the war? Where was the war? Nothing seemed to be happening. There were no bombs. No raids. I tried to make sense of the headlines in the *News of the World* that Mr Willock left lying on the kitchen table after checking the racing results. I wasn't sure what it meant but something called a *blitzkrieg* had happened in Poland. I didn't know where Poland was. I was sure it wasn't in England. Nor did I understand why this *blitzkrieg*, whatever it was, meant that I had to go on living out here. As far as I could tell everything was just as it had always been. I'd seen those German planes that day when I'd been out in the fields on my way back from the post office and they'd given me the willies. But since then, nothing. A few children had even gone home to Bethnal Green: the twins and little Molly, who'd had complications from scarlet fever. An epidemic of strawberry tongues, followed by a livid rash, had run through the school like wildfire. Most children got better but Molly's had turned to rheumatic fever. I probably escaped because Mrs Willock kept me off school so much.

But what was the point of being stuck out in the middle of nowhere when there weren't any bombs? Night after night I went to bed in a state of anxiety. Maybe tonight it would happen. Maybe tonight Hitler would bomb Nan and Mum. There were rumours that the Germans were planning to hit the cathedral cities. Liverpool and Coventry. To get there they'd have to fly over us. Would the planes be like those I'd seen over the field? Had those been carrying bombs? They'd flown so low I could almost see the pilots' faces. But since then there'd been nothing. Nothing at all. The war was like the scarlet fever epidemic: a danger lurking out there, but one that we couldn't actually see. Maybe Mr Chamberlain was right. Maybe Hitler didn't really want a fight. I was preparing to write to Mum to ask if I could go home when the letter arrived.

The postman rarely stopped at the Willocks' but today he came cycling up the lane carrying a white envelope with a blue 2½d stamp with the King's face in the corner and Mum's writing on the front. I'd never had a proper letter before. Just birthday cards from Dad. I slipped it under my cardigan and took it up to my room to read in private. I had to read it twice before the news sank in.

Nan's death was my first great loss. I can't easily express now how it felt. As though my world had imploded. As if I'd been hit in the solar plexus and couldn't breathe. Sitting on my bed in that cold room, the letter spread open on my knee, I sat watching the silverfish scuttle across the floorboards while the light slowly dimmed, trying to contain my grief. No one came to see where I was. No one came to see if I was all right.

On my last birthday I was eighty-seven. How did that happen? How did I grow to be so much older than my nan? My nan who'd always been, in my mind, as ancient as Methuselah. Sitting here with my afternoon tea, my slice of coffee and walnut cake, looking out at the laburnum, I think, surely, there must be some mistake. Wasn't it only yesterday that I was curled up on her brass bed under the paisley eiderdown above our crammed shop in Roman Road? Only the other day that I was twelve and sent away to that cold place? A few years ago that I was in my forties, running a library and teaching children how to search the shelves for the latest *Famous Five* or information on Anne Boleyn. Where did these liver spots on the backs of my hands come from? The lines around my eyes? What happened to my hair? How come I can't trust my legs when I step off the kerb? Then I think about you and realize it's been more than seventy years. The truth is, we never expect to grow old. Secretly believing that old age is not something that will happen to us, that it's a condition that only affects others because they've simply been careless or inattentive. We learn about the world in childhood, then life is broken up by tenses. The past, the present and the future. Simple gestures such as stirring sugar into this cup of tea or the breeze lifting these flowered curtains at my open window can disturb a thousand forgotten fragments.

*

Mum said I couldn't go home. She wrote that there were posters everywhere showing Hitler whispering to mothers to take back their children. But it was a trick, she said. Printed across the posters in big red letters was the clear message: 'DON'T DO IT, MOTHER—LEAVE THE CHILDREN WHERE THEY ARE'.

And anyway, Freda, Mum wrote, how could I manage the shop as well as you with Nan gone? There'd be no one to keep an eye. It'd be too much to cope with. I'll try and come and see you soon. I promise, ducks. But it's a long way and hard to get trains now. I hope you're being a good girl. That you're fattening up with all that clean country air and fresh food.

I put on my coat and wellingtons and wandered down the lane, turning left at the sea wall. An east wind was blowing off the Wash and I turned up the collar of my flimsy coat against the chill, listening to the flocks of geese drifting on the water, waiting to come in under cover of darkness to feed on the potato fields. Thin clouds raced across the face of the moon rising on the horizon and, as I sat huddled on the bank, the future lay spread out in front of me, mute, grey and cold. As far as the eye could see, the marsh was empty with no perceptible difference between sky and water. I'd never felt so alone. Every creek, every blade of grass sang of my isolation. How was it possible for Nan just to vanish? For her simply to fade away like the blue night fades into pale morning.

The cottage didn't have any running water, electricity or gas. Mrs Willock cooked on an old coal-fired stove, and the kitchen was lit by ancient paraffin lamps that gave off acrid plumes of smoke. The toilet was at the bottom of the garden beyond the vegetable patch. A long walk in the coal-black dark when you could barely see your hand in front of your nose. I tried to hold on in the small hours, worried that I'd wet the bed and be scolded for being dirty, but I was afraid of the screech owls, and the scuttering creatures hidden in the shadowy undergrowth. And the door of the lavatory didn't close properly, had to be hooked up onto a nail with a piece of string to stop it flapping open, and the place smelt horrible.

It was wet and blustery when I made my way down the garden path in the first light. I'd had pains all night. Cramps that kept me awake; my knees drawn up under my chin in a ball of misery. I wondered if I'd eaten something. But since the letter from Mum I'd been off my food. When I got to the privy hidden behind the bolted cabbages and collapsing frame of runner beans, I checked that no one was about, went in and hooked the door on the latch, giving it a shove to wedge it shut with the big stone. I was in so much pain, I could hardly pull my knickers down but when I did, they were soaked crimson. I thought I must be dying. Maybe the shock about Nan had done something terrible to my innards. I imagined something nasty growing inside me, like the dry rot under the shop floor in Bethnal Green. Maybe I had cancer too and would die before I could go home. A blackberry stain seeped across the back of my nightie and I started to cry. There was no one to tell. No one to ask what to do. How could I wash my nightie and knickers without Mrs Willock knowing? She'd tell me I was a filthy cockney. Hadn't she already said, when I'd dropped an egg on the kitchen floor, that if she'd known what I'd be like she'd never have agreed to have me, that I was nothing but trouble. Though I never knew what I was supposed to have done wrong.

I pulled a couple of leaves of newspaper off the nail on the back of the door to mop up the blood that had run down my leg but it was already dry, so I stuck my hand in the bucket kept for emptying water down the privy and tried to wash between my legs, stuffing my bloody knickers with balls of scrunched-up newsprint. After I'd cleaned myself up as best I could, I moved the stone and opened the door, hoping no one would see me as I made my way back to the cottage, though the newspaper in my knickers made it difficult to walk. Luckily, Mrs Willock was down feeding the hens with Billy. And Mr Willock out somewhere on the land. I pulled the handle of the pump and tried to rinse the back of my nightie in the cold water, slipping off my knickers and plunging them into the bucket so the water swirled in a vortex of red. Afterwards I fished them out, screwed them in a ball, then hid them under my cardigan with the extra sheets of newspaper I'd filched from the privy. I slipped back, knickerless, to my room. No one came up there much so I hung them on the hook behind my towel, hoping they wouldn't be spotted before they dried.

The next few days were full of watchfulness and deceit. I calculated the best times to make forays to the privy and inter the bloody sheets of newspaper in the compost. I only had three pairs of knickers, so had to wash them in rotation. I was terrified someone would discover my dirty little secret but, by the end of the week, the bleeding had stopped, though it wasn't until a few months later that I realized this might be something I'd have to put up with on a regular basis.

I was desperate to see Mum. When I went to the post office to collect the allowance for Mrs Willock, I managed to send her a letter, pushing the brown envelope marked 'EVACUEE' over the counter to the curious postmistress. I spent ages writing it. I had to pinch the paper from school as I had none of my own. I didn't really know what to say, so simply wrote that I hoped she was keeping well, that everything was all right in the shop and, that although I knew she was very busy, I would really like it if she could find the time to come and see me. Then I licked the envelope and sealed it, knowing that I hadn't really said any of the things that I needed to say. It was ages before I heard back.

> Freda, I hope you're being a good girl, now, minding your ps and qs and helping Mrs Willock. How's school? I'll try and come, I promise. But it's hard, with no one to mind the shop. And now, with the petrol rationed, well it's even more difficult. The trains are packed, and it'll cost me. It's not that I mind. I'd like to see you, love, honest. But it's so far and I'm a bit nervous travelling all that way on my own.

Recently a group of parents had come from London on a special coach, but Mum hadn't been able to leave the shop and I'd been broken-hearted. Then, out of the blue, I got a postcard with a picture of Big Ben on the front. She'd be coming after all. The last Saturday in October. Our neighbour, Mrs Baker, had offered to mind the shop. Any later, she said, and the days would be drawing in and it'd be too dark to make the journey. Could I get to King's Lynn? She'd meet me outside the station at eleven o'clock. Then she could catch the ten minutes past two train back to Liverpool Street before the blackout.

It was Thursday afternoon. She was coming in two days and I still had no idea how I'd get to King's Lynn. There was nothing for it but for me to tell the Willocks. I was nervous they'd be angry. Say that I was trying to get out of my chores or, worse, that I'd complained about them. But, to my surprise, Mr Willock said he had to see a man about a dog. I'd no idea what dog but he said he'd take me in on the tractor. I wasn't sure if the dog story was true or if it was just an excuse to gawp at Mum.

I woke early with the faces in the cracks of the wall leering at me. When it was light, I dragged the chair to the window to check the weather. It had been raining for days. Endless, driving rain, and though low clouds still lay banked on the horizon, at least it was dry.

I couldn't wait to see Mum. I brushed my hair and put in a Kirby grip. Polished my shoes with a rag and a gob of spit. I wanted to look clean and tidy so she wouldn't worry. Outside Mr Willock was waiting on the tractor. I climbed up beside him but still couldn't bear to look at his three-fingered hand.

We ground to a halt opposite the war memorial with its granite cross and list of names carved beneath the words: 'Lest We Forget'. The names of real men who'd lived in King's Lynn and fallen in the Great War. A wreath of red poppies, the petals limp with rain, lay on the step amid a collection of little wooden crosses. Mr Willock told me to get down and said he'd be back later to collect me after seeing about the dog.

Mum was waiting outside the station under a spotted umbrella, looking uncomfortable in her astrakhan coat. She was wearing a new felt hat and had hennaed her hair. I wasn't used to her as a redhead. She had on red lipstick to match. It made me shy with her. She looked impossibly glamorous. Not like Mum. More like one of those ladies on the front of one of those Butterick paper dress patterns. The ones she used to make her frocks on the treadle Singer with a bolt of fabric bought cheap in Petticoat Lane. I'd grown used to the villagers. To Mrs Willock's muddy wellingtons, her tweed coat that smelt of dogs and wood smoke, her greasy hair and missing teeth. I ran up to Mum, burying my face in her coat, and started to sob.

Come on now, luv, she said, standing back and holding me at arm's length to look me up and down. Cheer up, now, will you? I've come all this way. Don't want to spend the afternoon with a leaky waterworks, do I? My you've grown, girl. Look at you. Blimey you're thin. Look at them arms. You're like one of them stick-insect things. Don't you eat nothing? Anyway, I brought you a ginger cake. Made it yesterday. Put it in the Buckingham Palace tin. So it's all fresh. Where can we go? I'm dying for a cuppa.

Neither of us had been anywhere like King's Lynn before.

Blimey it's old, Mum said, as we passed the Corn Exchange and the Duke's Head Hotel. I slipped my hand into hers and we walked down Ferry Lane where we found a little tea room, Rosie's, with a copper kettle hanging outside and a bell that tinkled on a wire above the door when we went in. There were net curtains at the windows and horse brasses tacked to the dark beams. All the tables were laid with pink cloths and folded napkins. Flowered teacups and saucers.

It's a bit posh, Mum whispered under her breath.

We sat in the bay window and she took off her coat, ordering a pot of tea for two and two toasted teacakes from the waitress in a shiny black dress with a little white apron and crescent cap. We sat there, on our best behaviour, until the waitress brought our order on an aluminium tray covered in a paper doily with two dishes of strawberry and damson jam, a small jug of milk and a pot of tea hidden under a knitted tea cosy shaped like a lady in a crinoline. Though, as Mum poured the tea through the strainer, all I could think was that she'd soon be gone. I longed to tell her that I hardly went to school now but wasn't sure she would be interested and, anyway, I didn't want to worry her. How, even though Mrs Bint whacked us on the back of our legs with her ruler when we didn't get our punctuation right, I still missed going, that it was better than staying at the cottage when Mrs Willock kept me back to scrub the black frying pan, mind Billy and change his shitty nappies, and Mr Willock gave me funny looks and I had to collect the eggs, bring in the logs and hang up the washing. But mostly I wanted to ask her about the bleeding but was too shy and couldn't find the right words. I also wanted to ask about Nan. Whether she'd talked about me before she passed. If she had been in pain and what hymns they'd sung at her funeral. But Mum didn't mention her and I didn't like to ask. So I just ate my toasted teacake in silence while she chatted about the weather and petrol rationing. How the train had taken nearly three hours and been packed to the gills with noisy troops.

Honestly, Freda, you'd think one of them would have got off his skinny arse for a lady, wouldn't you? They just lounged around with their cigarettes and pimples. Bloody rude I call it. I had to stand half the way.

And then it was over. She had to leave. It was drizzling as I walked her back to the station and stood on the platform waiting to wave her off, aware that last time it had been her saying goodbye to me.

Cheerio, then, luv. Write soon, she said, kissing me roughly on both cheeks.

I hugged her stiffly. I'd longed to see her, but we hadn't talked about anything that mattered. Suddenly there was a mad scramble as people rushed for the train. Doors banged and arms waved from the half-open windows. Then the guard blew his whistle, and she was gone. Outside Mr Willock was waiting on his tractor by the war memorial. I climbed up and, as we bumped our way back across the black fields in the closing dusk, I hoped that he couldn't see I was crying. I didn't know when I'd see Mum again and had no idea where my dad was. He never wrote now and had forgotten my last birthday. There'd been no card with golden numbers.

Whenever I could I wandered down to the sea wall to be on my own. In that desolate place, made even more desolate by the cries of birds for whom those marshes were their winter home, I never felt afraid. There was solace in the silence. In the sleet-filled wind blowing off the Russian steppes. In the tide that breathed in and out of itself like the lungs of the world.

H E PULLED ON his heavy fisherman's sweater, picked up his binoculars and went to the window. It was a ritual when he woke, to go and watch the great flocks of sea birds take flight with the dawn. There were no other dwellings in sight. It suited him that way. He didn't want company. The tribunal had directed him to land work, but after the incident with the gang master he'd pretty much kept himself to himself, apart from the odd trip to the village for basic supplies, the occasional visit to the pub. His work for Mackman. No one seemed to care. No one checked up on him.

A storm was breaking in the distance. Great curtains of rain hung from the low slate clouds over the old windmill by the coastguard station. Oxford was now a distant memory. Another life. The Bird and Baby. Keble's polychromatic brickwork. The essays on Pauline doctrine and Christian orthodoxy. Peter and Jess. Touch.

He spent the morning digging up couch grass, thistles and bindweed in Mackman's field. Pressing the tines of his fork into the compacted black earth to dig out the white roots. He dug a spit about six inches wide, then lifted, turned and dropped the soil near the edge of the trench. With a tap of the fork, he knocked off the remaining dirt, picked out the trailing roots and dragged them, along with the brambles and thistles, to a corner of the field to burn. It was back-breaking work, yet there was something honest about his aching muscles at the end of the day that blotted out the moral dilemmas which had haunted him at Oxford. All he wanted now was to be a part of this flat landscape. To feel the wind on his face. The dirt caking his dry, cracked hands. He'd been struggling to write in his diary, to describe his feelings, yet every time he tried, they seemed to evaporate.

Since leaving Oxford he'd discovered a new relationship with time. He'd get up with the first light and go to bed like a peasant, when it became dark. His days were marked by these diurnal rhythms that carried him along like a leaf on a stream. He was grateful for these small rituals that made him less fearful of this lonely poverty, helped him to understand this solitary period with its chance to see things which, until now, he'd only half understood. Not speaking or speaking were equally valid ways of being in the world. There was, he realized, a time for interaction and a time for silence. And with this coming war, who knew what the future would hold. Another Somme? Millions of young men slaughtered, yet again? At least here, like a doctor who'd taken the Hippocratic oath, he was doing no harm. Simply doing what people had done since the beginning of time. Digging the land. Growing food. Surviving.

That day in Port Meadow everything had felt broken. His centre crumpled. He'd rejected his father's heroism and lost his faith. He'd been over and over the inconsistencies between a belief in the existence of God and a world where there was so much suffering, and few gave credence to the divine. Where self-advantage and hate so frequently eclipsed kindness and love. He was filled with a sense of longing. Desire even. But for what? He wasn't really sure. He knew he had an innate sense of the holy but that it had nothing to do with theology or creeds, that it was to be found, if anywhere, in the first primroses or the flight of whooper swans etched against the pale morning sky. He didn't need the burden of philosophy to appreciate these things. He just had to be a part of the world. To rely on his senses. On taste, smell and sound, but above all, on touch. He was beginning to understand that he was simply part and parcel of the living earth. Its wetlands and forests. Its seagrass and swamps, this matrix of interconnected tissues and living cells.

He had made the assumption that happiness could simply be disregarded, that he could press disdainfully on towards some higher goal. But now he understood that he had a choice. In each moment, in each day that unfolded in front of him, if only he decided to slow down and look. As a child, he'd been digging a hole in the garden when he realized that if he dug down far enough, he'd eventually begin to go up again and come out in Australia, under a clear blue sky. To bright stars, parrots and kangaroos. That there really wasn't a 'down', only an 'up'. Now he just did the small things. Rose with the sun. Brewed a pot of tea on the rusting stove. Walked and worked. Read and drew. Watched the birds. It was then he felt most alive. Most real. Connected to himself and the world around him.

Maybe he'd be able to start painting again. In hospital he'd understood what it meant to be alone and had finally accepted there was nothing out there that was going to save him. That his search for the divine was just a way of protecting himself from his darkest fears, from those moments at midnight when the wind howled round the lighthouse and he lay in his make-shift bed listening to the northerly gales prowling across the marshes, the moon flooding through his small round window. It was then he'd think of those meetings at the Bird and Baby and the consequences of a life without God. Eventually he'd plucked up courage to disagree with Jack Lewis, for whom the Bible remained a source of metaphor and meaning. Only two things mattered now. The natural world and painting. At Oxford he'd tried to fit in. A square peg in a round hole. But he'd always known that his decision to read theology had been mere expedience, that he'd never make a bishop. That he had simply been trying to prove himself to his Victoria-Cross-winning father and his beautiful, distant mother, to find a recipe for living and loving. Hadn't that been what Jess and Peter had been about?

In truth, he'd probably only ever loved one person. Before being sent away to school, his nanny had nursed him through whooping cough and measles. Read him *Robinson Crusoe* and *Peter Pan*. She'd been his Wendy and he, one of her Lost Boys. Of course, he had a mother. A beautiful mother, but it was Nanny who'd tucked him up in bed, the smell of her Imperial Leather lingering when she'd said goodnight, turning out the light, pulling to his door to leave a sliver of light from the landing. It broke his heart that she was dismissed when he was sent away to school.

At Oxford he'd fought so many conflicting emotions. His attraction to both Jess and Peter. To their family and way of life where thoughts and feelings were examined in forensic detail over the dinner table or morning coffee in the conservatory. Where everything was open to discussion. It had been the fascination of the moth to a flame. But he had to turn away. How could it have gone on? He missed them both terribly and their house in Holland Park with its bohemian chaos, its jumble of paintings and cat hair, its Bernard Leach pottery and piles of half-read copies of the *Criterion*. But, slowly, his strength was returning, reconnecting him to his body, giving it precedence over his ruminations. This place nourished him. Gave him resilience like the battered hawthorn that clung on against the odds, to the sea wall. And he was learning to look. Not just see, but to understand the need to be still and discover a world full of colour, texture and sound. He only had to stop. To use his eyes and ears. He was most at ease when walking over the marsh watching the great October flocks of migrating geese darken the sky, the air full of their beating wings as they headed down the coast from the cold wastes of Spitsbergen. He'd got into the habit of going out every day whatever the weather, of feeling the boggy marshland under his boots. Sometimes he'd come across a dead stoat in a ditch or a clump of shivering violets. He barely saw anyone. Just the odd wildfowler out with his gun dog. A lone oysterman.

Often he'd work all morning, digging and speaking to no one. Then, if he was lucky, Mackman would come striding across the field carrying a billycan of glutinous rabbit stew and a thermos of hot sweet tea.

Oreet now, lad, git this down you and shift out of the wind for a bit. This be me missus's special, now. You're doing a grand job.

When by four in the afternoon the light was beginning to fade, he picked up his fork and made his way back to the lighthouse. He'd made a rough bed of sorts from pieces of driftwood in the small round room at the top, hung up his few possessions on a nail hammered into a beam, moved the fishing tackle and rusting boat parts out into the yard. Now he had sufficient space for a table, he could lay out his paper and sticks of charcoal. His Indian inks and pigments. Begin to paint.

I WANTED THOSE WINGS. I wanted them so badly it hurt. They were made of silver card and white goose feathers stuck on with cow gum and had two green ribbons that crossed in an X in the front and tied round the waist, fastening at the back to keep them on. They reminded me of a painting I'd seen in a book that Miss Wilson had shown us in Scripture of the angel Gabriel by someone from long ago, whose name I forgot. But his wings had been more pointy, and he was wearing a pink dress. But still, I had to get to school before they were given away to someone else. They'd already started rehearsing. Brenda Stubbs had been given Mary, and Bert, Joseph, because he was tall, even though he wasn't a villager.

Gotta wear a striped tea towel on me barnet, he boasted. Like a pukka Israelite.

I tried to get my chores done. Not wanting to annoy Mrs Willock so she'd keep me off school. I got up early to give Billy his breakfast, change his stinky nappy and wipe his arse. To my relief Mrs Willock didn't try and stop me leaving when I put on my wellingtons. She was off into Sutton Bridge and had other things on her mind.

I did everything I could to help Mrs Bint. Filled the inkwells with newly mixed ink. Collected up the pencils at the end of the lesson. I could see the wings in her cupboard hanging limply on a wooden hanger. She'd made them herself, proudly guarding them as if they were the crown jewels, bringing them out year after year. The smaller children were sheep and villagers, but the main parts were given out to us older ones. It was an honour. When the bell rang and everybody rushed to the door with their coats and satchels to stumble into the cold, I hung back to sort out the reading books that hadn't been put back on the right shelves, clear up the pencil shavings dropped on the floor.

I suppose a modern child would think it strange. Rather babyish to want to be an angel at the age of twelve. Children now are so knowing. So worldly, with their video games, computers and mobile phones. But I was an innocent. There was so little to distract us, particularly in the middle of those flat black fens.

When Mrs Bint came up behind me and asked what I was doing I knew I had to risk it, so blurted out: that I knew Mary had gone to Brenda Stubbs and that I wasn't pretty enough to be a virgin and that it had to be a local girl but I really wanted to wear the silver and white goose-feather wings and stand on the kitchen ladder as if I'd just come down from heaven with the divine light all around me and announce greetings you are highly favoured among women and when Mary was scared out of her wits tell her she needn't be afraid because she was blessed and how I knew all the words and how our old teacher Miss Wilson had read us the Christmas story as well as the one about Shadrach, Meshach and Abednego who'd been thrown into the fiery furnace and how I couldn't really explain why it mattered so much but that the words were beautiful and made me feel all funny inside and though I felt shy I really wanted to be the angel Gabriel and if she let me I'd stay behind and tidy up the classroom every day and bring in the coal…

And, to my amazement, she said yes.

When everyone had gone, I wandered out of the playground and down the lane, feeling happy for the first time in ages. Mrs Willock wouldn't be able to keep me off school now I was going to be the angel Gabriel. And though I was still teased and called Rails, I preferred school to staying at the cottage looking after Billy, with the wolfish dogs and Mr Willock with his three-fingered hand. A sharp wind was coming in off the Wash as I walked down the lane. I was reading *Jane Eyre* and had to hold down the pages. I'd borrowed it from school and though I couldn't understand all the words, it didn't matter. At home we didn't have any books. Dad had one on racing tips with a picture of the winner of the Cheltenham Cup on the front, but apart from my *School Friend Annual* that Nan had given me for my birthday, I'd never had a book of my own. But when I found Jane, I knew she'd be my friend, that I'd be able to rely on her, tell her everything. After all, she had to live with her cruel aunt, Mrs Reed. I imagined us sitting heads together by the iron stove during break when everyone else was out in the yard, telling her about the greasy black pan and Mr Willock's fingers. Even the bleeding.

The light was beginning to fade and I'd just got to the bit where Jane was shut in the red room and thinks she's seen her uncle's ghost, when I heard a tractor coming up the lane behind me. It was Mr Willock returning from lifting beet. He slowed and leant down to offer me a lift, so I could feel his stale breath puffing into the cold air near my face. His stained Fair Isle sweater was stretched across his belly, which bulged like a newly risen loaf over his leather belt. One of the dogs was lying in the back of the trailer with the beets. One of the two wolfish ones that usually lay in the kitchen guarding the stove, its tongue lolling like a bit of cold spam over its yellow teeth.

Even though it was getting dark, I didn't want to go with him. I wanted to go on enjoying my angel Gabriel moment with Jane, but he told me to climb up and I couldn't say no. Couldn't be rude because I was living in his house and had to do what he said. So I clambered up beside him and tried not to look at his damaged hand. Then he said something that I didn't quite understand but knew he shouldn't have said.

I was never really sure whether the angel Gabriel was a he or a she. Rather like the man/woman who muttered under her breath while carrying her bucket of pigswill up the lane. But somehow I felt that whatever they were, they'd keep me safe. Since I'd got the part in the nativity play, Mrs Willock hadn't stopped me from going to school. I suppose she didn't want any criticism, was frightened of losing the 10s 6d. I hardly saw Mr Willock. As I was leaving for school one lunchtime, the postman came cycling up the track with a letter. It was for me. The envelope had my address in Bethnal Green written on the front. But it had been crossed out and underneath Mum had written, 'PLEASE FORWARD' and the Willocks' address. It was from Dad. I hadn't heard from him for months and had no idea where he was. I opened the letter and it said something about his having been assigned to the Pay Corps. I'd no idea what that was. There was no return address, so I couldn't write back but, he said, he had some news.

… Sorry Ducks not to have been in touch. Just wanted to let you know that Vera is in the family way, that you're going to have a little brother or sister. So, you see, I've got me hands a bit full what with that and the war. But I miss you, gal.
Be good. Dad.

I thought of him with a new bald baby. How he'd jiggle it up and down when it screamed and how, when it got bigger, he'd tell it stories when he came in from the pub with its name where mine had once been. How he'd buy it liquorice allsorts on a Sunday with his betting winnings and let it pick out the ones with pink and blue sprinkles. This girl/boy baby would grow up with my dad, while I was here in the middle of nowhere with the Willocks. I knew he'd left us, that he and Mum had fought. But I loved him. Not like Nan. Nan who'd have protected me against a plague of locusts. But because he was funny. Because he'd taken me to the zoo to feed the penguins in their black-and-white tuxedos and did tricks and showed me that life could be fun. I didn't know where his home was now. If he and Vera were still in London. When he'd first left I'd heard Mum whisper to Nan something about a boarding house on the south coast where no one would know whether or not Vera was his real missus. I thought of them by the sea. Vera in her fake fur and marcasite earrings, eating cockles and ice cream on the pier. A merry-go-round with painted horses. The big dipper and a shriek of gulls. I started to cry. Everyone was disappearing from my life. Everyone that mattered. I pulled on my wellingtons and went down to the orchard to peg the washing on the line before I left for school, even though I would be late. The overalls and towels were stiff as boards. I folded Mr Willock's long johns and shirt, Billy's vests, and put them in the basket, then lugged them back up to the house where I picked up the ginger tom that had started hanging around because, when Mrs Willock wasn't looking, I fed it. It had matted fur balls under its chin and purred while it kneaded my cardigan. Underneath its furry feet it had little pink pads where it hid its claws.

Mostly, I was left to my own devices. Stan Willock might be gone for hours, sometimes days. He took down anything with wings that had a bit of flesh on it if he could get his hands on the cartridges from under the counter at the pub, in exchange for the odd rabbit pie. Soon he was carting barrow loads of game up to the butcher who was always happy for a bit of cheap meat. The butcher asked few questions and neither did anyone else. Willock got 10s for a brent goose, 4s for a shelduck and 6d each for gulls. Pheasants netted £2 a brace. Hares 10s. Partridges and wood pigeons 4s. He'd never been so in the money.

I remember it was a wild night when he and Ernie Burton cadged an old Austin 7 and a gallon of black-market petrol. As dusk fell, they drove out to Terrington Marsh. The temperature had plummeted and the ground frozen hard on the upper saltings, the wind full of flurries of sleet and the stars icy and high. They knew it was hopeless to shoot flighting ducks against a clear sky but the wind kept the fowl low, and the thin cloud silhouetted them perfectly. There were wigeon, too, there for the asking, on their way in to feed before the creeks froze over. They had three boxes of cartridges. But the weather was so rough that when the birds took flight the men didn't bother to take cover in a creek. They knew they'd never be spotted. By the end of the night they'd bagged fourteen wigeon and sixteen ducks between them.

You all right, Freda? Jade asks, popping her head round my door. I just wondered if you're going to give us a hand with the decorations? All the others are in the activity room and asking where you are. There's a nice Victoria sponge today.

For a moment I'm taken aback, not sure who she is or what she's talking about. I've been so far away. But I'm in my room with the primrose curtains and blue crocheted cushion, looking out onto the laburnum.

I'll be right down, dear, I tell her. Just need a minute to tidy myself up.

I get up, go to the mirror and run a comb through my hair. It's as grey as a badger's. There are deep grooves either side of my nose, and my once bright eyes are pale and watery. And, for a second, I wonder who she is: this old woman. What has she got to do with me? What has she done with Fritha?

D USK WAS CLOSING IN cold as a steel trap. The wind stripping the flesh from his bones like a hunter's knife. He needed to get out. He couldn't work any more. It was Sunday and he didn't have to be out on the land. He'd been drawing all afternoon and was beginning to feel like a caged animal. Turning up the collar of his oilskin he made his way down onto the marsh. On the seaward side there was nothing but mudflats. On the landward, mile upon mile of neatly ditched reclaimed land, protected by the sea wall. A line of squat trees ran along its edge, bent by the force of the wind. Beyond lay a lattice of rich black fields dotted with glasshouses and small farms. He thought of Ely, with its towering cathedral, sailing like a great ship over the Fens. Of how he had visited it with his grandfather and been surprised by how many of the medieval statues had lost their heads. His grandfather had explained about Cromwell's campaign of iconoclasm and how Ely had been one of the great towns of England but had declined after the Napoleonic wars. How riots had broken out and the Royal Dragoons had rounded up twenty-three men and a single woman who were all tried at Ely assizes. Five were hanged, he said.

It depressed him to think about Cromwell. He was weary of conflict and of religion, of those who convinced themselves they had God on their side in order to justify the use of force. Cromwell's New Model Army had been terribly brutal and damaged relations between Ireland and England for centuries. But, it seemed, we never learnt, that each generation reinvented war. Now it was a game of wait and see. Warsaw had surrendered and the Allies were hoping to contain Nazi Germany until the war of attrition forced them to abandon the conflict, as they'd done in 1918. There was talk that the war could last for three years. Who knew? History had a way of creating its own stories. So far nothing much had happened here, though the Germans seemed to be bombing the shit out of Polish cities.

From his position on the sea wall he could see the network of muddy creeks branching out like capillaries towards the sea. The tide was coming in, flooding the saltings, as an orange moon rose in the east. Making his way across one of the tumbledown bridges, built by men who had business on the marsh, he could hear the unmistakable clamour of pink-foot, see the swooping black thread stitching itself, as if by an invisible hand, to the darkening sky.

And then he heard it: the whine of a dog, the swish of a black-pitched boat zigzagging its way up a creek, her bows mounted with a poacher's punt gun that was able to fire eight ounces of shot with a single ounce of powder. He soon spotted them: a man crouched behind the cockpit, the other holding a short pole to manoeuvre the shallow craft through the marsh grass, navigating a difficult gap in the spit. Then the crouched one stood up and, beneath the balaclava, Philip recognized Willock. From his own vantage point he was able to spot the silhouettes of the geese before the wildfowlers, watch as the two men stealthily flattened themselves against the bottom of the boat. Sensing predators, the geese spread their wings and took flight. Then there was a volley of shots and a brace of birds fell out of the sky.

He was up all night. Hunched over the rusty Valor stove, wrapped in an old tartan rug. He'd hoped that by leaving Oxford, by coming to this remote place where sea and sky merged, he would be able to find a sense of peace. He'd been thinking a lot about Jess and wondered whether she'd ever found out what had happened between him and her brother. He loved Jess. Loved her more than he loved Peter, and knew that she cared for him in return. But the love he felt for her wasn't the same as desire. It had been Peter he wanted. His hard white body pressed against his own. His urgency. There was an easy, seductive charm about him that drew both men and women alike into his orbit: Peter, the beautiful boy with his deep-violet eyes and long lashes. A witty, charismatic narcissist, he simply followed wherever whim took him, careless of other's feelings. He could be generous and compassionate but the next minute scathing and capricious, even cruel. Maybe if Philip was patient, his feelings would pass. Maybe, in time, he would be able to make a future with Jess, reconnect with his faith enough to find a living in some East End parish, set up a mission with her to help local women. Live a purposeful and contented life. He missed her spontaneity. Her laughter and warmth. Being with Peter was like walking on eggshells with the constant need to predict his moods. Jess took him out of himself. With her he could be silly as well as serious. He remembered the time she'd cut his hair. How she'd sat him in the chair in his college room with a white towel tied round his shoulders as if he were at the barber's. He'd worried that she'd snip his ear but she'd been careful and gentle and it was soothing having her massage his head and comb his hair. With the bits she cut off, she'd sticky-taped a little moustache under her nose, goose-stepping around his room pretending to be Hitler. But Peter? Peter was so demanding.

How he hated Willock and his accomplice for shooting those geese. And yet... Weren't they, somehow, closer to nature then he was? For them death was just an everyday part of life. It brought them nearer to the natural order of things than he'd ever be with his binoculars and sketch pad. He'd read of ancient cultures where the hunter thanked the animal he was about to kill for its sacrifice. Perhaps those quiet moments, when the predator's fingers froze and the cold air reddened his ears in the fog, were why he got up at dawn to sit in a cold creek downwind of a flock of wigeon. It was a communion of sorts, wasn't it? Then, for some reason, he thought of his father, how he'd only been a decade older than he was now when he'd been blown to smithereens on that blighted battlefield. What had been going through his head as he'd sat in a sea of mud with that young squaddie, his leg blown off above the knee, crying like a baby for his mother?

Did any of this change how he felt about joining up or killing another man? This war against the Third Reich could conceivably be called a just war, couldn't it? Already thousands were being threatened by Germany, at home and abroad. The reports he'd read of *Kristallnacht* had been horrific. How could the country of Beethoven, Brahms and Hölderlin descend to this? Didn't he have a moral duty to make a choice that, say, a fox tearing apart a hare didn't? He'd hoped that by coming to this wilderness he would find solace. There were no judgements in nature. It simply brought you up close to the realities of violence, the brutal aspects of yourself you most wanted to forget.

He got up and made a pot of tea. Yesterday his allowance had finally come through. He'd gone to the post office in Sutton Bridge he was using as a poste restante—not that he was expecting any post—and there the letter was from Edward Pemberton's solicitor. It was only a small amount and he recognized it for what it was. Conscience money. But still, it was enough to pay a peppercorn rent to ensure that he could stay in the lighthouse, secure his occupancy, whether or not he worked for Mackman, buy the time to paint. In the Warneford he'd drawn obsessively. Now he wanted to do something more challenging. To capture the essence of this remote place: the sudden squalls of rain, the rusty, ochre tones and wide skies, darkened with flocks of wild birds. He didn't want to be too literal—a camera could do that—simply to find meaning in the daily discipline of his craft. If he was going to be serious, he needed to explore his responses to the world through paint, understand its potential to express what couldn't be expressed in words. It sounded easy. But it wasn't. Everyone had feelings—the postman, the farm labourer—but the job of the artist was to articulate what others were unable to see or say. School and Oxford had taught him how to think, helped him to acquire a body of knowledge, but no one could teach you how to express your feelings. He knew he'd be taking a risk if he opened himself up. If he tore down all the defences built up by his education, class and background. But self-respect had nothing to do with the approval of his teachers, his dead father or his mother, Jess or Peter. Even God. He could waste what small gifts he had in constant bouts of anxiety and time-filling tasks, in endless broken nights. Or he could embrace the here and now, those moments, first thing in the morning, when he opened the front door and felt the wind grab him by the throat or the shock of the icy water from the pump on his cheeks. He could chose to allow himself to feel that ripple of night-fear when he lay in bed listening to a far-off vixen barking under the cold stars. To be a part of, rather than outside, the scheme of things.

He knew he was at a disadvantage as a painter. That he wasn't part of any of the discussions taking place in the pubs and drinking dens of Soho where artists met over a glass of cheap Algerian red and a packet of foul-smelling Turkish cigarettes to bitch, moan and discuss their work. He resented the time spent at Oxford when he could have been attending life classes at the Slade. While staying in Holland Park one weekend with Jess and Peter, Peter had taken him to the Fitzroy Tavern in Bloomsbury where Dylan Thomas and a drunken Nina Hamnett were propping up the bar. He'd watched in fascination as they'd stubbed cigarette after cigarette out into the overflowing ashtray, bickering amid the clouds of stale smoke. Nina had sung inebriated sea shanties in return for her next drink and Peter had gone over and kissed her, calling her 'darling', and the Queen of Bohemia. In return, she'd slapped him on the bottom. He'd also been introduced to Robert Colquhoun and Robert MacBryde, known always as the two Roberts—though he never could remember which was which—at a private view at the Leicester Galleries. It was a totally different world to any he'd previously experienced.

The next day Peter had taken him to lunch with his father at the National Liberal Club. With its Renaissance revival architecture, its wide staircase and arts and crafts tiles, the generous balcony that looked out with the certainty of privilege over the Thames, Philip had half expected Gladstone's ghost to appear at any moment. Lunch in the panelled dining room was mulligatawny soup and Dover sole, accompanied by grey potatoes and overcooked sprouts, served by an elderly waitress in a black dress and little white, half-moon cap. Peter's father was charming and loquacious but not much interested in his son. Let alone his son's friend. A psychiatrist, he was part of the same social circle as the art critic Adrian Stokes. It had been Stokes's analysis with the therapist Melanie Klein that had led to their association. Philip was intrigued by the Bohemian and literary circles that Peter moved in, so different to the world he had grown up in. He felt a twinge of envy.

*

He was impressed by the insouciance with which Peter was able to glide between these different worlds in a way that he, with his solidly middle-class upbringing, wasn't. Lunch involved a couple of bottles of claret and went on till late in the afternoon. When Peter's father caught a cab back to Holland Park, he and Peter, who enjoyed playing the *flâneur*, sauntered down the Embankment along the darkening river towards Soho and the French House. In the tiny smoke-filled bar painters and writers in gabardine raincoats and heavy jerseys smelling of fog and rain, chatted over their halves of bitter. That evening's talk was of the occult. The painter John Craxton had been reading Yeats and become fascinated by the Hermetic Order of the Golden Dawn. Producing a pack of tarot cards from the pocket of his tweed jacket, he explained the significance of the different symbols: the innocent wonder of the Fool, the talent and self-determination of the Magician. It was in the French that they'd bumped into Francis Bacon with his pimento-shaped face. He and Peter seemed to be on first-name terms. Bacon plied them with endless drinks, then insisted that they accompany him to Le Boeuf sur le Toit in Orange Street.

Best queer club in town, old fruit, he said, waving his arms to hail a taxi.

Philip had never been anywhere like it. The dim dining room with its soft pink lighting was packed with men in black ties and a smattering of crimson-lipped women, all drinking and smoking at small round tables covered in crisp white cloths. Chinese lanterns gave the place a louche, exotic glow. Bacon ordered champagne and Philip tried not to stare at the handsome young blond boy seated opposite on a velvet banquette, his tongue down the throat of a portly man in glasses.

Oh look, Bacon said, disappearing across the crowded room. Leonard's at the piano tonight. Such a dear old queen, even if he does look like an East End crimper.

Philip wasn't interested in academic painting, the sort of thing that students learnt in the life room at the Slade. He simply had an affinity with paint. He wished now he'd had the courage to ask Bacon about his work but the subject hadn't come up, and he was too shy to mention it. It was the materiality of the stuff that attracted him. Paint was a more visceral form of expression than words. But it was a continual struggle. He thought of Rembrandt's *Slaughtered Ox* hanging like a crucified Christ in an abattoir and Goya's *Dead Turkey*, both paintings he loved. Beast, blood and bone. Those painters would understand the lives of men like Willock.

BILLY, STOP! Stop it. Leave it alone now, the fox got it. There's nothing we can do. Put it down, it's all bloody. You'll get in a mess and it's got maggots.

But he wouldn't let go. He just stood there bawling and clutching the headless thing to his chest.

We'll bury it, give it a funeral. Come on now, stop wailing, please. There's an empty cartridge box in the shed by the privy. We can put Joey in there. Use it as a coffin.

Trailing the limp bird by the neck like a rag doll, Billy followed me, snivelling, into the shed where we filled the empty cartridge box with straw, then laid the inert body down as gently as baby Jesus in his manger.

Come on, Billy, get some berries and leaves. That's what the ancient Egyptians did. Gave people things to take to the afterlife, food and beads and stuff like that they thought they'd need so they wouldn't feel so lonely when they were dead. What d'you think Joey would like? Groundsel?

We picked a few clumps and a spray of red hawthorn berries, which we laid in a wreath over the decapitated corpse. Then Billy sprinkled it with a handful of meal as if it were confetti. After that we couldn't think what else to do so shut the box, dug a hole and buried it, making a cross with bits of wood lashed together with straw.

We have to say a prayer, Billy.

But the only prayer I knew was the Lord's Prayer, and after 'our Father who art in heaven', Billy got bored, grabbed my hand and dragged me back towards the house, complaining that he was hungry. Anyway, I didn't think the words were quite suitable for a chicken.

I spent as much time as I could with Billy. When Mrs Willock was out, I sat with him on my lap and showed him the pictures in my *School Friend Annual*.

That's a lady. That's a dog. What colour is that? Yes, that's right, blue. Clever boy. Give me a kiss.

I cut him a chain of paper dolls from the *News of the World*, made a paper boat and told him the stories that Dad had told me. Embellishing the details about the beautiful sea-green palace full of strange watery creatures that was home to the mermaid who walked on legs that felt like knives, and the handsome prince who slashed his way through the hundred-year-old thicket to wake the Sleeping Beauty. No one had ever played with Billy before. I cooked him breakfast, boiled him eggs, cutting the tops off and making toast soldiers for him to dip into the runny yolk, like Nan had done for me. As a result, he began to follow me everywhere, just as I wanted.

But I was always hungry. Mrs Willock never really cooked for me, slamming down Mr Willock's pigeon pie in front of him on the spread newspaper that had to do as a tablecloth. I hated the way he sucked the bones, wiping the middle finger of his three-fingered hand round and round in the gravy to clean his plate, poking his teeth with his dirty nail to loosen the trapped strings of meat. When he'd done, she'd eat, and I'd finish what was left, have a beetroot sandwich, a boiled egg or a slice of bread and dripping. Even though she said very little, I knew by the way she sighed and sucked in her cheeks that she was angry. Resentful at having to cook and wait on him, tidy up the dirty clothes he dropped on the floor, bring in the logs. He never did anything to help her.

The nights were growing colder, the windows icing over with fern-like patterns. I slept in my coat, the thin eiderdown pulled up over my head. When I woke in the morning my breath made clouds in the freezing air. The hedgerows were covered in thick hoar frost and an icicle hung from the iron pump. The path to the privy was covered with black ice so Mrs Willock gave me a bucket of cinders to sprinkle on it to stop us from slipping. Afterwards I picked Brussels sprouts from the vegetable patch at the end of the garden, twisting them off in one freezing hand, while hugging the other for warmth in my armpit.

That night it snowed. In the morning I woke to a numbing silence and everything covered in a white blanket. The only marks were those of the ginger tom who'd jumped from the privy roof, then padded off in search of something or other, and a fox that had been worrying round the chickens' pen. After my jobs, I wrapped up as warmly as I could and made my way over the snowy fields to meet Bert. I was going to get to school come what may. It was our last rehearsal. The snow reached the tops of the hedges and I followed the bird prints and animals tracks like an Indian tracker in the fresh snow. The dykes were frozen, and when I found Bert we slithered down the bank in our wellingtons so the thick grey ice creaked beneath us.

Come on, Freda. Race yer, he hollered, before falling with a heavy thud.

Ooh me arm. Me bleeding arm's broke. I swear it's broke.

I tried to haul him back onto the path, slipping and sliding with the weight of him on the ice. He was a big lad and much heavier than me. By the time we got to school he was moaning so loudly Mrs Bint got hold of his wrist and gave it a good twist.

That'll put it back, she said. You'll be as right as rain.

Bloody hell, he screamed. Me bloody Chalk Farm.

Afterwards she made a sling out of an old scarf she found in the back of the cupboard, complaining, all the while, that Joseph was now going to be a cripple.

On Sundays I walked with Mrs Willock and Billy the three miles to church. Inside were lots of carved slabs in memory of old dead people. Stained-glass windows cast pools of coloured light onto the stone floor and showed Jesus fishing on the Sea of Galilee or performing the miracle of the loaves and fishes. White petals from the vase of autumn chrysanthemums lay scattered on the red altar cloth. We always sat at the back by the door where we could see the front pew and the doctor, his wife and their two sons, who went to grammar school in King's Lynn, putting their half-crown on the silver collection plate. One Sunday the vicar read from Leviticus. Something about a goat being sent into the desert carrying the sins of the world on its back. He said that if we put our trust in Jesus our sins would be taken away and we'd be forgiven. He didn't say what would happen to the goat.

I couldn't believe that Mrs Willock had turned up. It was the day of the nativity play. She stood at the back of the classroom in her gumboots and tweed coat while the other mothers and carers pushed past in their winter hats and scarves—banging their mittens together to get the circulation back in their hands—and nab a seat at the front. I was terribly embarrassed. Why had she come? I hadn't asked her. Waiting nervously behind the improvised curtain, I could see the room filling up. There weren't enough seats so some people had to stand, crushed between the big iron stove and the nature table. The smaller children sat cross-legged on the floor in the front.

We'd spent the last two days cutting up strips of coloured paper, gluing them together with cow gum to make paper chains. We made snowflakes to stick on the classroom windows and picked holly from the churchyard to put round the candles on the windowsills that Mrs Bint was now lighting with a long wax taper. It was all so beautiful it made me want to cry. The candlelight. The greenery. My silver goose-feather wings. I didn't want Mrs Willock spoiling it.

As Mrs Bint began 'Silent Night' on the upright piano, the audience settled down and a hush fell in the classroom. The curtain was pulled back and there was Bert, a striped tea towel tied around his head with a pyjama cord. Taking a deep breath he stepped to the front of the stage and rattled off: Oh-what-woe-has-befallen-me-and-my-lady-wife-Mary-for-there-is-no-room-at-the-inn.

And the shepherds giggled.

After the performance we took our bows and the audience stood, while Mrs Bint thundered out 'God Save the King'. When it was all over all the children, along with their parents, trudged, flushed and excited, into the night, following the circle of torchlight up ahead towards the vicarage. Most of the mothers had on their best hats and scarves but Mrs Willock was still wearing her work clothes. I'd never seen her in anything else. I didn't want to walk with her so hung back with Bert.

The vicarage windows flickered in the dark. There was a wreath of holly on the front door, tied to the brass knocker shaped like a fox. In the hall gloomy paintings hung along the wooden staircase that was covered with a strip of crimson carpet held down by shiny brass rods. A blue-and-white tea set, decorated with little Chinese fishermen on a humpback bridge beneath a weeping willow, sat on the big oak dresser, and a mahogany barometer that Bert said could predict the weather hung by the front door. It had something to do with the pressure.

The grown-ups were ushered into the drawing room. Through the half-open door, we could see the vicar's wife pouring tea in front of the coal fire, the mothers awkwardly standing around stirring two sugars into their teacups, spoons clinking against the china. I hoped Mrs Willock didn't have mud on her wellingtons.

We children were sent to the kitchen where the housekeeper gave us each a glass of orange squash and told us to take an iced bun from the pile on the big white meat plate. The kitchen was huge, with a massive black range in the corner and shelves lined with large white jars marked 'FLOUR' and 'CURRANTS'.

When no one was looking, Bert snitched another iced bun and stuffed it into his pocket.

Then it was time to leave. Now the school holidays had begun I'd be stuck in the cottage with the Willocks, and only Billy and the ginger cat for company. I missed Nan. Every Christmas we sat in the scullery in front of the coal fire making Christmas decorations from old Lux boxes. Covering them with shiny paper and glitter. I thought of the Christmas before Dad had left to go with Vera. How one of his cronies had got hold of some tickets for *Aladdin* at the Hackney Empire that he let Dad have cheap. I'd never been to a theatre before. It was like a palace with its big swing doors, its vestibule of shimmering chandeliers and sweeping marble staircase, the three balconies that looked down over the huge auditorium filled with red velvet seats. The painted panels representing Tragedy, Comedy and Music. We sat in the front row of the circle so I was able to lean on the brass rail and look down at the stage. Mum was all dolled up in her best dress and Nan's rabbit-fur tippet. Dad bought her a box of Fry's Turkish Delight saying: Sweets for my sweet, though it was only a matter of months before he disappeared with Vera. I loved Widow Twankey. How the genie appeared when she polished the lamp so poor Aladdin could have his wish and marry the Sultan's daughter, the beautiful Princess Badroulbadour.

A bitter east wind was coming in off the sea, full of blustery sleet as we made our way back in twos and threes beneath the icy stars, past the great swing bridge. A hulking, hydraulic beast that swung open to let the ships carrying pig iron, coal and munitions up the River Nene to the Port of Wisbech. On weekdays, men would be unloading coal from the lorries onto the waiting ships but today was Sunday and the machines were idle. Beyond the boat yard and cranes, there was nothing. Nothing except empty fields and marshland, until you got to the Willocks' squat cottage where the Nene ran on in an unrelenting line towards the Wash, and the two old lighthouses with their flickering lamps flanked the mouth of the river like the dogs of Alcibiades.

THERE WAS A LETTER from his mother waiting at the post office. The first he'd received since he'd left Oxford. It had taken a long time to get to him. He'd been worried that she and Pemberton were stuck in Paris when war was declared. It was hard to know what was going on there. But the letter depressed him. It felt as though he hardly knew her any more; it was so long since he'd actually seen her, let alone lived under the same roof. A long time since he'd stood at that nursery window in Buckingham Palace Road watching the trains shunt in and out of Victoria station or pedalled the pianola for her to sing. A lifetime ago that he'd lain in bed watching the snowflakes swirl in his small glass globe as he drifted off to sleep.

He read the letter again:

Darling—

It's such an age since I've seen you. I do hope you're on the mend now. I'm so sorry I couldn't come over; it's just been too difficult. Everything's up in the air with this *drôle de guerre*. Nothing much seems to be happening, so we'll stay put for the moment and not come back to London. Anyway, Edward's flat in Kensington is let to someone from the Foreign Office and, of course, Buckingham

Palace Road has been sold. Paris was baking this summer, and everyone out in the cafés. It was glorious. But the government seems to accept that some sort of attack is inevitable now. We're all bracing ourselves. All around the city workmen are busy digging trenches in case there are any German raids. They've been tunnelling under the pavements right outside our apartment. It's been terribly noisy. So they're obviously expecting something any day now, and there are endless strikes and protests because the franc's so weak. Who knows what this nasty little Hitler man intends? Anyway, the shops here have become really dreary. You can't buy anything any more. I wanted a new pair of shoes recently and there wasn't a decent pair to be had anywhere, I traipsed all over the place. But we're making the best of it. We've become great friends with a charming American, Sylvia Beach, who runs a little bookshop called Shakespeare and Co. in the rue de l'Odéon. It's such fun. So many interesting people meet up there you could almost pretend this ghastly war wasn't really happening. Anyway, if necessary, we'll scoot across to Noirmoutier, I don't suppose the Germans will bother us there.

I do hope you're all right, darling. Are you in Oxford or London? Do let me know. Or maybe you're staying with friends. You mentioned a girl called Jess. Is it serious? Will I need to buy a new hat? Hopefully, things will settle down soon and we'll be able to come to London and see you. I can't wait!

Your loving Mama.

With his first allowance he bought the components to cobble together a cat's whisker radio. He was no engineer but had learnt the principles at school. There was no amplification but by fiddling with the wire antenna and using the second-hand earphones he'd managed to acquire, he could just pick up the Home Service crackling over the airways. He might be living in isolation but didn't want to live in ignorance. On 14th October he caught the tail end of an announcement that the *Royal Oak* battleship, anchored in Scapa Flow, had been torpedoed by a German submarine with 800 men and boys drowned. How on earth had the German navy been able to attack in British waters? Two days later, a Spitfire shot down a German Heinkel He 111 over a Lothian farmyard. Suddenly the prospect of combat felt very real. In between news broadcasts the BBC played carefully chosen gramophone records. Sandy MacPherson's lunchtime organ concerts seemed designed to lull people into a false sense of normality but they provided a bit of company in the cold silence of the lighthouse. While cruising the airways late one night, he heard a voice repeating over and over again: 'Germany calling, Germany calling', urging the British people to surrender. The treacherous Anglo-Irish drawl made his blood run cold.

He washed his face and made a pot of tea, drinking it black because he'd run out of milk. He could feel the dark comfort of the night giving way to the day's many uncertainties. He put down his tea and arranged his sticks of charcoal, pencils and pigments on the makeshift trestle, then lay down a series of colour washes on the canvas with a broad brush. As he did so, boundaries dissolved and a new sense of calm came over him that he'd never experienced in the lecture halls of Oxford. He thought of *The Light of the World*. Maybe in this remote place he'd be able to hear the knock at the door.

He knew he had to create a distance between his feelings and his work. Like Wordsworth, recollect his turbulent emotions in tranquillity rather than remain poised between paranoia and truth. He wanted to find a way of engaging directly with this bleak landscape. The horizontal black fields and grey zip of sky. Describe how it felt to stand in the wind and driving sleet. He'd start with what he had lying around him: a blue-and-white striped mug, the chipped yellow jug set against the circle of the lighthouse window. Real objects. Then he'd go outside and look for what nature could offer. Painting was a way of showing not telling. Emotions made concrete through marks rather than words. He wanted to go to bed at the end of the day thinking about the problems of the canvas he was working on, then wake with it resolved in his head. It was a meditation of sorts, wasn't it, this looking? A form of prayer. It mattered not one jot whether what he produced looked like the thing in front of him. What was important was that the marks he made were as integral to the bowl he was painting as its clay, or the texture of skin to his model. He wasn't concerned with perfection. What was perfection anyway except a denial of the vulnerable? What mattered now was mending what was broken.

Most people were afraid of being alone and filled their days with domestic chores. Trips to the grocer or the tailor to distract themselves from the despondency that threatened to overwhelm them. The sky and sea would become his touchstones.

He thought of the men on the pier down in Sutton Bridge, covered in oil and grease, loading coal and pig iron onto the waiting cargo ships, ready to set sail to the ports of England and Scotland. Men for whom the rhythms of work and sea ran though their veins.

But painting was a constant battle. When starting something new he felt as if it were the first picture he'd ever attempted. Then it would dawn on him that it was just that, simply a painting and he'd always be disappointed with what he produced. But it was this threat of failure that drove him on. The hope that with the next effort he'd get closer to his goal, to what he saw in his head. Perhaps, in truth, he was always painting himself, and the object in front of him just allowed him to invent more freely. This solitary life would give him the chance to dig deep. Colour, light and shadow. These would form his new vocabulary. And then, for no apparent reason, he thought of Jess, and was overwhelmed by a deep longing that he couldn't really call a sense of loss because there'd never been anything more between them than friendship. And yet... He remembered her in his Keble room. Her slender arms raised to brush her messy red hair out of her eyes, her small breasts straining against her thin summer blouse. And then he thought of Peter. His white body pressing again his. His insistent tongue exploring him in ways that set him on fire. And he knew then that he was better off here; alone with the wind, sky, and sea. In the company of birds.

T HE ELDERLY aren't supposed to need much sleep. Thoughts arrive in the early hours like uninvited guests. I'm lying under my flowered duvet watching the dirty London light break through the branches of the laburnum, listening to the first blackbirds and the carers trundling the tea trolley down the hall; the clatter of teacups and saucers. I can hear the concerned whispers of the night staff changing over with the day shift. Passing on information about those who've been taken ill in the night, though I'm not supposed to hear. They hate having to tell us someone has died. They know our first thought will be: me next? The staff try and make things as cheerful as possible with art and cookery classes, the share-your-memories sessions and weekly visits from the hairdresser who does a wash and set for a few quid (OAP rate). The manicurist who'll paint your nails a pretty shell pink. But we all know what this is... a prelude to the main event; we know there aren't any rewrites, any last-minute revisions to the old script; that most of us have overstayed our three score years and ten thanks to the NHS. Cobbled back together with a titanium hip, a pacemaker or a new knee. Age is a symphony of small losses.

Sometimes I wonder why I bother to write this journal when no one will read it. I can't imagine who'd be interested in what

I have to say. But it's a testament, of sorts, to a past that would otherwise evaporate like morning mist. Last night I had that dream again. The one where I'm being smothered by small feral creatures: their little teeth breaking my skin, their sharp beaks and claws holding me down, clumps of feathers filling my mouth, making me gag. And then: nothing. Nothing but darkness. Still. Still... after all these years.

A pink glow was breaking in the east, the heavy sky threatening snow. I pulled my coat tight over my nightie against the early chill, slipped on my wellingtons and made my way down to the privy, hoping no one was up yet. Spiders' webs hung like lace curtains in the frosted grass. At the bottom of the vegetable patch he was standing outside the privy, blowing smoke rings into the icy air. Usually Mr Willock shut himself in there for ages to do his business, have a roll-up and read the sports pages, so we had to wait or pee in a bush. But this morning he was leaning against the tool shed, a cigarette stub cupped between his thumb and forefinger, his flat cap pulled low over his face. When I passed the water butt he said hello. Normally he only spoke to me if he had to or I was a captive audience to hear about his exploits.

You're up early, gal. Come over here now. Would yer like to see t' smoke come out me eyes? It's a special trick. Not many can do it. Put your hand on me stomach, here, and watch me eyes very careful.

I shuffled closer and placed my reluctant hand above his wide leather belt, breathing in his stale tobacco breath. Then, before I realized what was happening, he'd grabbed my hand and shoved it into his open flies. I hadn't seen him unbutton them and tried to pull away, my heart pounding, but he held me by the wrist. I wanted to scream but no sound came out, so I turned away, concentrating on the icy leaves of the frozen kale, the straggling wigwam of frost-blackened runner beans, pretending that I was somewhere else, that this wasn't happening. Then he made a funny noise and let go of my hand.

Now, there, doant tha go telling no one, gal. You understand, he said buttoning up and straightening his braces. You git on back up to t' house now. Tha says a word and I'll be after thi. I'll catch thi, don't you worry 'bout that. I'll snip your fingers rit off.

As he disappeared up the path, I wiped my hand on the wet grass and went to the pump, letting the icy water run over and over my sticky fingers until they turned blue.

The organ pipes smiled down at me like a row of brass teeth and the wooden ceiling covered with golden stars seemed as unreachable as heaven. Above the altar Jesus hung nailed by his hands and feet to his wooden cross. I knelt down in front of the green cloth, the tall silver candlesticks and beeswax candles, trying to pray, but didn't know what to say. I wanted to tell him what had happened but felt too ashamed. Maybe he'd think it was my fault and I'd be sent away like the goat into the desert for doing something so dirty. The church was cold and musty. I wasn't sure if I was allowed to be in there on my own or if I'd be told off if someone found me. There was a wooden carving over the door. A golden lion standing on its hind legs next to a white unicorn, wearing a crown, balanced on a blue ribbon that said *Dieu et mon droit*. I'd no idea what the words meant, though I guessed they might have something to do with the King as his picture was nearby. I thought of his coronation, the streets of Bethnal Green hung with red, white and blue bunting. How we'd been given the day off school and each of us had a currant bun, and a Union Jack to wave.

I knew George VI was never supposed to have been king, that it was only because his brother had married a horrid thin American lady that no one liked who'd been married to someone else. It wasn't really fair of his brother to make him be king, because he stuttered. Everyone knew that. Though he tried to cover it up when he made speeches on the wireless. I thought it was lucky he was rich, that he hadn't had to go to school and be teased. He would have been in Mrs Bint's class or at my old school in Bethnal Green. Poor Iris. Everyone made fun of the Elastoplast patch on her glasses, calling her One-eye. Then I remembered the nursery rhyme about the lion and the unicorn fighting for the crown and wondered why, when the lion beat the unicorn and they were drummed out of town, some gave them white bread and some brown. I didn't think lions ate bread and everyone knew unicorns weren't real.

I went over to the Sunday school table and flipped through the pile of books. There was Jesus throwing the moneylenders out of the temple and a picture of him as a small boy helping to sweep up the wood shavings in Joseph's carpentry shop. Seeing that made me think of Nan. Of helping her fold the warm vests and blouses she'd just pressed with the heavy old iron, making sticky toffee together in the scullery while Mum was downstairs in the shop. We'd boil up the sugar, molasses and vinegar on the old gas stove, testing to see if the mixture was ready by dropping a teaspoonful into a glass of cold water, then stir in the butter and baking powder before pouring it onto a sheet of greaseproof paper to cool. When it was set, we cut it into squares, and I was allowed one piece. And all the while, Nan's smalls would be steaming on the rack above the stove, and Glenn Miller's 'Moonlight Serenade' pouring into the warm scullery from the big mahogany wireless.

Remembering those things broke my heart. Losing Nan was the worst thing that had ever happened to me. Worse than Mrs Bint bending back my arm in class. Worse than the girls at school calling me Rails or having to wash the black frying pan and Billy's stinky nappies. Worse, even, than the horrible thing Mr Willock had just done.

Coming up to Christmas there was an increased demand from the butcher for game. There may have been a war on, but still, Christmas was Christmas. Mr Willock left to spend two days with Ernie Burton in a derelict hut down on the marsh, a couple of packs of cartridges, bags of sugar, tea, cocoa and a blanket apiece strapped to the crossbars of their bicycles. The weather was foul. There was no one about and by the time they reached the sea wall the snow was falling so fast they had to get off their bikes and push them through the drifts.

How do I know? Because while standing at the sink doing the washing-up, Mr Willock was gutting his spoils at the kitchen table, ripping out the entrails onto the blood-soaked newspaper before throwing them into a bucket for the whining dogs, and he recounted every detail.

They'd woken to a blizzard, he said, the snow piled so high against the door they couldn't get out for the dawn duck flight. To pass the time he'd skinned a hare, shot the day before, breaking off bits of the hut for firewood to make a stew in the old frying pan with the snow that had drifted under the door.

Heers be easy prey, gal. You just calls 'em up from the bottom of the dyke with a suck of the lips, like this. It be a clever trick me dad learnt me. No one knows why they fall for it, but it were rit tasty that stew.

When the light broke, he wriggled out of the hole in the roof to dig open the door and let Ernie out.

But booger me, if he weren't lying there wrapped up like a babby in both them blankets and all he says were, I thought you was never goin' to git in here. Never you mind that, I says. You git on them white clothes and we'll go out after some more of those old heers and geese. Well it be cold, he says. Cold be boogered, I says. You git goin' now. Get on your ballyhava and stop your moaning.

As they walked back along the sea wall to their bikes, blood dripping onto the fresh snow from their bulging pockets, a flock of brent geese flew overhead. They could hear the rhythm of their wings—up-back-and-round, up-back-and-round—as goose called to goose, each flying in the slipstream of the one ahead following the lead bird. It was then he spotted it. A pink-foot, its feathers all puffed out at the bottom of the dyke. Pure white, casting a shadow against the snow.

Here quick, Ernie, I says. You doan't see many of them. Now Ernie's not much of a shot, so I says, see if you can give that old goose one, Ernie. Bet you can't. So Ernie slides down the bank on his arse and lets drive and that ol' goose flies off whining all over the marsh. I reckons it come down by the old sluice, but it were too dark to see.

When Mr Willock took the bucket of guts into the yard for the dogs, I slipped quietly out of the back door and down the rutted lane, cut past Willow Bottom Farm. Out on the sandbanks the geese seemed restless, gabbling among themselves, as the tide moved sluggishly up the gullies and little creeks. A dead dunlin floated past that had been hollowed to a feathered shell by a black-headed-gull, while out on the far sands I could hear the krank-krank of a heron digging for eels in the sulphurous-smelling mud.

Foolishly, I'd imagined that wearing those silver goose-feather wings in the nativity play would, somehow, protect me. It was a silly, childish notion, I know. But still. I began to pray, to ask God to stop Mr Willock doing horrible things and to let me go home. I didn't know what else to do.

I don't know how long I sat there watching the great flocks heading down from the frozen north, their high-pitched honking deafening as they swept in to graze on the ploughed sugar beet and potato fields sprinkled in a frosting of snow. I wondered how they knew the way. How such tiny hearts were strong enough to carry them on such a perilous journey from their distant homes.

Home. Would I ever go home? Nan was gone and Dad had more or less disappeared. And Mum? Well Mum seemed to find it easier to manage without me.

Dark clouds raced across the face of the afternoon moon. I couldn't stop shivering and pulled up the rabbit fur collar of my thin coat. I didn't want to go back, didn't want to spend a minute longer alone with Mr Willock and those whining dogs. He'd said the white goose had come down near the sluice, so I made my way back along the sea wall, my wellingtons slipping in the frozen slush. At first I couldn't see a thing, then I spotted it flapping by the rusty gate.

Scrambling over the spongy sea lavender, crunchy with frost, I realized that something was wrong when it let me walk right up to it without trying to fly away. It had milky, opalescent eyes and was snow white. One of its wings was hanging at a funny angle, and up close it seemed so large, it frightened me. I put out my hand and tried to stroke it, but it spread its good wing, hissed, and tried to peck me. I shrank back but knew that if I left it, it would die. Before going to that cold place, the only wild animals I'd seen were the mice in the scullery skirting, elephants and penguins at the zoo. But they didn't count. I knew from feeding the hens with Billy that I'd have to pin down its wings to catch it but I didn't dare, so, leaving it in the dyke, I clambered back up the bank in the sleety wind and made my way towards the window of the lighthouse, its warm beam gleaming invitingly in the gathering dusk.

H E WAS FIDDLING with the antennae, trying to catch the BBC through a pair of old headphones. He was a long way from the nearest transmitter and the signal was weak. The Soviets had just invaded Finland and the League of Nations had retaliated, expelling them for aggression. Philip needed to know what was going on. He could just make out the Home Service crackling over the airways announcing that in future, conscription would include all able-bodied men between nineteen and forty-one. He lit a cigarette, inhaling the blue smoke deep into his lungs, flicking the growing tail of ash into his saucer. He felt a pang of guilt, got up and pulled on his boots.

Despite his allowance from Pemberton he still felt obliged as a conscientious objector to do odd jobs even though he'd legged it from London and from official duties. Planting peas, clearing ditches, shifting fence posts. If Mackman didn't have enough work, he'd join one of the gangs of turnip pickers. Often there'd be twenty people waiting by the swing bridge to jump onto the back of a lorry to take them where they were needed that day. The work was hard. A flail on the back of the tractor went along the lines throwing up the potatoes and the pickers had to follow the spinner, picking them up before the tractor came back down the next row. He got to know some of those working the same patch: Roy Booker and Frank Walker from the other side of Sutton Bridge. Both were Quakers and had refused to join up. They were also tall, so got the job of loading the trailer, poking the long hiking stick into the bottom of the jute bags, then gripping the top with the other hand and slinging them onto the tractor. It was heavy, exhausting work.

When not working the land, he'd read and paint. He had found a wind-up gramophone in a second-hand shop in Sutton Bridge. It was a bargain and he wondered why the previous owner had got rid of it. Perhaps they'd died and the family that had cleared out the house had no interest in music. He still had a few of the gramophone records he'd bought in Oxford. Bach's cantatas. Chopin's études. A Scot Joplin rag. Music took the edge off the solitary evenings. Outside, he built a pen. A sanctuary for the injured birds he found when out walking. Birds with fishing hooks in their beaks or a damaged leg. It reminded him of school, when he'd nursed a jay and kept a pet ferret. He was comfortable in the company of animals. He helped them heal, then let them go.

He was putting on his waterproof jacket when there was a knock at the door. Few people came to the lighthouse. After the incident at the Anchor the locals tended to give him a wide berth. There was opposition to his being a conscientious objector, so he seldom went into the village except for vital supplies. Tea and bread. A bit of bacon. A packet of fags. Stopping for the occasional jar in the Jugged Hare, the pub favoured by field workers and poachers. He didn't go there often, preferring his own company away from the tittle-tattle and the fug of pipe smoke. Most of the regulars ignored him as he sat nursing his pint in the dark corner by the fire.

A young girl. Eleven, twelve, maybe? He'd no idea really. He knew nothing about children. She was standing on the step, her arms folded over her chest against the wind, her thin coat pulled tightly round her small frame. Her teeth chattering.

There's a goose. It's hurt, she whispered, one muddy wellington balanced awkwardly on top of the other, her chapped fingers picking at the stray threads hanging from the sleeve of her frayed coat.

Dunno what to do.

He asked her in out of the cold and she came in shyly, standing against the wall of his makeshift kitchen as if taking up too much room.

So, what's this about a goose? he asked, taking a final swig of his tea that was now growing cold.

I seen your light on, didn't I? Seen you out drawing. You're an artist, aren't you? It's hurt, the goose. Its wing's all wonky. It hissed and tried to peck me. I was scared. I didn't know what to do. But it'll die if I leave it. I don't want it to die, she said, her bottom lip beginning to tremble.

Her accent wasn't local. London? Cockney? She looked half-starved. What was she doing out here? He finished his toast and went in search of a towel and a cardboard box. Then pulled a chunk of bread from the loaf on the table and stuffed it in his pocket.

All right, then. You'd better show me where it is.

The girl said nothing as he followed her into the blustery wind in the direction of the iron sluice. At the bottom of the gulley, hiding under a clump of sea lavender, was the goose. It was pure white. Its eyes a milky pink. An albino? That would be rare indeed. He slithered down the bank and saw it was trailing its left wing, its snowy plumage spattered in blood. He climbed into the ditch and it raised its sinuous, snake-like neck to strike him. Fumbling in his pocket he felt for the bread, broke off a hunk, then threw it towards the bird, asking the girl to hand him the towel. While it was feeding, he crept up behind it, flung the towel over its head and lunged, grabbing it with his full weight, trying to pinion its wings against its body, careful not to apply too much pressure to the wound. But it was strong and hissed and honked, trying to turn its head from side to side to peck him. He could feel the mass of muscle rippling under his hands, sense its instinct to escape his grip and break free, but he managed to jam its tense body under his elbow to examine the damaged wing.

He couldn't tell whether or not it was broken. If he took the bird back to the lighthouse and nursed it, it might survive. It would take weeks, months even, for the flight feathers to grow back. But he couldn't just leave it. Other wild geese wouldn't tolerate it in their midst, they'd kill it. Nature had no use for cripples, he thought wryly.

Wrapped up inside the box, it seemed to settle. He closed the lid and carried it back in the direction of the lighthouse, the girl following close behind.

When he got in and opened the box, it had shat all over the inside. He picked it up and could feel its terror. Its heart pounding beneath its feathers as he spread out the damaged wing as gently as he could. He wasn't sure, but one of the bones where the wing bent seemed to be broken, where if it had been human, it would have had its elbow.

He had been nursing wounded birds for a while, but nothing as large as a goose. He told the girl to fetch the small first-aid box from the bottom of his haversack, fish out the tweezers, gauze and bandages, and hand them to him. Next he asked her to boil the kettle, telling her to put a handful of salt in the bowl and cover it with the hot water. She did as she was told, obediently bringing him the steaming bowl, setting it on the table. When the water had cooled, he told her to hold the bird's wing open, picked up the tweezers and rooted around for the shot, managing to extract it, before bathing the wound with the tepid saline solution.

The goose was calmer now, seeming to sense that they were trying to help it. He told the girl to fetch a paintbrush from the jam jar on his painting table, snap off the handle and lay it along a length of Elastoplast, then fold over the edges to make a splint while he held the goose. After that, he instructed her to cut up the gauze and place the pad on the wound, then the splint against the length of broken bone. He explained how to unwind the bandage and wrap it over the bird's back to lock the wing in place while he held it still. It had to be loose enough not to restrict its breathing but tight enough that it couldn't pull it off. When it was secure, he let go of the goose, trimmed the ends and asked the girl to move the coal scuttle and two stools together against the wall to make a makeshift pen. They had to keep the bird safe, he said, until he could figure out what to do next. He went in search of his hot water bottle, wrapped it in the towel, placing it gently inside the pen next to the bandaged bird. He knew it would be traumatized from being handled, that these next few hours would be critical.

Is it going to be all right? the girl asked, almost under her breath. It was the first time she'd spoken since they'd returned to the lighthouse.

All right? Yes, hopefully. But it'll take time. You look very cold, by the way. Can I get you something to eat? Some hot buttered toast?

He made her a couple of slices and she wolfed them down.

More?

She nodded.

So, what's your name?

Freda.

And what're you doing out here, Freda? You're from London, aren't you, by the sounds of it?

I'm with the Willocks. I got evacuated. Put on a train. My nan died and my mum's in our shop in Bethnal Green. Why do you keep them other birds in that cage outside?

Because they're hurt, Freda. They wouldn't survive in the wild on their own. I feed them and look after them, help them to get better.

Do you think the goose is going to get better? Will it die? I don't want it to die, she said, her face beginning to collapse.

No Freda. It won't die. Not if we look after it, but I'll need to change its dressing, go up to the village and get some medicine. But I think it'll be all right.

Can I help? Help look after the goose?

Of course, Freda. You found it.

He lifted the bike Mackman had lent him out of the shed, flung his leg over the crossbar and cycled up into Sutton Bridge. He needed iodine. He didn't want the wound to become infected. He'd washed it as well as he could but needed something stronger than salt water. He bought a small brown bottle in the chemist's, then went across to the general stores and post office to see if there was any post. The postmistress was getting to know him.

There's one letter Mr Rhayader with a London postmark. Just you wait there now while I find it. I know I put it over here somewhere.

The minute he saw the copperplate script he knew that it was from Jess. He shoved it into his breast pocket, clambered on his bike and headed back to the lighthouse. How had she found his address? After putting the bike in the shed he went inside, lit a cigarette and made a cup of tea, then sat down to open the letter.

Darling Philip,

I've been so worried. No one seems to know where you are. After you left the Warneford you just disappeared. I thought you might have gone to France to be with your mother or be staying in her Kensington flat. I rang the number you gave me but the woman who answered, the housekeeper I suppose, said you weren't there and that it was best to write to you via your stepfather's solicitor, that he'd be likely to know where you are. So, that's what I'm doing. Though God knows if you'll ever get this.

Darling boy. I spent all summer after finals with Peter at our godfather's house in Orvieto. It was bliss to be able to sit in the sun, swim and read for pleasure. We went to the cathedral. You'd have loved it. There are three huge bronze doors and a big rose window. The place is simply covered in gold, with some of the most beautiful frescoes I've ever seen and a ceiling by Fra Angelico. There's also a stunning painting, the Madonna della Tavola by Cimabue or, at least, one of his pupils. It would have been wonderful to hear your thoughts, for you to explain the difference in styles to me. You know so much more about painting than I do. As you know, I'm a bit of an ignoramus on that score. But I was particularly struck by the fresco in the San Brizio chapel by someone I'd never heard of called Signorelli: 'The Damned Cast into Hell'. I found it really disturbing. All those men and women screaming, their naked bodies contorted in pain and tortured by demons. It seemed terribly prescient on the eve of this horrible war. I so wish you could have been there with me to see it. For us all to have been together like the old days when we cycled down to the Vicky Arms and went punting. After our visit to the cathedral we had some wonderful local vino rosso under a vine in a little café opposite, and a delicious plate of spaghetti and ragu. The Italians certainly know how to eat.

It was then that Peter told me about you and him. Darling, do you think I care a jot? Everyone adores Peter and he always gets what he wants. But that doesn't have to spoil us, does it? And the truth is, Peter is now in love, which is rather amazing as he's so terribly fickle. He invited George Meredith from his tutorial group to join us in Orvieto for a few weeks. Since then they've been inseparable. There's no doubt George is very good-looking in a Rupert Brooke sort of way. I think he's a cad but Peter's obviously smitten. There's something a bit Maynard Keynes and Lytton Strachey about the pair of them. I think they rather enjoy hamming it up, wearing identical linen shirts, panama hats and matching cravats.

I do hope you don't mind, darling. You really shouldn't. The fact is, I don't think Peter really loves anyone except, perhaps, me. And that's altogether different. But it does seem to have lasted beyond the summer. Though, of course, now they'll both be called up. Peter has opted for the navy. He says they are the senior service and have the best uniform. I wondered whether he'd agree to serve or, like you, refuse. But he's not so principled. Happy to be bohemian and anarchic if it doesn't cost him too dear. Pacifism was, I suspect, always a bit of a pose to make him seem more interesting. He's my darling brother and I'd go to the ends of the earth for him, but I'm under no illusions. I do so admire you for sticking to your principles. It's one of the reasons I love you. Peter joining up is something that, sadly, we have rather fallen out about. It's the first time in our lives we've ever had a serious disagreement and it's all down to this ghastly war.

I feel dreadful that I didn't come to see you in hospital. But my parents practically forbade me, and I was too feeble to argue. They're all liberal tolerance when they want to be but not, it seems, when it comes to their only daughter. My God, you'd think that Daddy, being a psychiatrist, would have a bit more understanding. I think they were worried that I'd get too involved. Be hurt. And, though it's no excuse, I had finals coming up and was frightened if I saw you in that horrible place, I'd be upset and unable to work. Will you forgive me for being such a coward?

But Philip, darling, I'm writing to say how much I miss you. I miss being silly with you and talking to you in a way that I can't with anyone else. With everyone else I have to pretend, to fulfil their expectations, but with you I can just be me. Oh yes! And I went to the May Ball with Jack Forster. He's been after me for ages, but it wasn't the same as being with you. He's charming and attractive, but really a bit of an ass.

Please tell me where you are. I'm in London sharing a flat with a girl from my year at Lady Margaret Hall. Working at the Ministry of Defence. It's all supposed to be hush-hush. There are several of us from my year at Oxford. A couple from Cambridge and one from Birmingham. But really, we're just glorified clerks. No one knows what's going on. Everyone is on tenterhooks wondering if tomorrow will be the day that they hit. But I keep telling myself that at least I'm not actually killing anyone, not doing any harm. Or should I have refused?

Oh Philip, the idea of this war is just too ghastly. I don't think I can bear it. I know the Germans are being quite foul but how is mass killing going to solve anything? I've always been so sure of my beliefs. Now I'm just confused as to what's the right and moral thing to do. Philip, please tell me where you are and I will leave London tomorrow and come to you. I have my small allowance from Granny, so don't really have to work, and I haven't been called up yet—just doing my bit—so presume I could leave. It would mean living like a church mouse. But I don't care. Please let me come to you. We can be together. Sit up all night drinking cocoa and putting the world to rights. Turn our backs on all this horror.

Do write. Do let me know where you are, my darling. I can't wait to hear from you.

Your loving,

Jess

He could hardly bear to read it. Part of him longed to sit down and write straight back, to tell her where he was and ask her to come to him. They could live here together; read, cook. Take long walks along the coastal path. Birdwatch. He imagined her stockings airing above the stove. The smell of her scent as she lay naked beside him on the makeshift bed. Her milk-white skin and mass of red hair tumbling in the dark across his chest. Maybe, with the horrors of war that were bound to come, he ought to snatch any chance of happiness that came his way. He knew further preparations were being made on the home front, that more children were being evacuated out of the cities, that soldiers were being posted abroad, even as others were returning on Christmas leave from France.

But no. If he was honest, he knew it wouldn't work. He loved Jess but could never be what she wanted or needed. He'd always let her down and he couldn't bear to hurt her. To be thinking of Peter, wanting to fuck Peter, while they made love. He was better alone. He remembered, at Oxford, reading Pascal's assertion that humanity's problems stemmed from an inability to sit quietly alone in a room. He lit another cigarette and looked out of the window. It was raining. He could see a skein of pink-foot looping across the sky above the lighthouse. Maybe here, away from everything, he'd discover what he really wanted. For a long time, every meeting with another person had been a trial of sorts and left him exhausted. He felt too much, was too open to the world. His skin too thin. His whole life had been spent trying to prove himself to a father he barely remembered and a mother occupied elsewhere. Every drawing, every painting he did was for that purpose. Solitude gave no guarantee of protection from the darkness within. Yet maybe he could finally face that void, painful as it was, and find some sort of resolution, a sort of peace.

The reasons for his breakdown no longer interested him. What mattered, now, was how he dealt with things, the choices he made, how he responded to events going on around him. He fetched his jacket. An evening walk would do him good. Take him out of himself. His work wasn't going well. He'd scrubbed back the canvas twice already, dissatisfied with what he'd produced. He felt angry with his failures, his inability to capture what he saw in his mind's eye. It was only when out walking that his thoughts began to fall into place, that he was able to find a sense of balance. Solitude gave him a sort of clarity. When he returned to the lighthouse, windblown and soaked after hours out on the marsh, he felt revived and ready to work. He never walked with any purpose or took a particular direction. He simply followed his nose where whim and intuition led him. Sauntered. The word was derived, he'd read, from those who had roamed the countryside asking for alms in the Middle Ages. Often their requests were bogus, a pretence that they were going *à la Sainte Terre*—to the Holy Land—and were in need of funds. Children would shout: 'There goes a *Sainte-Terrer*' and run after them throwing stones.

But solitude was beginning to suit him. Everyone seemed terrified of being alone, filling their days sitting on committees or playing bridge. Learning Spanish. Things that made them feel connected, important, their life meaningful. We lived in a society where achievement was a badge of honour, yet he'd never had an anchor to hold him fast, never felt entitled to happiness. His life had been circumscribed by what was expected of him: common entrance, matric, prelims, finals. Joining the right societies and making the right friends. With no father to guide him and a mother busy with her own concerns, he'd had to find his own way. Now, through this immersion in silence, he was slowly beginning to discover himself in the sound of the wind and sea birds.

He thought of the painters he admired—Rembrandt, Vermeer, Turner—and wondered what he, untrained as he was, could hope to achieve as an artist. But getting depressed would only lead to a downward spiral. The answer was to stay focused, to work and avoid pessimism, to stop being so easily discouraged. After all, he had his paints and books, the freedoms offered by this wild place. Wasn't that enough when Europe was about to descend into a bloodbath?

The light was fading. The receding tide leaving frothy suds in the creeks. The water levels dropping and making strange gurgling noises as they drained through the mud. A gull's feather was drifting out to sea, the salty rivulets leaving wavy lines on sandbanks. He walked on, feeling the squelch beneath his boots, stopping to listen to the faint cheeping of a flock of pipits, watch a pair of snow buntings tossed like scraps of paper on the wind. He could see the body of a black-headed gull floating in and out of a clump of samphire on the receding tide as the pale moon rose over the Wash.

The wind was brutal. He turned to make his way back to the lighthouse, towards the small porthole of light glimmering in the distance and, as darkness fell, he realized that his presence here was justified, that everything was beginning to make sense. When he got in, he hung up his jacket, lit the stove and sat down to reread Jess's letter. When he'd finished he folded it along the creases, put it back in the envelope and slipped it behind the clock. Then he went out to see to the goose.

S CHOOL WAS FINISHED. The local children were busy helping their mothers make plum puddings and pick holly. People didn't go out much unless they had to. I was desperate to get back to London and wrote to Mum begging her to come and fetch me for Christmas. But, she answered, the government was giving out leaflets telling parents to keep their children where they were, out of harm's way. Her *Woman's Own* was advising mothers to put 'the happiness of their children first and spare them the sorrow of another parting'.

But I hated being at the Willocks'. And the worst was that Bert had gone back to Bethnal Green. His dad said that as there hadn't been any bombs, he might as well be at home. Bert was big, loud and silly but I'd miss him.

Now that I wasn't at school, Mrs Willock made it clear she didn't want me under her feet. So as soon as I'd done my jobs I put on my wellingtons and headed along the sea wall to the lighthouse. I didn't know if you'd send me away with a flea in my ear, but when I knocked, you invited me in. I thought you sounded incredibly posh, like the doctor who'd looked after Nan. The goose was still in its chair-and-coal-scuttle pen, the floor streaked with trails of chalky shit. Though it seemed to have perked up a bit and was waddling round in its bandages. You'd given it some cabbage leaves and a bowl of water.

Can I feed it?

You can try, you said. But geese can be aggressive if they feel threatened. They stick their necks out and hiss like she did when we tried to catch her. You need to be gentle. She's a young bird. Maybe that's why she was shot. She has less experience than older birds. And being white, she's very visible. It makes her a target. Here, try this, you said, handing me some kale. Tear it into bits so she doesn't choke. Let her come to you.

I ripped the leaf into shreds, laid them across my palm and crouched down. At first she hissed, but after a little while came up and snatched a strip.

Look, look, she ate out of my hand! Can I hold her?

Not yet. Soon, maybe. Wild birds don't like being handled. Imagine how you'd feel if you were picked up by a giant. Leave her for now until she gets used to you. Would you like some toast? You look freezing. Don't you have any gloves?

You made me hot buttered toast and sweet tea. It felt cosy by the Valor stove, like being with Nan in the scullery in Bethnal Green on a smoggy winter evening. The place was littered with books and you'd pinned your drawings around the walls. There was also a big map of Great Britain showing all the rivers and mountain ranges. There weren't many mountains in England but lots in Scotland and Wales.

I asked if you'd read all the books.

No, Freda. A lot, but not all of them. There are always more books to read. New things to learn.

We never had no books at home. Nan gave me a *School Friend Annual* for me birthday. I'm reading *Jane Eyre* now. I borrowed it from school. It's sad and has lots of long words.

What about the family you're with? Don't they have any books?

Nah. I just do jobs there, and mind Billy.

Well you can come and look at my books anytime. I've lots with pictures of birds. You can learn their names. Those on that shelf over there have poems in them. And those, you said, pointing to a large pile on the floor, are paintings by famous artists. You might enjoy looking at those. And the goose, Freda? What are you going to call the goose?

Me?

Yes, you found her. You should name her.

Can I call her Freda?

Well, you can if that's what you want. She's a pink-foot and in the autumn left her home in the Arctic to fly here. That's a long way for one small bird to travel. Pink-foot normally have grey-brown bodies and dark heads with white-tipped tail feathers but she's an albino. That's why she's white and has pink eyes. It makes her vulnerable. She's special because she's different. So maybe we should give her a special name? A Norse name to remind her where she's come from. What do you think of Fritha? It sounds a bit like Freda, doesn't it? It means 'fair' and 'beautiful' as well as 'protector of peace'. I think that might be a good name for a goose in wartime, don't you?

Yes, yes, I like that. But can I be Fritha too? Will you call me Fritha?

I don't see why not, you said, smiling.

And what's your name. What do I call you?

Philip. Just Philip.

I don't know why I asked you to call me Fritha too. Maybe I sensed that it would mark a new beginning. That by taking a different name I could become someone else. It'd be a secret that no one—not the Willocks, not Mrs Bint, not even my mother—would know about. Fritha would only exist when I came to the lighthouse. I'd leave Freda behind, hanging on the back of the door in my room like an old coat, and slip my arms into the sleeves of my new name. Pull it up round my shoulders and hug it tight. I would be whatever I wanted. Strong. Brave. Beautiful. I'd no longer be Freda from Bethnal Green, or Rails who didn't know where her dad was and had to put up with Mr Willock doing horrible things. I'd be a girl from a faraway land of sparkling glaciers and frozen stars, where everything was shimmering, white and clean.

I slipped up to my room, got out a piece of paper and wrote: F R I T H A across it in big letters and knew then that that blank white sheet was covered with secret paths like the tracks in snow, and that all I had to do was to follow one of them, and wherever it led, that would be my life.

I thought Mrs Willock wouldn't let me go. But the invitation came from the vicar's wife, so I don't think she liked to say no. It was for a Christmas party at Sutton Bridge RAF mess, organized by the Mother and Baby section of the WVS for local children under fourteen. The Mother and Baby section met in the village hall to help the district nurses weigh newborns. They gave advice to first-time mothers and dispensed food vouchers and clothing to those bringing up children alone, and whose husbands were invalids or out of work. The knitting circle met on Tuesdays where, over a cup of tea and a slice of Victoria sponge, they turned out gloves and socks for the troops.

The airbase was surrounded by high barbed wire. There were notices everywhere that warned 'TRESPASSERS WILL BE PROSECUTED'. The base had been built after the First World War. Now it was being used as a training ground for pilots to practise firing machine guns and dropping bombs along the coastal marshlands of the Wash. With the declaration of war, activity had been stepped up. We'd seen the airmen in their distinctive blue-grey uniforms down in Sutton Bridge.

The invitation said I should be ready and waiting near the swing bridge on Saturday at four o'clock sharp. Clean, tidy and in my best clothes. The WVS had organized for those with cars to collect us and drive us to the party. Then drop us back when it was over.

I took a saucepan of hot water up to my room to wash my hair in the big porcelain bowl. I didn't have any shampoo, so the sliver of Wright's coal tar left from the piece Mum had brought when she came to visit had to do. I had nothing new to wear but at least I could be clean. At three o'clock I walked up to the swing bridge. I was sorry Bert wasn't with me. Especially as the girls who were my class tormentors, the ones who called me Rails, were. But they seemed to have forgotten the pleasure of teasing me in the excitement of going to a party.

The mess was decorated with coloured balloons and home-made paper chains. The tables were groaning with food: plates of jam tarts, currant buns, sausage rolls, jellies and mince pies. We were all told to take a cardboard plate and help ourselves. The airmen had organized a Punch and Judy show in a little striped booth. It reminded me of being in Southend with Mum. But I didn't like it much and wondered why the others found it so funny when Mr Punch, squeaking 'That's the way to do it', beat Judy senseless. There were musical chairs and blind man's bluff, along with a great deal of showing off and giggling. One girl became so overexcited that she was sick. Before we left, we were each given a hunk of Christmas cake, wrapped in a paper napkin, to take home. And, for a moment, I almost forgot that I'd be spending Christmas more or less alone.

For days after the party Mrs Willock gave me piles of jobs to do, as if making me pay for being allowed to go. I had to wash Billy's stinky nappies. Carry the wet pile down to the orchard to hang on the line propped up with a forked stick that snapped under the weight, so they had to be washed again. I brought in the logs. Picked sprouts and kale. Scrubbed the shit off the bowl in the privy with a big bristle brush. Then, when she couldn't think of anything else to make me do, I ran off to the lighthouse. The sun was low, and the cattle huddled by the gate blowing steam from their pink nostrils, their muddy hoof-holes covered in sheets of ice. A fog was coming in on the morning tide disorienting the tweeting pipits as they flew up out of marsh hedges. In the distance I could see a pair of wildfowlers trudging back towards the bank so as not to get caught on the sands in the murk. And further out I could hear the bellow of a foghorn, a ship moving nervously as a pregnant heifer, slowly through the mist.

I realize that I've said very little about you in this journal. The truth is, I didn't know that much about you. I'm trying to remember your grey eyes and straight nose. But somehow you remain just out of reach like someone trapped behind an old mirror. It's all such a long time ago. You weren't particularly tall, I seem to remember. A rather boyish frame, with something strained about the eyes that, even as a young girl, I felt I understood. Your hair was sandy. Quite long. Not at all the fashion for those days, with an untidy fringe that kept falling in your eyes. But it's your fingers, with their square nails, I remember best. A painter's hands.

And you always wore the same thing. A blue sailor's jersey over a flannel shirt and heavy, working men's trousers like those worn by the local stevedores. I'm sure you had other clothes. Smart clothes. Suits from made by a tailor in Savile Row. Good shirts. I didn't realize it at the time—how could I have known?—that you came from a comfortable middle-class family. I understood nothing about Oxford and punting. Tutorials on the existence of God. Nothing of that long hot summer you'd spent in France, dressed in shorts and white plimsolls, eating *tarte tatin* at the iron table on the terrace of your stepfather's house.

All these things were beyond my experience. Until I was sent to that cold place my life had consisted of St John's infant school and the back scullery of our hardware shop. Sink plungers. Nails. Brooms hanging in the shop doorway onto the street. I knew no one other than my immediate neighbours. My teachers and those in my class. Mum, Dad and Nan. While you were punting on the Cherwell, I was with Iris watching loonies shouting from the top of soapboxes in Victoria Park.

Reading this it strikes me that my handwriting looks very old-fashioned. People don't write like this any more. Miss Wilson taught us how to do cursive script between two black lines, to make the downward and upward strokes thick and thin, the tails of the 'g's and 'y's drop and curl beneath the bottom line. The vowels sit like sparrows along a telegraph wire. I write exactly the same way as I did then. But my hands are old. Covered in liver spots. They remind me, if there was ever any doubt, how much time has passed.

Bernadette pops her head round the door to ask if I want some more tea. I invite her in and offer her one of my chocolate Bourbons. She plops herself down in my easy chair with the blue crocheted cushion, pleased to take the weight off her feet. She's a nice girl and chats away about her wedding plans. Tells me the reception for sixty is going to be at the golf club in Co. Leitrim, that her wedding dress is, to use her words, 'very Ginger Rogers'. That her twin nieces are going to be bridesmaids and her sister-in-law the maid of honour. Her mam, she says, is making them a three-tiered wedding cake.

Sure, I'll bring you a slice, Freda. I'll be back after the honeymoon for a bit before I'm finally off. We're lucky the house we're moving to belongs to my Uncle Pat. So we'll only have to pay a peppercorn rent. It will make a grand B & B. The Americans are mad for Ireland, Freda. You should come and stay one day.

H E HEARD THE ROAR of the three RAF squadrons setting out across the North Sea. Next day the BBC announced that a tightly flown bomber formation had been sent to destroy German U-boats taking their toll on Allied shipping in the Heligoland Bight. The Air Ministry had launched an attack to prevent German surface ships supporting U-boats in the North Atlantic. But reading between the lines, it seemed the Germans had inflicted more damage on the RAF than the Luftwaffe had received. Glued to the radio he learnt it had been a daylight raid and that the casualties had been high, rather undermining the RAF's mantra, he thought wryly, that 'the bomber always gets through'. It hardly constituted a victory.

So this was it. After all the weeks of waiting and false rumours, the fighting had finally started. All hopes that the Treaty of Versailles and the new League of Nations would prevent a further European conflict, now shattered. Hitler's ambitions for German expansion, despite his cynical disavowals, increasingly evident.

He was in despair. How could any good come out of what would be another bloodbath? He'd always had a vision of a Europe at peace. A continent where people were free to roam from the Swiss Alps to the Bay of Naples. He remembered his first visit to Jess and Peter's house in Holland Park. How among the Clarice Cliff china and smelly Siamese cats, the piles of *Punch* and *London Illustrated News*, there'd been a small arts and crafts glass cabinet full of curios from the family's frequent travels to the Continent. A carved Bavarian wooden spoon from Munich. A little spyglass that enlarged a microscopic view of Notre-Dame. A miniature tin leg—a healing votive from some dark Italian church. Upstairs on the landing, a photograph of St Mark's Square taken at sunset hung beside a black-and-white etching of Chartres cathedral, and on the big oak chest there'd been one of Jess and Peter as children, standing in sun hats in front of some Etruscan ruins. His first visit to Europe hadn't been until he was twelve, when he'd gone to France to visit his mother and Edward Pemberton.

For the first time, he was having doubts. Questioning his right to stay holed up in the middle of nowhere while other men risked their lives. He could no longer deny that Hitler was a threat or be blind to the fact that civil liberties, personal freedom and the rule of law were in jeopardy. The RAF had been dropping propaganda leaflets on Germany warning of the evils of the Nazi regime, reminding the citizens that they were vulnerable to bombing raids. But, he thought ruefully, we were well past the leafleting stage now.

The December wind was savage. He went out to check on the birds. Recently he'd taken in an oyster catcher and a couple of redshanks. He fed them, changed their water and then went back inside to see to the goose's dressing. When the bandages came off he'd move her into the pen with the other birds, get her acclimatized to being outdoors again.

He was running low on supplies and that would mean a trip to the village. He needed candles. Paraffin. Milk, bread and tea. He heated up the last of the potato soup he'd made the previous day. In the pub, when he'd recently stopped for a quick pint, he heard talk that bacon, butter and sugar were all going to be rationed after Christmas. Maybe he should write back to Jess after all. Accept the offer of companionship and warmth she held out in these dark times. It would be different living here with someone else. They could cook together instead of his surviving on boiled eggs and toast. Cultivate a garden. Read and walk. When he moved in, he'd done very little other than clear a space for a bed in the top room. Put the junk in the yard. But you could hardly call the place homely. With Jess here, it would be different.

He wondered where she'd be for Christmas. Holland Park? And if Peter would be there too. He imagined them around the big oak dining table. A log fire in the grate and the Siamese cats curled up on the Persian rug, their father in his velvet smoking-jacket and silk cravat. A hamper from Fortnum's full of stilton and port on the sideboard. Candles. *The Times*, which he was able to pick up when he cycled into the village, had recently published pictures of the young Princesses Elizabeth and Margaret doing their Christmas shopping in Woolworths. Presumably to make people feel that we were all in this together. There'd also been an article on how to make the most of a wartime Christmas. Oxford Street, it reported, was chock-a-block with men in uniform on leave from France, and Marshall & Snelgrove had received numerous inquiries for evening and party dresses to 'welcome back our men'. While the lingerie department, it added coyly, had been 'particularly busy'. And for those looking for 'an inexpensive but practical gift for their sweethearts', a luminous flower-shaped badge that glowed in the blackout to prevent bumps from other people, was 'the perfect gift'.

He couldn't bear the triviality of it all.

The paper also carried a report of a police raid on the flat of Norah Elam, one of ten women the British Union of Fascists had chosen to stand as candidates in the forthcoming election. A member of Archibald Ramsay's Right Club that had introduced a private member's bill in Parliament to prevent aliens gathering to 'propagate blasphemous or atheistic doctrines calculated to interfere with the established religious institutions of Great Britain', this Dublin acolyte of Oswald Mosley's, he realized, was proof that Germany wasn't the only enemy we needed to fear.

He wondered if the girl would come back. He worried that the Willocks weren't being kind to her. She seemed young and vulnerable, and both times she'd been to the lighthouse she'd appeared hungry. He had no idea how old she was. He'd led such a sheltered life. What did he know about how most people lived? What challenges they faced. At Oxford he'd sat in the Bird and Baby or in his rooms with Peter and Jess putting the world to rights but it had all been theoretical. Just talk. Jess was more in touch than most of them. She had a natural empathy and frequently visited the East End with her mother to help needy women. If Frith—as he was getting used to calling her, while the goose seemed to have become Fritha—did come back, he'd lend her some books. Encourage her to read and draw. Teach her the names of the different local birds. It would be good to have something to think about other than his own emotional maelstroms.

It was a few days before she appeared again, wearing the same thin cotton dress and lilac hand-knitted cardigan. She looked freezing and he wondered if she had any other clothes. Her hands were red and raw with chilblains. She came in and went straight to the goose. This time, it took the cabbage leaves direct from her hand and she asked if she could pick it up. He told her to sit down, then reached into the makeshift pen to fish out the bird and placed it on her lap. He was touched by her gentleness. How pleased she was it didn't struggle to break free. When they put it back, he offered her some soup and bread. He suspected that she was really hungry.

After she'd eaten, he asked if she'd like to choose a book for them to look at together. She went to the shelves and ran her fingers along the spines, stopping at N.H. Joy's *How to Know British Birds*. He showed her the Passeri: the blackbirds and choughs. The song thrushes, wagtails and nuthatches. The blue tits and great tits. Then he turned to the waders, the ringed plovers and common sandpipers. Followed by the ducks and terns. He explained that the easiest way to recognize birds was to divide them into categories: those that lived on the land and those that lived on water. The land birds had special feet with curved claws for grasping their perches. Whereas water birds' feet were webbed and adapted for swimming. As he sat in the glow of the paraffin lamp explaining these simple facts to this child, he felt a new peace.

She came back the following day and, after she'd had her toast and tea, he asked if she'd like him to read to her. He leafed through his *Palgrave's Golden Treasury*, stopping at William Blake's 'The Tyger'. A poem he'd loved as a child. She sat enthralled while he read. Then asked him the meaning of 'immortal' and 'symmetry'. He explained and suggested that she might like to borrow the book to read the poem for herself.

After that he didn't see her for several days. He wondered what was keeping her away. Whether she'd lost interest. When she did return, she gave no explanation for her absence. He suggested that they go for a walk and take the bird book to see if they could identify any of the different species in the wild. He found an old hat and scarf and told her to put them on.

It's cold out there, Frith, but good weather for birdwatching.

He fetched his jacket, picked up his binoculars and they set off down the track to the sea wall to find a spot out of the wind. He handed her the binoculars, explaining how to move the little wheel on the top to bring things into focus. At first, she couldn't see anything.

Look towards the mudflats, he suggested. Over there. And then adjust the eye piece till things became clear. Can you see the flock of wheeling knots flashing their pale underwings, twisting and turning in the wind like acrobats? If we sit quietly, we might see one up close. Knots are dumpy, short-legged wading birds. In winter they're dull grey with white breasts. But in the spring, their faces and chests turn brick-red.

He could see she was shivering, that she didn't have enough warm clothes to protect her against the wind, and suggested that they go back. But she wanted to stay, to go on watching the knots twirl against the whitening sky.

Come on now, Frith, it's freezing. I don't want you to catch cold. Anyway, I think it's time for you to go. I don't want you to get into trouble. We can come again another day. I promise. Come up to the lighthouse now. I'll make you some toast and tea before you go. I've just remembered I've got a pot of raspberry jam somewhere.

He didn't see her again until Christmas Eve. He was vaguely worried about her. Had a sense, for which he had no real evidence, that she was being neglected by the Willocks. He didn't like to say anything. Anyway, what could he do? But she always seemed highly strung and anxious, inadequately dressed against the harsh east winds. So grateful for the tea and couple of slices of toast he rustled up.

He wanted to give her something. A small Christmas gift, but had no idea what. He searched among his things to find something suitable for a young girl. There wasn't much. At the bottom of his trunk he'd had sent on from Oxford was the glass snow globe he'd owned as a small boy. He hadn't seen it for years. He picked it up, shook it, and a blizzard of artificial snow swirled around the miniature village. And then he remembered all those years ago, lying under the paisley eiderdown in his nursery. The white flakes twirling beneath the nightlight when his mother, dressed in black lace for some concert or other, had said goodnight and left his room in a cloud of Blue Grass. In the same trunk he found a scrap of blue wrapping paper decorated with stars. If Frith came back, he'd give it to her.

It was the coldest winter for forty-five years. Snow gathered in deep drifts. The Thames froze over, as well as sections of the Mersey, Humber and Severn. Torrential rain turned to ice storms. Telegraph and power lines sang in the wind, then sagged and collapsed under the weight of ice, cutting off power supplies and creating further misery for those already burdened by war. A photograph in *The Times* showed troops shovelling the knee-high drifts so that people could still get to work. It was a constant battle to keep warm. For days, swirling blizzards blew across the fens. Mackman dropped by to lend him another paraffin stove. But the place was still freezing. He slept in his clothes under a pile of rugs and coats. When he woke the windows were covered in thick sheets of ice. He hardly went out unless forced to go up to the village for supplies. The snow was too thick for him to cycle. So he had to trudge back through the knee-deep drifts carrying potatoes and turnips, sugar and tea in his rucksack, trying not to slip under the weight of the paraffin can, as gusts of blinding sleet blew into his face. And all the while he thought about Jess. How it would have been to have her here with him, but he still hadn't been able to answer her letter.

He tried to tune into the BBC, though the bad weather seemed to make the signal even fainter. There was nothing but a snowstorm of white noise. When he did manage to catch the Home Service, it was clear things were getting worse. After Christmas, the newsreader announced, the government would be introducing price controls on coffee, rice, biscuits and jelly to discourage profiteering.

He was worried about the girl and wondered if she was warm enough. If the Willocks were taking care of her. He'd no proof but suspected they might be using her as cheap labour. He'd spotted Willock a couple of times in the Jugged Hare. One evening, when he was sitting in the corner sipping a pint of pale ale, Willock had walked in with another man, both of them dressed in filthy green oilskins, balaclavas, sea boots and thick stockings. They were carrying guns and looked as if they'd just come in off the marsh. Philip felt an instinctive distaste for the man's rheumy blue eyes. His ginger stubble. There was something unsavoury about him that he couldn't put his finger on, though he didn't hang around to find out what.

The dove-grey cashmere sweater from Galeries Lafayette was wrapped in fine tissue paper. She was sending it *poste restante*, his mother wrote, and very much hoped it wouldn't get lost. What was he doing out in the middle of nowhere, anyway? She understood that having been 'unwell', he wouldn't be called up. Was he with friends at the moment? If so, why hadn't he given her their address so she could have sent the present direct? Would he be spending Christmas with them? She'd hoped to give him the jersey herself, but it was too difficult to leave Paris at the moment. Still, she sent it with her love and hoped he'd have a lovely Christmas and that she'd see him early in the New Year.

She and Edward had been invited to the embassy Christmas dinner. A real treat. The food was always divine. Foie gras. Boeuf Wellington. Bollinger. The tables laid with crisp white linen and napkins, the embassy silver and gorgeous-smelling freesias. It would be hard to believe, among the chandeliers and vases of long-stemmed lilies, that there was a war on. Really nothing much was happening. A few skirmishes on the Western Front. But that was miles away. Admittedly the authorities had taken out the stained-glass windows of the Sainte-Chapelle. Their friend, Pierre Lapicque, a curator at the Louvre, had said packers from the department stores La Samaritine and Bazar de l'Hôtel de Ville, had been packing away the museum's major art works. *The Winged Victory of Samothrace* had been hoisted onto a truck used to move scenery for the Comédie-Française and trundled, with dimmed headlights, down a series of small country roads to some secret destination in the Loire Valley. But, she supposed, this was just a precaution. Really *cette drôle de guerre* was getting on everybody's nerves. When the weather was better, no doubt everyone would come to their senses and things would be back to normal soon. No one would want to fight in the spring when the lilac was in bloom. Then they'd come and see him.

Maybe the bad weather was keeping the girl away. It was too cold to do much. He trudged out through the deep snow to tend to the birds, breaking the ice on their water bowl. Back inside, he cut the fingers off a pair of old woollen gloves and began a series of landscapes. Painting allowed him to see the world from another perspective. To imagine living in a different skin. He leafed through a pile of old maps to get a feel for the local topography. He'd been looking at Turner, trying to catch something of his immediacy, and began laying down a layer of gesso, then painting over the top to give a rough, elemental texture. It was as if he were seeing the place for the first time in the olive greens, the stains of umber and near blacks he produced. The flashes of titanium white. He wanted to express his feelings about this war and being in this place that was neither land nor sea. A feeling which had nothing whatever to do with patriotism, but something deep-rooted and elemental he couldn't even name. At Oxford he'd been surrounded by would-be future leaders. Foreign secretaries. Civil servants. Prime ministers. That's what their education—the tutorials and debating societies—trained them for. But it wasn't for him.

He'd been reading Thoreau and, like him, wanted to divest himself of everything but the basics: food, shelter, clothing, fuel. With just a modest house and a garden in which to grow his food. But most of all he wanted to learn to listen to the silence, to hear the screech of a barn owl, the distant ring of a church bell across the flat fens, the wing beats of migrating geese, stars of water dripping from their hanging paddles.

He missed Frith. As an only child, he'd never had much to do with other children, except the boys at school, and had no idea, really, what interested them or how to talk to them. She seemed young for her years. Lost. He was surprised how much he enjoyed her company, teaching her simple facts. Reading to her. Her thirst for what she didn't know touched him. He knew very little about her life and didn't want to interrogate her, but had gleaned that she'd been brought up in the East End by her mother and grandmother, that they ran some sort of hardware shop, and that the father, a bit of a waster by all accounts, had gone off with another woman. This approximation he'd pieced together from the small fragments she'd offered.

If she came back, he'd ask if he could paint her.

A SMELL OF BLOOD and guts filled the cottage. There were feathers everywhere. Ducks, pheasants and geese. Mr Willock was preparing them for the butcher. While Billy amused himself in the corner teasing the dogs, he and Mrs Willock were at the kitchen table plucking the dead birds. It was Christmas and people wanted their game ready for the oven. With the threat of war, they seemed happy to splash out. To spend a bob or two to take their mind off things. It might be their last chance and they weren't going to go without their roast dinners with all the trimmings if they didn't have to. Who knew what the following year would bring? The village shop had run out of dried fruit and suet, and many were complaining they couldn't make their Christmas puddings. The rumour in the pub, where Willock went to share a pint in the snug with men in muddy boots and bloodstained jackets, was that rationing was due any day now. It was only a rumour, mind. But still. Once Christmas was over people would be cutting back. He had to cash in now. Come the New Year it would be back to clearing ditches and planting potatoes. Maybe no work at all.

Other than gutting and plucking game, there were few Christmas preparations at the Willocks'. Mum sent a parcel with a blue shop-bought cardigan and a card with a robin on the front. She wrote that she'd be spending Christmas Day next door with Mrs Baker. I hated not being at home and couldn't stop thinking about Nan. How I'd always woken on Christmas mornings to find one of Dad's socks at the end of my bed stuffed with a marzipan pig, a jigsaw and a tangerine. I knew they were from Nan, though she always insisted they weren't. Mum paid into a Christmas club for the extras. The bottle of sweet sherry that sat gathering dust for the rest of the year. The box of dates with a camel and a palm tree on the lid. Even so, money was tight. On Christmas Eve we went down to Roman Road and hung round the butcher's stall waiting for the prices of the turkeys to come down. The stalls and barrows stayed open late. The pressurized paraffin lamps lighting up their wares, the vendors vying for custom as they shouted out a constant stream of sales patter.

On Christmas morning Nan would put on her best dress and pour a small glass of sweet sherry, which she'd sip while making the bread sauce. When Dad was at home, he did card tricks and Mum would get tipsy. Normally she didn't drink much. Then she and Dad would get all lovey-dovey. But that was before Vera.

On the afternoon of Christmas Eve I put on my coat and wellingtons to go and see Fritha. I didn't care if the Willocks said I couldn't, but they didn't say anything or notice me leave; if they did, they didn't care. The light was already fading. When you opened the door, the Valor stove was giving off a smoky glow. You took my coat and hung it on the back of the chair as if I were a lady. There was an upturned book on the table by the oil lamp and a half-eaten box of Turkish delight on the arm of your chair. You told me to help myself, then made me a mug of sweet milky cocoa.

I was getting used to spending time at the lighthouse. To the small routines we established. Drawing. Looking at books. Feeding the goose. There was a calm about the place I'd never experienced before. That Christmas Eve you asked if you could draw me. I didn't know what to say. I was embarrassed but didn't like to offend with a refusal. You sat me down on the stool by the window, telling me to keep very still, to find something to let my eyes rest on so I didn't keep moving. It was strange being looked at. Not looked at, exactly, but examined with a scrutiny that felt as if you could see right inside my head. I sat there for ages. After the light went, you put down your paints and told me I'd better go, that you didn't want to get me into trouble. I asked if I could see the painting and you said not until it was finished. That meant I'd have to come back. You didn't offer me any toast but handed me a small packet wrapped in blue paper covered with stars. I didn't know what to say, so hid it under my cardigan, muttering my nervous thanks, and made my way back to the Willocks' in the freezing dark.

Mr Willock spent most of Christmas Day down at the Jugged Hare with Samphire Charlie who scraped a living gathering samphire on the marsh, which he sold in the market for pickle making. Charlie liked a drink. So while the church bells were ringing out across the fens, he cycled the four miles up to the village with his dog in the basket of his old errand boy's bike for a jar with his mate Stan Willock.

I was left with little choice but to go with Mrs Willock and Billy to the morning service. I'd never thought of her as a believer, but the need to keep up appearances demanded that she show her face in church on the last Sunday of each month and on Christmas Day. Many of the congregation were dressed in the new scarves and gloves they'd received that morning as gifts. The vicar wearing a spotless white surplice stood in the porch after the service, shaking hands with the congregation as they trailed out into the blustery sleet. But it was too cold to linger. Everyone was eager to get back to their roast dinners and trifle, their mince pies and board games. The chance to sit bloated by the fireside next to the wireless, tuned into the Home Service, listening to Tommy Handley's fast-talking Liverpudlian twang in *ITMA*.

For the rest of the day Mrs Willock sat pulling labels off the fabric samples for her rag rugs, while Billy lay on his stomach by the stove, poking the dogs and making them growl. No one had any presents but when Mr Willock came back from the pub the worse for wear we had a pigeon pie and a bowl of mashed swede, which I was allowed to eat with them.

PHILIP SPENT CHRISTMAS DAY alone with a bottle of Johnnie Walker that he had spent a good chunk of Pemberton's allowance on. It was his only indulgence apart from a box of Turkish delight. He poured a measure of the oaky golden liquid into a glass and rolled it around his mouth, feeling the burn on his tongue. As the paraffin stove spluttered and Chopin's '*Capriccio*' crackled on the gramophone, he realized he'd begun to relish these moments of isolation. He thought about his mother and Edward Pemberton got up in evening dress at the British embassy in Paris. The large Christmas tree, the international guests, the *foie gras* and handmade *petits fours* prepared by the kitchen's *pâtissier*. He took another sip of whisky and watched the large flakes outside swirling and drifting in the high wind, piling up under the telegraph wires, carpeting the black fields and frozen creeks in a white blanket. Apart from the circle of light from his paraffin lamp, it was pitch black. No moon. No stars. Nothing but the silent, muffling snow.

None of his childhood Christmases had been particularly happy. He wondered what it would have been like to have had siblings. To hide under a big paisley eiderdown whispering in the early hours, daring each other to get up and investigate the stockings hanging on the bedposts at the end of their beds. Perhaps that's what Peter and Jess had done. His own childhood had been overshadowed by the loss of his father. He thought of Tolstoy's happy families and wondered what it would have been like to have a different life. To have been born the son of a baker, say, rather than an army officer. To have left school at fourteen to work in the family bakery, up early each morning to light the oven, prove and knead the dough. A nutty smell of warm bread wafting through the bakery. Would such a life have been any less meaningful than the one he'd been expected to lead?

When he was sent to the Downs at six, he wondered whether he'd inadvertently done something wrong. If he was being punished for some misdemeanour that he didn't know he'd committed and that's why he was being sent away, banished. After he left, his nanny was dismissed. It broke his heart when he came home from school in the holidays to find her gone, with no chance to say goodbye. His teachers and mother were more concerned with his attainment than his comfort. Trying to regain an emotional footing after his breakdown had tested his resolve. Now, if he was to be serious about painting, he had to accept the possibility of failure. Nothing worthwhile was ever achieved with absolute certainty. Doggedness and perseverance would have to get him through. He was reading Zola's *Germinal*. The story of a coalminers' strike in northern France in the 1860s. Zola had made a visit to a French mining town and gone down the pit and witnessed the crippling effects of a local strike first-hand. He knew about hardship. The daily grit needed to get through. It seemed an appropriate book to be reading in such dark days.

Twenty past three. He didn't need to look at his watch. He woke at the same time each night. Cold and stiff. Attacked by anxiety. Anyway, it was practically Boxing Day. There was nowhere he had to be. Nothing he had to do. He got up and lit the paraffin lamp that puffed out a cloud of acrid smoke before settling to burn with a steady flame. Then he pulled on his thick jersey, his fingerless gloves, and picked up his brush.

Would he be able to remember her face, that vulnerability he'd seen the first day when she'd stood on his doorstep, plucking at the frayed sleeves of her thin coat to tell him about the goose? He'd done a few charcoal sketches the last time she was here, now he wanted to work them into a painting.

He started with the eyes. Trying to catch that evasive disquiet lurking behind them. He supposed she must miss her mother and the grandmother who'd recently died. They had obviously been close. She was still so young and far from home, far from all she was used to. He couldn't put his finger on it but there was a fragility there. He had so little experience of what was normal for a child of her age; even so, he felt a nagging concern. Their backgrounds and interests couldn't have been more different, yet there was something that reminded him of his younger self. Like him, she seemed to belong nowhere in particular. He spent a long time trying to capture her face before realizing the needle of the gramophone had got stuck and was slipping backwards and forwards in the final groove of Chopin's 'Waterfall' étude, so the concluding arpeggio's ascents and descents were being repeated over and over again, the notes tumbling like a cascade of falling water. He went to lift the arm, then returned to his canvas, working through the night until the first break of morning.

It was two days after Boxing Day, and he'd run out of everything. He trudged through the knee-deep snow up to the general stores and post office. There was hardly anyone about and a post-festive gloom hung over the village. He was paying for his bag of sugar and cigarettes when the postmistress handed him a letter. It was from Jess.

Darling boy,

Why don't you write? It's just too cruel of you not to tell me where you are. Are you all right? That's all I want to know. At least alive and well? How was your Christmas? Mine was ghastly. Mostly because Peter insisted on bringing his new 'friend' George Meredith to stay and Mummy found them in bed together. Really, he is such a dunderhead. He can do what he likes when he's not at home but why rock the boat? She went to call him down for breakfast, which we always have in our dressing gowns on Christmas morning—scrambled eggs and smoked salmon, with a glass of Buck's Fizz—only to find them, to use her phrase, 'at it'. It's ridiculous, of course. My parents shouldn't mind. They have liberal stamped through them like Brighton through a stick of rock. If he were anyone else's son, they'd make a show of accepting it. But their own? Well, it seems, that's a whole different kettle of fish. Christmas Day was all banging doors and dark scowls. Daddy just shut himself in the conservatory refusing to talk to anybody, reading Freud's Totem and Taboo which, frankly, struck me as pretty ironic, though no one else seemed to notice.

The rest of us had a go at charades but no one had their heart in it. Then, when Mummy's guest, some woman she'd picked up at the Fabian Society in a ghastly homespun dress dropped in for Earl Grey and Christmas cake, and came up with Noël Coward's Private Lives, Peter stormed off. It was as though the very mention of Coward was a deliberate dig. How on earth was Miss Homespun supposed to know he's queer? Anyway he seems to have gone to the country with George. No one has any idea where. He only has a few more days leave before having to go back to his ship. It's all hush-hush, of course, but I gather they're off somewhere near Iceland to hunt for German commercial ships and minesweepers. Peter didn't say exactly, just hinted, but I think they're carrying mysterious cargoes to top-secret ports. I suppose all this cloak and dagger stuff rather suits his soldier-of-fortune nature but I feel distraught that I might not see him again before he disappears into those northern waters filled with German mines and I hate that he's leaving with this bad feeling between him and Mummy and Daddy. He's impossible, of course, but he's MY impossible.

You won't believe it, but I'm trying to write a novel. Don't laugh. Something about a woman working for the Ministry of Defence. She has an affair with her married boss and gets pregnant. He, of course, won't leave his wife. And before you ask: no, its not autobiographical but sort of based on a girl I do know, who works with me and *is* having an affair with her boss. I go to the office every day but there isn't always that much to do—I suppose that'll change if this beastly war hots up—so there's time to look around, observe and take notes. I want to explore what a real, modern woman would do in such circumstances. How she'd cope. No one seems to deal with these things in novels, least of all female writers. And I need something to occupy me, to take my mind off things. Everything's so grim. It's hard to look ahead and believe in a future. I heard from an Oxford friend, who's married to a very nice German psychiatrist, that it's really terrible there, that there are things happening that most Germans don't have a clue about. But they have a small daughter and are afraid of speaking out of turn. They've seen what happens to those that do. My friend, Claire, said that the SS Untersturmführer, Herbert Lange—why do the Germans have such pompous titles like something from Ruritania?—is overseeing this euthanasia programme of mentally disabled patients at the psychiatric hospital in Gniezno, Poland. She wrote that they're being gassed in special vans loaded with carbon monoxide. Can you imagine anything more horrific? Her husband, Dieter, only found out by accident because he's been conscripted onto some awful psychiatric committee and it was too dangerous to say no. But Dieter's a lovely man and wouldn't hurt a fly. He came to visit Claire in Oxford when she was reading modern languages. They'd met on some walking holiday in the Tyrol. I'm sure she took a terrible risk writing to me and I dread to think what would happen if her letter had been intercepted. I'm sure much of the post is censored. Perhaps her letter got through because she's the wife of a 'trusted' doctor. I'm worried about writing back in case I get them into trouble. But she wants me to tell people here, for the world to know what we are up against. So, you see how bad things are. I'm terribly depressed because I've always been so sure of my pacifism. And now? Well, now I just don't know how human beings can do such terrible things to one another. I'd so love to talk to you. I know you'd understand. I feel so lonely now that I've lost my beloved Peter. It's the first time we have been at loggerheads and it's this ghastly war that's created the rift.

Philip darling, please write. Please tell me where you are. What you're doing. I may never be destined to be Mrs Philip Rhayader, but I do love you. Honestly, I do, and whatever happens in the future, I will always be here for you.

Your loving,

Jess

It broke his heart not to be able to tell her to come to him. He'd write soon. He owed her that, at least, honesty in these terrible times. He loved her deeply but not as she loved him. Perhaps he should have become a Catholic priest instead of giving up on the Church. That, at least, would have given him the excuse of celibacy. A framework to live by. He thought of the poet Gerard Manley Hopkins, of his unrequited love for the would-be young poet Digby Dolben he met at Oxford, who'd wandered around barefoot, posing as a medieval monk, hardly noticing poor Hopkins's existence. Hopkins had been so troubled by the sexual arousal he felt at the images of a half-naked Christ that he took to flagellating himself in punishment. It was poetry that saved him, the fevered repetitions of his syntax that gave voice to his pent-up passions.

Philip didn't have to go to such extremes, but this time away from everything would give him a chance to discover the relationship between body and mind. To find a greater balance. Mend the Cartesian split. He'd desired Peter but knew he didn't love him. Not in the way he loved Jess. One day, maybe, he'd find both things in one person but he knew that he'd never have children, that his name would stop with him. There were times when a heaviness came over him that prevented him from working. That was how he'd felt just before his breakdown but he knew he'd be lost if he gave into it now. He had to keep going. One footstep at a time. He went to fetch his coat and scarf to go for a walk down on the marsh, to feel the sleety wind blowing against his face, his boots disappearing into the deep drifts. If he was lucky, he might see a pair of snow buntings, and the watery sun rising over the Wash.

PART 2

1940

THE WASH WAS GRIPPED BY WINTER, the foreshore littered with cakes of ice, some a foot thick and three feet high, the dawn an icy orange, with that smokiness that comes only with a hard frost. There were few pink-foot now. There were hardly any potatoes left for them to eat and the frozen fields were too hard to for them to land on. Though, on the way to school, I still saw the occasional skein flying low against the sky, lines of birds gabbling one to another as they disappeared over the mist rising from the marsh, their plumage brilliant against the hard white snow. And further out, hundreds of mallards and wigeon floated on huge bergs of crystal ice.

But the coast was changing. Naval defences were springing up everywhere. Guns mothballed since the First World War were being brought back into service and placed at vulnerable points along the coast to defend against a German invasion. Red-eared soldiers stood on the snow-blown beaches clapping their chilblained hands, constructing concrete pillboxes to hold the light-aircraft guns needed to shoot down the Luftwaffe. There was talk in the pub of German planes coming in over the Wash, of the Nene being used to navigate their way to bombing raids on the Midlands.

Now Bert had gone back to London, I had to walk to school by myself. The grass along the dykes was bent beneath the snow that came up to the top of my wellington boots. When I crossed the drain by the sluice where we'd found Fritha, I searched for clues as to the whereabouts of King John's lost treasure. Fantasized what I'd do if I found it: where I'd go, what I'd buy. We'd been learning about England's monarchs. King Alfred burning the cakes. King Cnut trying to turn back the tide. Henry VIII's wives. We had just read about Bad King John. He wasn't popular because he'd lost so many of England's lands in France and, after he signed the Magna Carta, broke his word to the barons, so they revolted. While travelling from Spalding on the River Welland in the South Holland district of the county to Bishop's Lynn, as King's Lynn was called then, he was struck with dysentery. When he got better, he sent his baggage and jewels on ahead by what he thought would be a quicker route across the Wash. The bay then, Mrs Bint explained, was much wider. The sea reached as far as Wisbech, and Long Sutton was a port. Up to three thousand courtiers set off carrying the royal wardrobe and the whole of the kingdom's treasury across the sands. The tide was low, the causeway wet and muddy, so the heavy wagons kept getting stuck. Men struggled to hold on to the trunks. Others pulled at the reluctant horses trying to get them to move but eventually everything—men, animals, wagons and jewels—was lost to the incoming tide. Warming to her theme, Mrs Bint described how the ground had opened up in the midst of the waves and bottomless whirlpools had sucked in the chests of coins, necklaces and golden goblets. Nothing, it seemed, was safe in this world. Not even the riches of kings.

*

In the end, it wasn't treasure I found, but the burning wreck of a Spitfire that had crashed just some miles from the Willocks' cottage, at Gedney Drove End. Plumes of smoke rising from the fuselage scattered over the frozen fields. According to the postman, who'd been cycling up the lane when the aircraft broke from its squadron, it appeared to recover before taking a nosedive, then hitting the ground and bursting into flames.

It hadn't been so long ago that I'd seen those German planes over the spinney. I'd been scared stiff, but then no one had been hurt. Now someone had been killed. I heard the crashed plane was being flown by a young pilot on his first training flight. I clambered over the frozen furrows to have a look. Everything was smouldering. Shards of charred and twisted metal poking like black bones from the snow-covered ground. The left wing was shattered, as if some great bird had been brought down by a poacher.

So, this was war.

I hadn't been to the lighthouse since term had started. I was either at school, bringing in the logs, washing nappies or minding Billy. Home and London seemed further and further away. I hadn't heard from Mum, let alone Dad. When I could, I read the book of poems you'd lent me. In my head you were always *you*. I never could get used to calling you Philip. It just didn't seem right, somehow. Mostly I didn't call you anything. I'd learnt Blake's 'Tyger' by heart, and his poem about a lamb. But the poem I liked best was by someone called Thomas Hood, describing the house where he was born, the early sun coming in through his bedroom window. It made me think of my own small room above the shop in Bethnal Green. The narrow iron bedstead and peeling paint. The patchwork quilt made by Nan. The shelf with my Buckingham Palace tin and china doll with a broken arm. I'd never realized that's what poetry could do, tell you how you were feeling. I lay in my narrow bed and wondered what it would be like to really belong somewhere. To walk down the street as I'd done in Bethnal Green and know the people you passed. People who'd stop and ask how you were, if your cough was better or you were over the mumps. How your Nan was keeping. What it would be like to be at the centre of your own life rather than watching from the sidelines. To collect memories I could keep like newly ironed handkerchiefs in a drawer to be brought out when needed.

Now Christmas was over Mr Willock was back spreading slurry on the fields. Getting them ready for the silage and hay that would be gathered later in the year. Repairing broken farm machinery. Soon he'd start to wean the calves onto sugar beet, and it wouldn't be too long till calving was underway, so I didn't see much of him. He'd get called on to give a hand wherever it was needed. Those who kept ewes would soon be wanting extra help with the lambing. But he hated the work. Earning so little for so much effort.

Early one morning, while out on his rusty bike, he glimpsed a flock of geese grazing in Farmer Brady's orchard. Next day they were still there. That afternoon he rode into Sutton Bridge to see his old friend Harry Reece. He and Harry had been at school together, gone bird-nesting and hotching for hedgehogs. Now Harry ran a little barber's shop in one of the backstreets. Occasionally he fenced the odd pheasant or brace of ducks, did a little under-the-counter business with Willock. There were no customers when he opened the door to find Harry sitting with his feet propped on the mantle among the cracked shaving cups, enjoying a cup of tea and reading the newspaper.

Don't often see you 'ere, Stan Willock. No good you bringing me pheasants this time o' year.

No. It's eel hooks I be after, Harry Reece. Got any?

You going fishin'? Thought you were a game man, Reece said, rummaging through an untidy drawer and pulling out a bundle of galvanized hooks.

Going to look in that ol' middle drain. There be some rare big eels down there. Two penn'orth'll do.

Slipping into the orchard under the cover of darkness, Willock fastened the hooks to a length of wire, tying it to the fence and covering the hooks with leaves. With no noise of gunfire, there was little chance of his getting caught. He'd just wait, then slip back in the dead of night to claim his catch. Fixing a lump of bread on each hook, he buried the barbs up beyond the hilt. If the geese came, they'd swallow the bread and be held fast until he could get back to ring their necks. He worked quickly, laying down a line of hooks, before slipping back into the shadows of the ditch. It was deathly still, and his breath made small white ghosts in the freezing air. In the moonlight he could hear the men singing as they tumbled out from the Jugged Hare.

After several hours, the geese still hadn't turned up. From the bottom of the ditch he could hear a car coming along the lane. See its headlamps sweep across the neighbouring field like searchlights. Blowing on his icy hands, he heard Brady switch off the engine, slam the car door and make his way across the cobbled yard towards the farmhouse. A dog barked. Lights went on, and someone shouted, 'Quiet, Molly' before coming out to let her off her chain. Willock knew the dog, a lurcher. She'd tried to bite him once.

A rat rustled in the ditch. Then he heard what he'd been waiting for. The call of a goose from over the far potato patch. Soon the flock was coming in all around him, landing in the middle of the field. If he'd had a gun, he could have bagged the lot. But he had to be quiet. No one must know he was there. One by one, the geese began to eat the bread on the baited hooks when, suddenly, a barn owl screeched in the coppice and the flock took off towards the sea wall. It was then he saw Molly, silhouetted in the moonlight, wolfing down the lumps of bread.

Then there was a sharp yelp, followed by a series of howls. Molly was writhing on the ground, trying to free herself from the wire. For a while it held, then snapped with a twang as she fled, dragging it behind her, yowling back towards the farmhouse. Lights came on. Doors slammed. Angry voices were heard in the yard. Under the cover of darkness Willock slipped noiselessly back into the ditch, then slunk back to his cottage.

*

Of course, I wasn't there to witness it, but it soon became common knowledge. There was a great to-do in the village when Farmer Brady took Molly to the vet to have the hook cut out of her mouth. And it was me who answered the door to PC Watson standing on the doorstep in his helmet, asking if Mr Willock was at home. Before I could answer, he'd taken off his bicycle clips and marched into the kitchen where Mr Willock was sitting at the table, checking the odds for the Lincoln Handicap.

This be yours, by any chance? PC Watson said, pulling a bent, bloodstained eel hook from his pocket.

What would I want with a hook like that? I'm a gunner not a fisher.

Well, suppose I was to say you bought two penn'orth worth from Harry Reece? What would you say to that, Stan Willock?

The magistrate was severe. No doubt mindful of all the other petty crimes and misdemeanours for which he'd been unable to touch Willock, he sent him down for a fortnight. When he came home, he was in a foul mood. Not only did he have to pay a fine, but he'd lost two weeks' work and was worse off than ever.

While he was away, Mrs Willock took to her bed with a heavy cold. Her nose red and raw. Her head bunged up with snot. She did little but trail downstairs in her tweed coat, woolly socks and grubby nightdress to make cups of tea, before padding back upstairs. She'd never been the most diligent of housekeepers. Now the place was cold and filthy. Unwashed clothes strewn everywhere. Dirty pots and pans. The stove unlit. Billy smelling.

While I was getting ready for school one morning, she came down and told me to bring in some logs.

It was as if he'd been on the lookout, waiting for me behind the wood stack, his hand deep in his unbuttoned flies. As soon as I saw him, I dropped the wet logs and began to run back to the house, my heart racing, but he came after me, grabbing me by the hair.

You best git on out of here, gal. You be gone now, he hissed, buttoning up.

I let the icy water from the pump stream over my cheeks until they were numb. That day I didn't go to school but hid in the nook of the sea wall, sheltering from the icy wind. For days I'd been carrying around a sliver of glass in my pocket. A brown shard I'd found in the compost heap from one of the bottles of Newcastle Brown Mr Willock drank while cleaning his guns. I ran my fingers over the amber surface, holding it in my palm like something precious, tracing the sharp edge with my thumb. Then I pulled up my sleeve and slowly, very slowly, dragged it across the thin white skin on the inside of my wrist, so a crimson trickle ran down into the frayed sleeve of my coat. And with it came the relief; for a moment, I felt it all drain away: the fear, the disgust, the gnawing misery and chaos in my head. The voices telling me I was dirty and useless.

THE YOUNG AIRMAN'S CRASH was the talk of the Jugged Hare. Had he been trying to bail out? If so, why hadn't he used his parachute? Though the chatter was soon eclipsed when the first enemy aircraft was brought down up the coast near Whitby. Three 43 Squadron Hurricanes based at RAF Acklington shot down a Heinkel III. Village gossip had it that the formation had been led by a young flight lieutenant, a Peter Townsend who was said to be a friend of the royals and had limped back to the airfield after a dogfight despite the five bullet holes in his fuselage. Even so, the following day he managed to visit the young German rear gunner recuperating in hospital to wish him well.

More and more Philip wondered whether he could justify living in comparative safety while other men put their lives on the line. He'd been excused military service because of his breakdown, along with his claim to be a conscientious objector, and directed to land work, which had its own quiet rewards. The sense of achievement at a ditch cleared. The satisfaction of aching muscles after a day's digging and the chance to live in his body rather than his head. Still, he knew that many of the locals saw him as a fifth columnist. His fellow field workers had jeered when he'd ironically wished a group of muddy, carrot-pulling internees 'a happy holiday' in his schoolboy German. When he tuned into the wireless, he'd switched between the early morning prayers of *Lift Up Your Hearts*, the daily physical exercises encouraged by *Up in the Morning Early* and the mindless stream of *Music While You Work* for the Home Service series, produced by Laurence Gillam, *The Shadow of the Swastika*. Based on real documents, it gave him the closest insight that he was likely to get as to what they were really up against.

At Oxford he'd been so sure of his views, but then it had largely been theoretical. Something to argue about over tea and crumpets or amid the pipe smoke in the Bird and Baby. In truth, he had never really had to face the choices implicit in being a pacifist. Never had to ask what he'd do if push came to shove or what sort of person he really was. Rhetoric was one thing, action another.

He began to spot heavy gun lorries trundling down the sleepy Lincolnshire lanes, new faces filling the pub. Young sergeants and corporals from Birmingham and Coventry loudly downing pints in the smoke-filled snug. Meanwhile, the news was full of Chamberlain's meetings in Paris. Britain had just announced that all merchant ships in the North Sea would now be armed and Germany had retaliated by classifying them as warships.

He wondered how his mother and Pemberton were faring. Perhaps being 'in' with the British embassy gave them a degree of protection but he'd heard things were becoming increasingly difficult in Paris. Since Daladier had signed the Munich pact, along with Chamberlain, the French minister had found himself in a precarious situation, added to which, the French army was decrepit, unmodernized since the Great War.

He received his buff-coloured ration book and would now have to hand over the coupons to the local shopkeepers for his basic supplies. He knew it would be much worse for those in the towns whose only access to any little extras—a slab of butter, an ounce or two of sugar—was the black market. Small luxuries to be had from slipping a bob to the spiv on the corner. Out here he could always filch the old spuds left after the harvest at the corner of the fields. Cadge the odd rabbit or pigeon from Mackman.

Again he wondered what had happened to the girl. He never knew if she was going to turn up or not. Sometimes she came regularly. Then he'd not see her for days and find himself looking out of the window, waiting for the small, huddled figure in the thin coat to appear along the sea wall, silhouetted against the curdy sky. He spent a good deal of time staring out of the window when the weather was too bad to get out and walk. There was always something different to see. A bank of slate clouds hanging over the far windmill. A 'V' of mallard etched against the wall of white sky like the porcelain ducks in flight above the dining-room fireplace of his childhood home. The last time Frith had come, they'd done a jigsaw together. Frans Hals's *Laughing Cavalier*. He'd had it since he was a boy and spent many long wet weekends at the Downs sitting in the bay window of the common room looking for the last piece of the waxed moustache while the other boys flicked paper darts from elastic-band catapults in the long Sunday afternoons. Now it lay half finished on the small round table by his armchair, anticipating her return. Fragments of lace and black silk waiting to take up their rightful place in the scheme of things. Even in this cheap puzzle version, the soldier's eyes had a piercing quality, an uncanny ability to look right through you, and he realized with a shock that he missed her, this skinny young girl, her bones light as a bird's.

He hadn't shaved for days and had barely changed his clothes. When he came in from the fields, he was too exhausted. He'd pull off his caked boots, have some tea or soup, then get down to painting. Often working far into the night. He was moving between figuration and abstraction, trying to get to grips with the grid of creeks covered in grey ice that criss-crossed the marsh, when there was a knock on the door. She just stood there on the step without a word, her face pinched by the wind, her left hand wrapped in a grubby bandage. He didn't ask what had happened or if she'd had an accident, and she offered no explanation, slipping quietly inside and heading for the goose in the corner. She picked it up out of the makeshift pen and took it over to the stool by the stove, where she sat cradling it on her lap. The bird didn't resist as she buried her face in its white feathers. He could see that she was crying.

He couldn't sleep. All night the wind moaned across the marsh. He couldn't put his finger on it but there was something differ- ent about the girl. Her nails were bitten to the quick and she seemed even more withdrawn than usual. He wondered, yet again, if he should speak to Willock. But how could he? What business was it of his? He was only here under sufferance as it was. Just about tolerated by the locals if he kept himself to himself. It wouldn't do to stir things up. Anyway, she'd been officially billeted with him and his wife. But he'd never much liked the man. Still, someone must be keeping an eye. A teacher? The vicar? One of the ladies from the WVS? He worried the Willocks were stingy. Not feeding her properly and working her too hard. But what was it to him? Yet, when he watched her drawing beneath the beam of the storm lantern he felt—what? He didn't even know the right word.

But her hand. What had she done to her hand?

M R WILLOCK had put half a crown at 5 to 1 on Bogskar at Doncaster and it had won. Now he was down the pub with Samphire Charlie spending his winnings. The weather was so rough that I'd missed a good deal of school, unable to make it through the deep drifts to the village or even up to the lighthouse. I hardly spoke and tried to make myself scarce. As if by being silent I might make myself invisible. A wraith on the edge of my own life. Unless I absolutely had to, I only talked to Billy, who trailed round after me waving his arms in the air, whining for me to pick him up and give him a hug. When I could, I escaped to my room and sat huddled in bed in my coat, reading the *Palgrave's Golden Treasury* you'd lent me. The poems brought me back to myself. Made me feel as if I wasn't the only one struggling, that others were as adrift as I was. But the loneliness sat in my chest like something swallowed that I couldn't digest. I gnawed at my cuticles until they bled. Picked at the sleeve of my cardigan till it became even more frayed and tattered, and I still had the piece of amber glass for when everything threatened to overwhelm me.

Then the snow began to melt, to slide off the privy and hen house to form a muddy slush. As I made my way along the sea wall for the first time in weeks, I saw a clump of early violets shivering on the bank and, approaching the lighthouse, could hear the notes of a piano blowing in the wind like a flock of wheeling birds. When you let me in, I saw you had a gramophone. I hadn't noticed it before. I always felt shy with you after a time away, but after you made me tea and toast with gooseberry jam, I settled by the stove with pens and paper to do some drawing. I'd never done much before. I tried to draw Fritha hiding in the dyke under the sea lavender where we'd found her, and to do a picture of me sitting on Nan's bed in Bethnal Green with her row of elephants lined up on the mantlepiece.

What's that music? I asked.

Chopin.

Who's Chopin?

A Polish composer, you answered. This is one of his études. He wrote the first one when he wasn't much older than you.

What're études?

It's the French word for studies. They're a way of exploring musical ideas. A bit like you practising drawing. But how are you, Frith? I haven't seen you for a bit. How's your hand? Last time you were here I noticed you'd cut it. Is it better now?

I didn't answer, asking instead where the goose had gone, as she wasn't in the kitchen.

She's outside. In the pen with the other birds. The weather's getting better, and so is she.

April. I was going to be thirteen. I wondered if Dad would remember and send me a card with a golden 13 on the front. Or would he forget now the new baby was due? I wondered if I'd ever get to see it, this half-brother-sister. If it would look like Dad or have red hair like Vera. Mum sent me a fruit cake tied up in brown paper and string. Plus two new hankies with an F embroidered on each in pink cross stitch, and a card with Popeye on the front eating a tin of spinach.

Goodness, ducks! Are you really 13? Makes me feel like an old lady. Only one more year of school and then you'll be off out to work. How's it all going? I'll try and come to see you sometime now the weather's getting better. London's been bloody cold and miserable, I can tell you, what with the blackout. All the pipes froze. The ones in the outside lav burst and the price of coal has gone up. Anyway, enjoy the cake and hope you like the hankies. Happy Birthday.
    Love, Mum

Just one more year of school and then what? Not that I wanted to stay at the Willocks' but even if I did, they'd throw me out when they stopped getting their 10s 6d from the government. Where would I go? Would Mum have me back in London? What if there were bombs? Maybe I could find work in Sutton Bridge. Though where would I live?

You told me to come to the lighthouse the Saturday after my birthday. It was a bright and windy day and when I'd finished my jobs, I slipped out of the cottage with Mum's cake in a basket. You'd promised to take me birdwatching. When I arrived there was a bunch of primroses in a jam jar on the table and, propped up against it, a card with a goose you'd painted on the front.

Is that for me?

Yes, of course, it's for you, Frith. Happy belated birthday.

After a pot of tea and some hot buttered toast, we set off. The rooks in the sycamores behind the lighthouse were flinging themselves on the wind, wheeling round and round in the gusts. We could hear lambs bleating in the lane and a pair of sedge warblers chattering in the thickets. The blackthorn was coming into bloom and goldfinches darting in and out of the white flowers. But it was still very cold. When the sun peeped from behind a cloud it disappeared just as quickly in a sudden downpour. Running for shelter in a nearby barn, we stood among the bales of straw looking out through the heavy curtain of rain at the distant farms nestling between the flat black fields. Just then a rainbow appeared above the marsh.

Look, Frith. That's for your birthday.

After the shower stopped we continued our walk. Dead reeds rustled in the dykes and new green shoots were pushing up among the brown. A drift of geese rose over the bank. But the flocks were smaller than in winter. Most of the birds had gone north to breed, leaving only a scattering of unmated juveniles hanging around on the mudflats.

Get out the binoculars, Frith. There should be lots of new spring migrants for you to see. Redstarts and stonechats. Maybe some chiffchaffs and godwits. See if you can tell me which is which. Did you bring the book? Quick, look up. Can you see? The geese are leaving, heading out across the North Sea to their summer home, that's why Fritha's so restless. She can feel the call to migrate. It's why she keeps trying to flap her wings, though they're not strong enough yet for her to leave. No one knows how they find their way, Frith. It's like a magnet: the same force that moves the tides and winds seems to call them away.

Oh look, the sun's come out again. Think I'll risk a quick dip. It's really too early, mind. Bet it'll be freezing but I fancy blowing off the cobwebs.

You slipped off your thick jersey, pulled your shirt over your head and unbuttoned your flannel trousers. Underneath you were wearing a pair of black woollen swimming trunks. The water by the sluice was dark green, and you dived in, leaving a stream of bubbles trailing up behind you as you disappeared under the reedy water.

Brrr. It's cold, you said, your head breaking the surface like a seal's.

Then, grabbing the iron post by the sluice, you hauled yourself back onto the bank, the muscles in your back rippling with the effort, and shook yourself like a wet dog, sending drips flying everywhere, tipping your head from side to side to get the water out of your ears. Your teeth were chattering, and your skin covered in goosebumps. You didn't have a towel, so rubbed yourself down with your vest, mopping up the beads of water caught in the glistening hairs of your chest, the dark line that ran from your belly button down into your swimming trunks. You didn't seem very dry to me but pulled on your shirt and heavy fisherman's sweater, and your tweed trousers over your damp trunks so they left a wet patch on the seat.

Think we need a snifter of this, you suggested, unscrewing the thermos of hot cocoa and pouring it into the two Bakelite cups you'd put in the basket along with the cake.

Happy birthday, Frith, you said, raising your mug in a toast. So, what does it feel like to be thirteen?

We sat for a long time in the lea of the wall, your hair dripping water into your collar, sipping cocoa and eating Mum's fruit cake. We didn't talk much. Far away over the marsh I could see the black dot of a skylark, its high notes piercing the single patch of blue, but the weather was closing in, dark storm clouds gathering on the far horizon.

T HE NEWS WAS BAD. When he tuned into the wireless he heard that German forces were advancing in Norway. The problem for Norway, he could see, was that though the country was officially neutral, its ports were strategically important to both sides. The Allies were worried that occupying neutral Scandinavian countries would drive them into an alliance with Germany.

He felt impotent. What could he do other than watch from the sidelines? Trust, that now Churchill had taken over, there would be a more positive outcome. During Neville Chamberlain's premiership there'd been endless diplomatic defeats and humiliations. He'd wanted to believe, when Chamberlain returned flapping his piece of paper on the tarmac, that he'd brokered a lasting peace, that that would be the end of the matter. But in his heart he knew it wouldn't be. There seemed to be a terrible inevitability to unfolding events, like watching a car with broken brakes career towards the edge of a cliff. You could see what was going to happen but could do nothing to stop it other than just stand in open-mouthed horror. Was there a tipping point, he wondered? A final failure of the human imagination when war simply became inevitable? Was this inability to live and let live, without the need to be top dog, hard-wired into the human psyche? Hunting and war were as old as civilization, he reflected, thinking of Willock and his mate out with their guns on that punt, but now there were heavily armoured tanks and aircraft. All the paraphernalia of modernity the more efficiently to obliterate those we didn't even know and towards whom we had no personal animosity. Who knew where things would end?

And Peter. He was worried about Peter. He was out there, somewhere in the North Sea. He had no way of knowing whether he was in danger. They hadn't spoken since Oxford. The only news he'd heard had been via Jess. He tuned into the Home Service several times a day, hoping to hear something that would give him a clue. He knew Peter was no longer his business. Still, he thought about him a good deal, tried to picture him, handsome in his navy-blue uniform on the bridge of HMS *Hood*, staring out across the frozen wastes of Spitsbergen or Bear Island. The sky a rosy pink in the daytime night. He wondered what it would be like to be a naval officer disrupting enemy logistics and destroying merchant shipping out on the North Atlantic, having men under your command. What his ship was really doing in those cold grey wastes. Did he believe in what he was doing or was he just a pragmatist, carrying out the tasks assigned to him? Peter was a shape-shifter, a chameleon with the ability to be whatever others wanted or needed him to be. Yet, still, he lay dormant as a virus in Philip's bloodstream.

He knew that his emotions were inherently ambivalent, that they shifted backwards and forwards between desire and anxiety. Yet if he was honest, didn't he have to admit that he was jealous of, even angry with Peter for moving on so quickly to George? But that only increased his feelings of desire. Or was it simply human impulse to crave what we couldn't have? He couldn't bear to think of a life in which Peter didn't figure at all and tried to convince himself that he really only wanted him to be happy, that he was fine about his relationship with George if only they could stay friends. But he knew that he was fooling himself. Perhaps the way we loved people dictated why we grew angry with them. But Peter had changed him. Their relationship had made him more self-critical, more unsure of the rightness of his actions.

He tried to tune into his radio. But out on the fens the reception was bad. He'd just managed to make out that on 15th May, one day after the Rotterdam blitz, RAF Bomber Command had been authorized to attack German targets east of the Rhine and had hit oil plants and blast furnaces in the Ruhr. But what else had been damaged?

He couldn't bear it. The pointless devastation. The incendiary assaults on an old man winding his clock in the evening shadows or a young mother putting her child to bed. The senseless incineration of innocent people going about their day-to-day lives.

He went to the window. The creeks were shimmering in the May sun. Above, puffy cumulus floated in the high blue. Why wasn't the world in tears? Why wasn't it screaming? Ever since he'd been a boy, he'd known that he didn't want to fight. He could still remember the nightmares he'd had about his father in the trenches. The mud and jumbled corpses of men and mules flickering like a black-and-white film on the nursery wall. The acrid stench of death. Now he was all at sea. He was tempted to write to Jess, to ask her to come to him but knew, as he pulled on his boots and went to feed the birds, that wasn't the answer.

Y OU TOLD ME you hated everything to do with war.
Explained that's why you were living in the lighthouse,
digging fields and sowing carrots, instead of being a soldier.

Because, Frith, I believe that killing people is wrong. It solves
nothing. War is a failure of the imagination. An act of the
petty-minded. We live in an advanced industrial society yet have
hardly developed emotionally since we lived in caves. Peace and
love, Frith, are skills. A choice. Not just feelings. That's something I'm slowly beginning to learn. Most catastrophes between
people and nations occur from a lack of emotional intelligence.
We can choose to escape our fate. Write our lives differently...

Do you understand anything I'm saying?

Your face comes back to me now—sitting here in my room
looking out at the laburnum—half hidden in the shadows of
that rusty Valor stove, trying to explain your views on pacifism
to a confused thirteen-year-old girl. I realize how young you
were. Twenty-two? Twenty-three? A boy, really. I remember
that you'd decorated the lighthouse with the drawings ripped
from your notebooks: the flat fen fields, geese in flight against
the moon. Lapwings. I can still see your ration book lying on

the broken arm of the old burgundy armchair, bursting with horsehair stuffing. The makeshift shelf with your tins of tea, sugar and Bournville cocoa. I try not to think of those times too often. Frightened, after all these years, of wearing away the last precious memories, of leaving nothing but a faded patch like a bleached negative. Perhaps the truth is that there are only ever beginnings, rarely ends. And the sea…there's always the dark, dark sea…

I can't get the sequins to stick. I'm not bothered but Jade's keen that I help with the bunting, and it seems churlish to say no. I've always wondered why our flag is called the Union Jack. The Union bit is obvious, but Jack? So I looked it up. Years of being a librarian, I suppose, and found that it's the naval term for a flag mounted on a warship when not in harbour. You can still learn new things, even at my age.

Jade's a sweet girl, with spiky blond hair—dyed, I presume—and a penchant for leopard-skin tops and silver rings, worn with fingernails that are usually painted black. Sometimes we do real art. Not just kindergarten stuff: set up a still life in the window or a vase of daffodils next to a cup and saucer. A bowl of russet apples. One day Joe, the groundsman, came and sat for us in his overalls and big boots. Normally he's out and about raking leaves or trimming the edges of the flower beds. I enjoyed that, the slow looking, the coordination between hand and eye. But today we're finishing the bunting.

There are only five of us who went through the last war. Joan, Sheila and Heather. Heather was a Wren but she's in a wheelchair now. She often talks of being a child in Newlyn, Cornwall. Of rushing down to see the fishing fleet dock. The silver mackerel being packed in ice on the quay to be sent by train up to the fancy restaurants in London. After the war, her husband worked for the council while she stayed home to look after her two girls, Shirley and Jean—Shirley comes to visit sometimes. She became president of her local WI. Heather's a pleasant enough soul. Always friendly, though we don't really have that much in common apart from being in here. But you have to make an effort to get on. Then there's Neil. He's the quiet one. A bit of a closed book. I think he finds it hard being the only man. And his memory isn't what it was. A fireman during the Blitz, he must have seen some terrible things, but he doesn't talk about them.

Jade says she's planning to borrow a wind-up gramophone from somewhere so we can listen to Vera Lynn with our tea, as if the war were no more than 'There'll be blue birds over the white cliffs of Dover...' But she means well.

After lunch I go back to my room and turn on my little portable Roberts radio. I like listening to Radio 3's afternoon concert. I'm particularly happy if it happens to be Chopin. I go to my chest of drawers and lift out the shoebox full of my bits and bobs, then sit down on the bed. I don't look at them often, but all this talk of Dunkirk has put me in a pensive mood. There's the brown paper name tag I had tied to my coat when I was evacuated. The birthday cards from Dad, the one from Mum with Popeye on the front that I got for my thirteenth birthday. There's also a postcard from Iris, sent after she got married and moved to Scotland. A black-and-white photograph of the High Kirk in Glasgow that she sent just after the war. We lost touch soon after that. I don't remember why. She's probably dead by now. Buried beneath all these is the souvenir programme from *Aladdin* I saw that Christmas at the Hackney Empire. There's a tea stain on the cover. I've no idea where that came from. I remember the day so well. Dad's brilliantined hair. Mum in her best frock. Climbing the brick stairs at the back of the theatre to the upper circle. The heavy red curtain drawn across the stage, the plush seating and the ceiling covered in plaster cherubs. Maybe that's why it's called 'the gods' because it's closer to heaven.

And I've always kept significant train and bus tickets. I still have the itinerary from the Cook's Tour I went on in 1970, to Oberammergau, where they have the Passion Play. It's not that I'm religious, I just liked the idea of all that Alpine scenery. The clean air and sound of cow bells. The edelweiss and little wooden chalets with their flower boxes of red geraniums nestling beneath the snowy peaks. First performed in 1634, the play was a result of a vow made by villagers during the bubonic plague that if they were spared, they'd put on a play every ten years. Hundreds from the village get involved. Carpenters. Butchers. Local farmers. I was shocked to learn Hitler had been a keen advocate. It was on that trip that I met Brian. It was his first holiday alone since his wife had passed away. She'd been ill for several years and he'd looked after her in their bungalow in Bexhill-on-Sea. Wouldn't hear of her going into a home. He was a good man.

We sat next to one another on the coach, got talking and stayed in touch. He was ten years older than me, a solicitor with a practice on the south coast. It's hard to say why we became involved. The truth, I suppose, is that despite my job in the library and my Tuesday bridge, I was lonely. And he was kind. Grateful to have someone to drive out with in the Vauxhall Victor on a Sunday afternoon, to ride the Hastings funicular and eat the other half of a cream tea on the seafront. Yes, I shared his bed. But he didn't want much and that suited me, though it was nice to be brought a cup of tea in the morning, read the Sunday papers together and do the crossword. But when he asked me to move in, I had to say no. My heart wasn't really in it.

At the bottom of the box I find the card you painted with a white goose. The paper is yellow now, the angular writing faded to sepia. It says:

'Happy thirteenth birthday, Frith. From your friend, Philip.'

Luxembourg had fallen, and now Belgium and the Netherlands too. Could things get any worse? He walked out into the night, threading his way through the creeks and tough fen grass. A light wind was blowing off the Wash, the tide coming in over the sandbanks. Above, the sky was littered with stars: Orion, the Milky Way.

He strode on, hunched inside his jacket, trying to collect his thoughts. He needed to clear his head. To settle the arguments raging inside him. All the values that his life had been based on for twenty-three years were crumbling. There was a hole at the centre that he'd attempted to fill, first with faith, then, when that failed, with sex. The cold seeped into his bones and a pockmarked moon shimmered on the anthracite surface of the dykes. Walking brought him back to himself. Grounded him. The repetitive rhythm of placing one foot in front of the other, his weight shifting between heel and toe. The slow inflation and deflation of his lungs like the swell of the night tide. Out here, in the wind, he was suddenly acutely aware of his fragility. This wilderness provided an antidote to the battle going on inside him. Every dyke, every clump of reeds calmed him. Human consciousness, he realized, was both a thing of beauty and bittersweetness, a continual negotiation between optimism and despair. Lacking the instinct of animals we were wracked with doubt, unlike salmon that know with certainty the river to return to in order to spawn or birds that find their way back unerringly to their summer homes. Our decisions were made not *for* us but *by* us. And the price? Insecurity, to which hope was the only counterbalance. We'd be lost, he thought, without any sense of reverence, with no feeling that there was anything beyond us to inspire awe. The world could only be understood through close attention—noticing the small changes in the weather or the first spring violets nestled on the bank, not through strength of will. God, he had to admit, didn't exist in the sense of something out there that could save him either from himself or from this bleak moment in history. Yet was the divine really any more of an illusion than falling in love?

He'd read that the word 'silence' had its root in the Gothic verb *anasilan*. A word used to describe a dying wind, as well as reflecting the Latin *desinere*, to abandon or stop. Silence, he was beginning to understand, was a form of letting go. An abandonment of the chase, which allowed us to see the world more clearly. He thought of those Chinese monks who practised *kinhin*, a form of walking meditation, picturing them in some remote, snow-covered mountain temple moving slowly clockwise around a silent room, their eyes half closed. One hand gently closed in a fist, covered by the other.

As a child he'd always felt that real life was just out of reach. That somehow he was not, and didn't deserve to be, a part of it, that, in some way, he wasn't worthy. One evening he'd gone into the conservatory in Buckingham Palace Road to look for his mother but she hadn't been there. For a moment he'd been flooded with anxiety, then had noticed a large fern in an earthenware pot. It must have been there for years as it was quite big. Though he couldn't remember ever having seen it before. He went over and looked more closely at the curling fronds, the prehistoric-looking nodules, when it became clear that the plant, earth and the pot in which the plant was growing in were all interconnected, that each gave the other point and purpose. It was winter and although only six o'clock, very dark. He presumed his mother must be out somewhere and had forgotten to tell him, his nanny upstairs in the nursery, darning socks by the gas fire. The pot was made of rough, grey-green earthenware. The fern ghostly in the beam of the street lamp shining through the window. He stood there for a long time in his blue dressing gown and striped pyjamas, too young to give a name to what he was feeling, but the experience stayed with him.

The night was cloudless, with above a trillion stars—the Plough, Corona Borealis, Ursa Major—all shining in their faraway galaxies. Across the marsh, a barn owl screeched and he knew then that he couldn't just turn away, that he was accountable. That he couldn't simply hide safe on the peripheries but had to enter the dark heart of his times. He walked on, his boots pushing into the sandy mud, feeling the epochs and aeons beneath. The stalactites and drift of tectonic plates. Millions would die in this war. Yet in five billion years the sun would become exhausted, the Earth fall dark. We all stand on the brink, he thought, with our toes hanging off the edge of the world.

He was glued to the wireless and couldn't paint. It would seem disrespectful to those in danger to be worrying about form and colour while they were fighting for their fragile lives. The reception was weak, and the voices faded in and out of the ether on the crackling airways. The Germans, it seemed, were marching relentlessly towards the English Channel. The Battle of Arras had only halted the *Wehrmacht* for twenty-four hours. Disaster appeared to be looming. When Churchill and his aides had flown to Paris just a few days before, the Prime Minister had apparently looked out of the window onto the French diplomatic headquarters on the Quai d'Orsay to see frenzied officials burning documents in an attempt to keep them out of German hands. Now the French defences at Sedan and the Meuse had been broken and it looked as if all would be lost. The German army had swept like a scythe around the right and rear of the northern Allies, severing supply lines for food and ammunition that ran through Amiens, Abbeville, then on up the coast to Boulogne, Calais and Dunkirk. As far as he could make out the enemy was attacking on all sides. Nearly 400,000 troops were stranded on the beaches or stuck in surrounding villages. Outnumbered, outgunned and outmanoeuvred.

He was cleaning his paintbrushes when he heard the order over the airways 'to all owners of self-propelled pleasure craft between 30' and 100' in length to send particulars to the Admiralty', followed by Churchill's message that we would defend 'our island' whatever it took. He took a deep breath. Albion: ancient, beautiful, imperfect. These fenland marshes and black Lincolnshire earth. Oxford and the Bodleian. Christ Church meadows and late winter afternoons with Jess and Peter when, after a walk, they toasted crumpets in front of the gas fire in his Keble rooms. Hyde Park where he'd walked with his nanny. The seedy Soho pubs filled with a crush of writers and painters, many of them homosexuals. The relaxed bonhomie of bohemia he'd experienced when staying with Peter. Surely these were things worth defending from the jackboot and the Gestapo.

He dipped his fountain pen into the bottle of blue Quink, filled the barrel and wrote to Jess.

My dearest Jess,

Will you forgive my unforgivable silence? There's no excuse I can offer for not answering your warm and loving letters before, except cowardice and a feeble inability to find the appropriate words. But now I must write. I don't know what the next days have in store for me. If I still believed in God, I'd say my fate lay in his hands but the truth is, I've been in turmoil over the last weeks, listening to the news about this escalating war, obsessed with following every detail as closely as I can. I wish I could talk with you because what's happening is challenging every belief I've ever held dear that pacifism is the only right response against aggression. Now, reluctantly, I don't think I have the right to continue on that course or live in this remote safety while other men put their lives on the line.

That I'm holed up, here, in this lighthouse on the edge of the Wash is pure serendipity. I came here after leaving the Warneford. I'd hoped Mother might come and get me, or at least offer me a place to stay while I found my feet, but she had other things on her mind. I remembered Lincolnshire a little from visiting my late grandparents. They had a home here when I was a child. It seemed as good a place as any. I live here like some backwoodsman, like Thoreau, without electricity or running water. I do some land work. Try to paint. I'm calmer and happier, I think, than I've ever been. It's wild and bleak but the place has a savage beauty.

But I must admit I've been sorely tempted by your offer to come and join me. I miss you, Jess. Your warmth, your playfulness and your integrity. I'm lonely. Yearning for a sense of connection and intimacy that's always eluded me. If things had been different, I believe we might have made a life together. I can't think of any woman I'd rather be with than you. But it wouldn't work, because as I think you know in your heart of hearts, it's Peter whom, even against my better judgement, I desire. You deserve so much more, Jess, than a husband who'd give you second best. Hide behind your skirts. You have so much to offer. I wish with all my heart that one day you'll find a good, companionable man who'll value who you are and with whom you can have children. You will be a fantastic mother, and if I do come back, I'd like to offer myself up as number one godparent to your firstborn (if you don't mind one who's become so godless). I also think it's wonderful that you're writing. Please don't be dismissive about it or come up with any of that silly 'lady novelist' rubbish. You've always been by far the brightest of us three. I hope to see your name on an orange Penguin spine any day now.

As I said, I'm living like a peasant but one thing that's given me unexpected pleasure is a strange little friendship I've developed with an evacuee from the East End. A child called Freda. She is just thirteen. It was her birthday recently. Our meeting came about through our mutual care of a wounded goose. A rare albino pink-foot. You know me and wildlife. It's always been a bit of a thing, ever since I was a boy. I like doing simple things with her. Teaching her things. Perhaps she's the younger sister I never had. She borrows my books and likes drawing. It's interesting watching her develop. I don't think she's had a very good start in life but she's a bright little thing, though, I sense, vulnerable, and billeted with an unsuitable family. I worry about her and do what I can to help. It's not much but there are, I've come to realize, many ways of connecting. The truth is, I'll probably never have children of my own, and she's taught me something of the pleasure of giving. I hope that doesn't sound too worthy or sanctimonious. I want nothing from her. I simply enjoy her company when she chooses to give it to me. Though Freud might suggest (and your father as well, I've no doubt) that she represents the wounded child in me. And it's certainly true that in some ways, my feelings for her have helped to heal those towards myself.

But my real reason for writing, dear Jess, is to tell you that I've decided to go to Dunkirk. I can't enlist. Unsurprisingly they wouldn't want me. But I have a little knowledge of how to handle a boat, acquired in Noirmoutier as a boy, when I learnt to sail with the local fisherman the summer I was twelve. I shall go alone, of course. Probably at night, as I will have to 'borrow' a boat. But this feels like something I can do that involves saving rather than destroying life. I may have lost my faith in God, but I've come to believe that we're all part of the cosmos and—if it doesn't sound too high-flown or bombastic—all interconnected.

I don't know what's going to happen. Whether I'll even come back. But this, now, is the only thing that seems to make any sense. Believe me, my dear friend, I've loved you as much as any person can love another. Live a good life, Jess, and wish me Godspeed.

Forever,

Philip

He folded the letter, put it in an envelope and propped it behind the clock. Then went to the shelf and took down his copy of T.A. Coward's *The Birds of the British Isles*, with its tan cloth and board cover, the gilt robin embossed on the front, and wrote on the flyleaf:

'For Frith. On my going away. Affectionately, Philip, May 1940.'

Nine o'clock. The evening was already fading when he scrambled up the ladder to unhook his canvas rucksack from its nail, stuffing it with two of pairs of thick socks, a flannel shirt and warm sweater, before pulling on the grey cashmere his mother had sent from Paris for Christmas. It amused him to think she'd almost certainly have imagined him wearing it in rather different circumstances. At a casual country house weekend or Sunday lunch with friends in some quaint pub. He climbed back downstairs and cut a pile of cheese and pickle sandwiches, wrapping them in newspaper and putting them in the bag, then he went to check his modest store cupboard. There wasn't much. A couple of tins of corned beef. Some sardines, half a jar of Bovril. While searching for matches and his torch he came across a bar of Fry's Chocolate Cream and put that in his pack too.

High tide was just after midnight. He needed to get to the quay before then. He wasn't sure what he was looking for but would know when he saw it. He put on his heavy boots and waterproof, picked up his rucksack and set off down the track towards Sutton Bridge quay where the Nene ran straight as a die down from Wisbech, past the South Holland main drain under Crosskeys Bridge, to the outfall just above the lighthouse. It was pitch black. Recently, a couple of stevedores had been knocked into the harbour by a crane emptying a cargo hold in the blackout, and a naval reserve officer was fined for striking a match in a telephone kiosk whilst helping his girlfriend to see the dial.

The wind was rattling the cleats and stays of the open fishing smacks, snapping the burgees backwards and forwards. He switched on the torch, shielding it with his hand, directing the beam down onto the ground in front of him. Every few minutes the arc of a searchlight from Boston, the inland port some twenty miles away, swept across the sky, obliterating the stars. Recently, the small port of Sutton Bridge had been closed to all passenger traffic and continental shipping services suspended. Many of the local boats had been requisitioned to transport guns and heavy equipment across to France.

Slowly his eyes adjusted to the darkness. He could just make out the fleet of small fishing boats bobbing on the tide, silhouetted in the moonlight. He had to act fast, before he was noticed, and it had to be a boat that he could handle alone. He'd learnt basic sailing skills the summer he'd spent in France with his mother and Pemberton. Could read a nautical map. But the Wash was notorious for its channels and sandbanks, and he had no real experience of ocean-going, though the weather was calm and, hopefully, would be kind.

Then he spotted her. A little wooden motor launch, not more than twenty-five feet, with a couple of sails and a small single engine. He didn't think she'd be too hard to handle. He could see her clearly in the moonlight and clambered down the iron ladder on the wet quayside wall to the deck. The wheelhouse wasn't locked. Though small, it would keep him dry if the weather deteriorated. There was a gas hob and a kettle, and the starter motor seemed quite straightforward with a basic forward and reverse movement. The needle on the fuel tank pointed to full. It looked as though she'd been used for delivering timber, then refuelled for work the following day. He dropped his bag on the floor and searched around. In the cubbyhole beside the helm he found a compass and a local chart showing the channels through the sandbanks. He spread it on the varnished table, lit the lamp and began to plot a course. He needed to leave soon to avoid running aground on the mudflats at the mouth of the Wash. It was too dark and too still to go under sail so, very slowly, he pulled back the throttle and the engine spluttered into life.

It was just past midnight.

He set the compass, taking a steady pace of ten knots, keeping to the central channel of the Nene. He calculated that it would take the best part of an hour to get back to the lighthouse at the mouth of the river. He needed to reach the Wash before the tide turned or he'd be in danger of getting stuck. The wind was light. The sky cloudless and full of stars. He wasn't sure what he expected. What it would be like if he did eventually make it to Dunkirk. He was just glad to be under way. To have made a decision. Now he had to forget his doubts, the voices in his head telling him that he was mad, and concentrate on the task ahead.

He looked at his watch. It was nearly three thirty. As he slipped out of the Nene, the buoys Big Tom and Big Annie bobbed on his port and starboard, indicating that he was holding the right course. It would be a challenge to make it through the shallow channel over the sandbanks and mudflats to the Outer Wash. He moved the compass to 10 degrees north. He needed to head for the Old Lynn Channel. Keep an eye out for the white flash of the Roaring Middle lightship that would indicate deeper water. Then he felt a dull thud and knew the keel had hit a sandbar. For a moment he panicked, uncertain whether he had the seamanship to get afloat on an ebbing tide. Placing the bow at 30 degrees to the lightship, he reversed slowly. The engine stalled. Then, on the roll of a big wave, the stern lifted and he opened the throttle. He was free.

Ahead there were still the shell banks of the Woolpack. He'd have to navigate these before he could drop down to hug the coast due south. He needed to cross before low tide. Eventually, he could see Gore Point on his starboard. With luck, he'd make it past Holkham to Wells-next-the-Sea by early morning and be able to moor for a short time, make some hot Bovril, have something to eat and put his head down for a couple of hours. And he needed fuel. If the gods were with him, there might be a can lying around in a deserted boathouse, and if there wasn't a strong offshore wind he should be able to drop anchor in a deserted creek. He didn't want to go into the main harbour. It was unlikely, but someone might recognize the boat. Looking at the nautical chart, he could see there was a reasonable amount of deep water but that coming in from the west of the Wash he had to be careful of the shallows. He hoped his navigation skills were up to it. He was getting tired.

The sun was slowly rising over the port side, staining the slate sea pink. He could see the pine woods to the west further down the coast. He left the green buoys that marked the run over the sandbar on his starboard, feeling exposed now that it was getting light. It would, though, be easier to navigate past Blakeney and Cromer. To pick up some speed as he headed towards Harwich, before dropping down towards Ramsgate.

I'VE BEEN PRONE to migraines all my life. The acute pain relieved only by throwing up, as if ridding my system of some ingested poison. What once was impossible to bear lurks deep in aching muscles and throbbing arteries, flashes across my brain in the early hours like forked lightning against a night sky. The body remembers even when the mind chooses to forget…

Mrs Willock had gone up to the village to take three of her rag rugs to the haberdasher. He sold them on commission and Billy had gone with her, leaving me to get in the washing from the orchard. The sheets and nappies. Mr Willock's stained vests and long johns. When I carried the basket back up to the kitchen, he was taking potshots at the rooks in the trees behind the cottage when there was a loud bang and a bird fell out of the sky, twirling like a black smut, before landing with a thud in the vegetable patch.

Well that be the end of him, he said, grabbing the bird by the claws and slinging it into the compost heap, while the rest of the clamour flew off, cawing overhead.

Blighters won't be back any time soon, he said, hitching up his belt and going indoors.

While I sorted the clothes, he spread sheets of newspaper on the deal table, sitting down to his favourite pastime, cleaning his gun. Picking up a piece of oily rag he threaded it through the cleaning rod, pushing it slowly up and down the breech, before pulling it out covered in filth, all the while looking at me.

That barrel be quite clean now, he said, peering down it with one eye closed and lowering his head to the sight as if about to take aim.

Put the kettle on, gal. I'm parched.

I went and filled the heavy aluminium kettle and was standing waiting for it to boil when he came up behind me. I didn't notice at first, then felt his sour breath on my neck, his weight pushing me onto the broken chaise longue that Mrs Willock was supposed to be upholstering for the haberdasher but hadn't got around to doing yet. The coiled springs and horsehair stuffing poked through the canvas into my ribs, his rough ginger bristles rasped my face. There were yellow stains in the armpits of his vest and I thought I'd choke from the unwashed smell of him pushing me into the pile of filthy socks and underpants. The bag of dog biscuits.

The rest is a blur. I know only that my mind went blank. That later, much later, I found myself alone in that cold kitchen, my knickers round my knees, my dress all crumpled, and something sticky between my thighs. I've no idea how long I lay there, the clock ticking into the cold silence, before I crept up to my room.

I hardly dared breathe and didn't cry. For tears would have made too much noise and, besides, what relief would they have brought with no one to comfort me? There was a drop of water in the bottom of the bedroom pitcher which I poured into the enamel basin, washing myself the best I could but it stung, and I realized that I was bleeding. I went in search of a pair of clean knickers, stuffing them with bits of rag, straightened my dress and fished out the pillowcase rucksack from beneath my bed, neatly folding the rest of my underwear, the blue cardigan Mum had sent me for Christmas, the hankies with an 'F' embroidered in pink cross stitch and packed them, along with the snow globe and card with the goose on the front, carefully inside. Then I put on my coat with the rabbit-fur collar, tiptoed downstairs and, checking that Mr Willock wasn't about, slipped out of the house.

The rooks were back, cawing angrily above the spinney. Without a backwards glance, I ran through the vegetable patch, the bolted cabbages and wigwam of runner beans, past the privy, my heart racing, on down towards the sea wall. I don't know how long I sat there huddled against the wind, far from myself, watching the shivering reeds. I knew only one thing—that I had to leave. To get away. That I would rather live as a wild child with burrs in my hair than ever go back. I wasn't sure how I'd explain or what I'd say but knew you and the lighthouse were my only options.

When I knocked, there was no answer. I thought you might be out digging in the fields or off drawing somewhere as the weather was fine. You never locked the door and always said I should make myself at home if I ever came by and you weren't in. I went over to your work table and inspected the tubes of vermilion, cadmium and ochre—recognizing the names you'd taught me—laid out beside your pencils. The little sketch books filled with the charcoal drawings you did when out walking. Your home-made wireless set with its earphones and the wind-up gramophone on which I'd first heard Chopin, sitting silently beside your shabby armchair. The wooden lid of the gramophone was open and the needle resting in the last groove of the record. Beside it lay the discarded brown paper sleeve, a picture of a little white terrier with brown ears on the front, his head cocked to his master's voice coming from the big horn.

Even though it was fine outside, it was still cold. The stove hadn't been lit and a deathly hush hung over the room. I climbed into the armchair and wrapped myself in your tartan rug, then waited while the afternoon slipped into evening and the light began to fade.

It was barely daylight when I woke with a crick in my neck and still you hadn't returned. I wondered if maybe you'd gone to meet someone but you never seemed to go anywhere other than up to the general store and post office, or talk to anyone besides Mr Mackman and me. I knew nothing of your life. Where you were from. What you did before you came to the lighthouse. Nothing about your family. Only that you were different from the locals, that you read books and listened to classical music. Painted. I wondered about your parents. If you had brothers and sisters. And why, if you were so posh, you had chosen to live in this draughty old place instead of somewhere nice and warm and comfortable, even though you'd said something about it being to do with not being a soldier. I'd never really thought about you having a life of your own. A life beyond the lighthouse. This was simply the place I came for tea and toast, to escape the Willocks and see Fritha.

I wasn't sure if you'd mind me looking around at your gramophone records and art books. It felt wrong somehow but I was desperate to find out about you. It was then I spotted the envelope propped behind the clock addressed to someone called Jess, beside the copy of *The Birds of the British Isles*, with its tan cloth and gilt robin embossed on the front, that we'd taken on our walk. When I opened it, I saw you had dedicated it to me. Suddenly I was frightened that you might have gone for good, that I'd never see you again. Why would you have left without telling me? Where would you have gone? Everyone seemed to leave: Nan, Dad, Mum. Even Bert. There was a dirty teacup in the washing-up bowl and a book with the name Kierkegaard on the spine lying on the floor, the corner of a page turned down to mark your place. Your painting shirt was hanging on the back of the chair. I picked it up and put it on—it was much too big—burying my face in your smell mingled with turps and oil paint, feeling I was doing something wrong.

There was a dark bruise across my shoulder and my legs were covered in mauve and yellow marks like maps of small countries. I'd no idea what to do. Whether to stay or go. But I was really hungry. There was a bowl of eggs on the shelf, so I put the kettle on the stove and placed an egg inside, boiling it in the water for my tea. After a few minutes I fished it out, placed it on a saucer to cool and warmed the brown pot. While the tea was brewing, I peeled the egg and dipped the white dome into a hill of salt. It felt strange being in the lighthouse without you. As if playing house. I worried the Willocks would notice I'd gone by now and was afraid they'd come looking for me and take me back. After my tea and egg, I went out to check the birds. They needed feeding. You did it night and morning. Often I helped, filling their water trough, picking handfuls of fresh grass, giving them grain. Fritha knew me now and waddled towards me, guessing that I'd brought her some food. When I finished, I went back inside, sat down in the armchair again and waited. But still you didn't come.

A T THE MOUTH of the Thames estuary Philip fell in
with a growing number of other motor launches, fishing
smacks and pleasure craft making their way down the coast,
entering Ramsgate harbour in the late afternoon. A fleet of
boats was already assembling, being organized into convoys.
The police had sealed off all the roads to the harbour where
the navy had requisitioned many of the buildings to form
the base HMS *Fervent*, only letting through those on legiti-
mate business. With its marine engineering facilities, its rail
links and proximity to Dunkirk, Ramsgate was an obvious
assembly point for the little ships gathering from all around
the coast.

The town was bristling with ambulances, lorries, stretcher-
bearers and civilian volunteers. Swarming with military and
civil police, with boats being refuelled and hosed down, patched
up ready to be loaded with drums of fuel and jerrycans of
water. Some had already set out across the Channel and were
returning with their cargos of bleary-eyed soldiers to be met
by the Salvation Army doling out jam sandwiches and mugs of
tea. The manager of the Olympic Ballroom had bought up all
the men's underwear in town and was handing out clean socks
and underpants to the exhausted men.

Groups of women stood on the pavement waving bars of chocolate and packs of cigarettes, offering an encouraging, 'Well done, lad', along with a pat on the shoulder as if the men were returning heroes, rather than an army in retreat. Each returnee was told to register and deposit his weapon on the quayside. A fleet of buses, their doors removed to accommodate the wounded on stretchers, was waiting to ferry them to the town's train station where WVS volunteers were giving out postcards rubber-stamped with 'ARRIVED SAFELY' in purple ink, to send off to their anxious families.

Get these down you, son, a woman in a flowered apron cajoled as she handed Philip a mug of sweet tea and a currant bun in the refreshment tent. An able seaman standing in the queue behind him offered him a cigarette. He and his mate, he said, were dossing down in the Merrie England Ballroom just up the road. Philip should join them unless he fancied trying his luck up at the yacht club with the officers. Philip thanked him, finished the cigarette, then drained his mug, before making his excuses and heading back to his boat. He didn't like to be gone for too long. Just as he was about to snatch a couple of hours sleep, the skipper of the fishing trawler moored next to him called over.

Hey lad, can you give us a hand to strip this girl out? We need to get her unrigged.

Philip got up and clambered on board. The fisherman and his son were local and usually made their living catching lobsters and crabs. He worked for a couple of hours helping them to shift nets and lobster pots from the hold, removing anything that might catch fire, to make space for as many men as possible. They stripped the cabin and filled a tank with fresh water. Took down the mast and removed all the equipment stowed on the deck. In a couple of hours she was ready to sail.

Thanks lad. Good luck to you. It's not going to be any sort of picnic out there. Try and stay close to us, the fisherman said, holding out his hand.

Back on board his own vessel, Philip collapsed onto the hard bunk and tried to grab a few hours' sleep.

He woke at ten o'clock to the sound of the first convoy preparing to leave on the turning tide. Eight launches and an escorting motorboat were headed for De Panne. He got up, splashed cold water on his face and checked the fuel gauge, then pulled on his waterproof. A second convoy was leaving soon for Dunkirk. He would sail with that.

There was a rumour that the concrete mole protecting the outer harbour of Dunkirk had been damaged. Never designed to dock ships, most of the men, it seems, were being taken off this way. Now, the only alternative was evacuation direct from the beaches. The news was jumbled and contradictory from those returning on the first boats out but some said the dunes were covered with trapped and desperate men being heavily targeted by the Luftwaffe. Picked off like grouse on a moorland shoot. The big ships weren't able to get in close enough to the shallow beaches, so the smaller craft had to take the men off and then taxi them out to the waiting vessels. He could see a long line of boats stretching away into the distance. Near the quay, several smaller craft had been roped together to form a flotilla. Others, like him, would go under their own steam. With traffic moving in both directions, the place was as busy as a high street on a Saturday morning. Just past midnight he hooked up with a group of barges, lifeboats and tugs led by a Belgian ferry, heading out the fifty miles to Dunkirk. Among them was a Leigh cockle boat and a Thames river launch that had never seen the sea. With its slatted wooden seats he imagined families on a summer day trip floating downstream past St Paul's and the Tower of London with their ice cream cones, dressed in their summer best. There were boats from Newhaven, Portsmouth, Tilbury, Sheerness and Gravesend. From all along the south and south-east coasts. From ports and fishing villages, shipping towns and yachting harbours. Equipped with tea, bread, tinned meat and drums of water.

It was calm when he followed the flotilla out of the harbour. He didn't know what to expect but wasn't too worried about the route, knowing he just had to follow the boats ahead. The sea was 'crinkly', the corrugated waves hitting hard against the bow, so he could only do around eight knots, though the sky was clear and cloudless. With luck, the weather would stay fair. He estimated that it would take around three hours to make it across to Dunkirk.

As they came close to the French coast, the early morning mist was beginning to lift, the sky lighten. A heavy pall of smoke was drifting over the harbour mouth, turning everything black. In the distance orange flames from the burning oil tankers licked the dawn sky and all around him were the skeletons of torpedoed and sunken ships. One had a red cross just visible above the waterline. How many, he wondered, had gone down when she'd been hit? All those young doctors and nurses. Those boys who'd lost eyes and arms, longing to get home to their childhood beds, crying and praying as the water rose around them. He couldn't bear to think about it. The place was a hellhole. But what had he expected?

Suddenly, there was a high-pitched whine and he was aware that he'd attracted the attention of a Stuka. The blood began to pound in his ears, his heart race and, for a moment, he couldn't move as the plane dived at a steep angle, swinging downwards and outwards, so its propellers would clear the detonations from the bombs it was about to drop before it broke away. What was he doing here? Why wasn't he in the lighthouse, miles away, safe on the fens? What was he trying to prove with these theatrical heroics? His stomach lurched and his bowels began to loosen, so he thought he'd shit himself. Then, without thinking, he pulled the boat hard to port and she turned sharply, just as a bomb landed with a huge explosion in a column of water and flames on his starboard side.

Shaking, he tried to gather his thoughts, but the Stuka was coming around again for another go, worrying at him like an annoying black mosquito. This time, charged with adrenaline, he used every ounce of strength to fling the boat starboard as bullets rained down into the sea beside him. Then, just a few yards to his port side a bomb detonated, sending up a great wave that swamped the deck and threatened to capsize him.

How many out there? he yelled across to the skipper of a small launch overflowing with wounded soldiers, coming back in the opposite direction.

Thousands. Bloody thousands, came the reply.

Every inch of the dunes was swarming with men. Some had dug themselves into bunkers. Others were playing cards as if relaxing on the beach in Southend on a warm May Saturday. One fellow had a small mirror balanced on his backpack and was shaving. Another was heating a billycan of water for tea. And everywhere there were bodies. Boys without arms or legs, their heads blown off into a bloody pulp. Scattered rifles and kit bags spilling out bars of Bournville chocolate, dirty underpants, a mouth organ. A tattered photograph of a now bereaved sweetheart. The planes overhead continued to wheel and screech like angry seagulls. A wild-eyed young lad, not more than seventeen or eighteen, was kneeling up to his waist in water, muttering and pleading with no one in particular when, suddenly, he was felled by a direct hit. And all the while, the Allied destroyers were pumping shells into the air, trying to hit the Stukas, only to disappear behind huge walls of spray thrown up by their near misses. He was completely exposed, so manoeuvred his boat into the lea of a wrecked steamer to sit out the raid. When he dropped anchor, he realized he was shivering uncontrollably and had wet himself. He was praying...

So, that was the point of prayer. A comfort blanket in adversity.

In the clamour his mind slipped back to the marshes. To the twig-snap of his boots against the frozen ground. The vast, elemental silence. He thought of his mother. Of Peter and Jess. Of Frith's innocent delight in the unfolding world, and wondered if he'd ever see any of them again. Had that been the sum total of human interaction and love due to him? If he didn't make it back, no one would know what had happened to him. He wondered if Jess would ever find his letter or Frith the book he'd left her.

The bombing continued for what seemed like hours. He hadn't anticipated the terrible noise. The shelling from the French cruisers. The guns letting off their pom-poms. Boats were scrambling to get in and out of the harbour, but no one seemed to be in charge or giving directions. It was chaos.

In the distance he could see the bombed railway tracks. The old crane derricks smashed like shattered spines. Hear the constant droning whine of the Stukas coming down in vertical dives right on top of the men. Some men fired back but it was as useless as trying to bring down a plane with a peashooter. Where was the RAF? There only seemed to be destroyers with anti-aircraft guns. As the bombs hit the beach, men scrambled to safety behind blasted tanks. Huddled under tin helmets in foxholes, they emerged after the strafing was over, covered in sand. Others took shelter in bomb craters created by previous explosions but these were so deep that another blast would mean being buried alive. Even so, they stood a better chance on the beach. Unlike a road where shrapnel from the blast ricocheted into a thousand lethal smithereens, the sand took some of the impact.

He'd had no idea that things would be this bad. Those on the home front hadn't the foggiest. After hours of explosions he was becoming dulled to the pounding blasts. Death no longer frightened him. Either a bomb would hit him or it wouldn't. There was nothing he could do about it. When, after what seemed like an eternity, the Stukas flew off, a ragged line of men began to wade and half-swim out towards him, the water lapping round their waists, rifles held high over their heads. Behind them an enormous column of black smoke billowed from the burning tanks, so they looked like wraiths emerging from the mouth of some terrible inferno. He thought of Dante's circles of Hell, of the lower edge of Malebolge guarded by rings of titans and earth giants chained together in punishment for their rebellion against God. And then below and beyond the giants, Hell's final depth, Cocytus, with its frozen lake of infidel tears. And everywhere there was the stink of cordite. The stench of blood and death. And along the surf's edge, a line of bodies pulled from the sea, lying like a row of fallen tin soldiers.

There was clearly no way to get all the men out to the waiting frigates. There were too many and not enough boats. Ten or twelve queues, stretching like lines of ants over the sands, ran for a quarter of a mile back behind the dunes. Nobody seemed to be in command. Yet most of the men were orderly. Like people waiting for a bus into town. Though as he drew close to the beach, he could see a few sporadic fights breaking out.

Get back, you fucking cunt or I'll shoot, a sergeant was bellowing at a wild-eyed young private. But the shell-shocked lad just kept on screaming and running into the sea, trying to grab the back of a nearby dinghy that threatened to capsize under the extra weight.

I said fucking get back, the sergeant shouted again, pulling out his pistol and firing into the air.

And still they kept coming. Pushing and shoving, panic-stricken men, breaking free, now, from the previously ordered queues. Some flung their rifles into the sea before trying to clamber aboard. Others took off their boots. Philip let the engine idle to allow the last few to scramble on board. As he started to pull away from the beach a group of Scots squaddies dressed in khaki and kilts came down to the tide's edge, where one of them called out:

Whaur ye gaun, min?

Off out to those waiting boats, he yelled, then in again and back to Blighty.

Well fuck yerself. W'ur nae bloody comin', then. W'ur aff tae rammy th'Bosch.

The boat was packed with men. Filthy, stinking, wounded men. Crammed in the cockpit, huddled in the wheelhouse, piled on deck. He couldn't say how many there were. Fifty, sixty maybe? Certainly more than the boat's capacity. With so many men the boat was dangerously low in the water. He reckoned there was only about three feet below the keel. The slightest swell would swamp them. As he opened the throttle, a squaddie with a dog in his arms began to wade through the waves, calling out for him to wait.

The places are for the fucking men, shouted an officer. Not fucking dogs. But the squaddie simply went on paddling towards the boat with his mutt in his arms. Back, the officer bellowed. Back, you cunt, before pulling out his pistol—and to jeers from the men on the beach—shooting the dog through the head.

Philip watched aghast as its inert body drifted in and out, in and out on the reddening tide.

I COULDN'T FIND THE LAUGHING CAVALIER'S BEARD. The puzzle lay unfinished on the small round table next to the arm of your chair. I'd managed the cuff and some of the sleeve but was finding the rest difficult. All the embroidery looked the same. How had anybody painted all that intricate lace? I wondered who he was and why he was called the Laughing Cavalier. In the picture on the lid of the box he didn't seem to be laughing very much to me. Just smiling a funny little smile under his big moustache.

That night I slept in your bed. The one you'd made from bits of driftwood. The chair was too uncomfortable. I'd never been up to the top room before and the bedding smelt of you. I could feel your shape imprinted in the mattress, the curve of your shoulder, the dent from your knees. Your striped pyjamas still lay folded under the pillow. But my sleep was broken by dark dreams. Beating wings, the scratch of tiny claws. Sharp talons breaking my skin and clumps of feathers clotting in my throat, making me gag. At first light I was woken by the cries of gulls squawking on top of the lighthouse but was too afraid to get out of bed.

*

I'd been at the lighthouse for two days and two nights. But still you hadn't come back. I spent a lot of time crying, wondering if what Mr Willock had done to me had in some way been my fault. I'd tried to help Mrs Willock. To do what was asked of me. To mind Billy and keep out of the way. Yet I always felt jumpy and ill at ease. I thought of that time in church when the vicar had talked about sin and transgression and the goat that was sent away into the desert carrying all the wickedness of the world on its back and wondered if perhaps I was like that goat. I wondered, too, if I should write to Mum. But I had no way of getting to the post office and was frightened of being seen by someone who'd tell the Willocks where I was.

And what would I say? Anyway, she might not believe me. Say I'd done something filthy and that it was all my fault.

I got out of bed, keeping my eyes half closed, trying to pretend that I was still asleep. I didn't want to face the day. Suddenly it was all too much, and I felt overwhelmed by shame and anxiety. Where were you? You were my only friend. The only person I could rely on. You never asked for anything. Just fed me toast and tea. Showed me your art books full of fiery Turner sunsets and ladies in silk dresses by Joshua Reynolds. Taught me the names of plants and birds. No one had paid me so much attention before. No one had ever been interested in me except my nan. I sat down on the bed and sobbed and sobbed. My face wet with snot and tears, I pulled my knees up to my chest, wrapped my arms over my head and tried to muffle the horrible noises escaping from me like the wailing of a wounded animal. I'd no idea what to do. No idea where

I belonged or who I was. I wanted Nan and the reassurance of her big brass bed. Her bedroom with its plaster horses and naked ladies with roses in their hair. The smell of coal dust and Parma violets. I didn't know where Dad was and, though I loved him, I could never tell him what had happened. Dad played with me, entertained me and made me laugh, but we never spoke about anything important. Least of all why he'd left. And Mum? Well I didn't think Mum would want to know.

I boiled a couple more eggs in the kettle. Made some lumpy porridge with water and the oats from the stone jar. Drank my tea with sugar but no milk. I didn't dare go out except to see to the birds. Back inside, I invented games to pass the time. A version of pelmanism, where I closed my eyes and had to remember all the objects in the room. A ball of string. A blue jug with a yellow flower painted on the side. Your books and the painting you'd done of me that hung above the stove. I played patience and did the washing-up. Tidied the shelves in the makeshift kitchen. Cleaned your muddy boots and placed them neatly by the door. Lined up your pencils according to the hardness of their lead. Sitting on the arm of your chair was a box of matches and the saucer you used as an ashtray. I picked up a stub and lit it. I'd never smoked before and the tobacco tasted bitter and burned my lips. After a few puffs I began to cough. Still, I smoked it down to the very end. Trying to keep it alight gave me something to do but when the butt began to singe my fingers, I crushed it out in the ashtray, leaving a wisp of smoke and a stale smell.

I opened the *Palgrave's Golden Treasury* by your chair and flipped through the pages, stopping at a poem by John Keats. I'd never heard of him and there were lots of words I didn't know. 'Winnowing' and 'swath'. And I had no idea what a gourd was. But I could picture melancholy Autumn like a girl with long golden tresses, sitting on the barn floor. I was trying to read it out loud, struggling with 'o'er-brimm'd' and 'drows'd', when there was a knock on the door. I froze. It couldn't be you or you'd have walked straight in. I was frightened Mr Willock had come to get me.

And what might you be doing here, young lady? I'm looking for Mr Rhayader. Any idea where he might be?

I shook my head, whispering that I was waiting for him too. That he was my friend and had said I could come here whenever I wanted.

Well that's as maybe, Mr Mackman continued, but did I happen to know anything about a boat? Someone heard a rumpus on the quay the other night. A boat had gone missing. He'd just come by to have a word. See if Mr Rhayader knew anything, had any clue as to what might have happened. It was odd he wasn't here because he wasn't up in the field, and friend or not, I couldn't stay in the lighthouse on my own.

You're billeted with Stan Willock and his missus, aren't you? Better run along now or I'll give 'em a shout to fetch you.

After he left, I sat picking the ragged skin off my cuticles until they bled. What if Mr Mackman did tell Mr Willock where I was? I wouldn't go back. Not on any account. But where could I go? I had no money and knew no one who could help me. I wished Bert were still here. He'd have known what to do. I considered my options. There weren't many. Maybe I could go and talk to the vicar. Ask if anybody needed some hired help in the village. A girl in the year above me at school had recently left and now got 5s a week working for the dentist's wife. She had to be up at half past six to clean the dining room, light a fire and have the breakfast ready, but I worked that hard for the Willocks and got nothing. But if I went to see the vicar, I'd have to explain why I wanted to leave. And I just couldn't. Perhaps I could go back to London and help Mum in the shop. I was tidy and good at adding up and wouldn't get in her way. Maybe she'd be pleased to have some help, glad of the company. I didn't care about the threat of bombs. If there was an air raid we could sit under the stairs and play patience.

I packed my toothbrush and cardigan in my pillowcase rucksack. Put *The Birds of the British Isles* and the Palgrave anthology on the top, then went and took the painting you'd done of me off the wall. Somehow, I knew, I'd never be coming back. Before leaving, I found a piece of paper and wrote:

I ran away from the Willocks'. I had nowhere to go. I thought you'd let me be here, but you seem to have gone away. I borrowed your poetry book and took the painting. I hope you don't think that's stealing. I'm not sure where I'm going but if you do want them back you can write to my mum at 16 Roman Road, Bethnal Green. Thank you for being my friend and learning me things.

Fritha

I left the note behind the clock next to the one you'd addressed to someone called Jess. Put on my coat and picked up my things. Then I shut the door and went out to open the gate to the bird's pen. The redshanks and oystercatcher waddled out curiously. I picked up Fritha, and she stared back at me with her beady eyes. I wondered if she knew that we both had the same name. I held her close against my chest, feeling the weight of her in my arms, the webbing of her big paddles, her sinuous neck momentarily laid against my shoulder, then I opened my arms:

Go, Fritha. Go…

For a moment she hesitated. Then, stretching out her muscular neck, she spread her white angel wings, flapping them a few times before managing to take off. It was the first time I'd seen her fly. I stood in the wind on the bank near the lighthouse, watching her head north, a pale dot growing smaller and smaller on the horizon, my eyes filling with tears, until I thought my heart would break.

I T UPSET HIM, THAT DEAD DOG. The poor beast had as
much right to escape the mayhem as anyone else. He turned
away from the bobbing carcass. A nearby paddle steamer had
just taken a direct hit and the noise was horrendous. Everything
whited out in a pall of acrid smoke. All around him men were
sitting on deck, shivering and shaking from shell shock. One
quietly playing a harmonica. Another groaning in pain. But
Philip was powerless to do anything to help other than attempt
to get them to a larger ship heading back to Blighty.

He was trying to keep a steady course out to the ferry that
was waiting to leave—he could see that it was overloaded—when
he heard the teasing whine of a Stuka overhead. There was a
massive explosion. An ammunition ship up ahead had been hit
and he could feel the blast juddering through his bones.

By nightfall things were getting desperate. He could see up
ahead on the beaches that the boats intended for the wounded
were being seized by little gangs of men who'd lost their nerve
and broken ranks from the waiting queues. He could feel the
tide beginning to turn. Realized that loading would soon have
to be abandoned. He'd been on the go for hours without rest,
food or drink. The light was fading and the water vivid with
phosphorescence. All the wet ropes brilliantly illuminated.

Every damp footstep on the deck glowing. Why the hell was he here? What possible difference could he make? What was he trying to prove and to whom? Thousands would still die whatever he did.

He helped the last man to board the waiting ferry. Then paused and lit a cigarette, inhaling slowly, as if he had all the time in the world, taking a few seconds to decide whether to head for home or go back in again. As a species we'd gone, he thought, drawing the smoke deep into his lungs, from bacteria to Beethoven. We had learnt how to make fire and music. Had understood the secrets of mathematics. Built great cities and libraries. Invented the piston engine and penicillin. Yet still the same questions remained. What was all this for? Was there, really, something out there rather than nothing? He'd doubted his faith but had he been right? Now, here among all this mayhem, he was being tested. What a comfort it would be to believe that there was a divine presence watching over him. Is that why he was here? Not heroism. Not even duty, but a search for meaning. The only thing that mattered now was to find a sense of purpose beyond himself. Nothing good or true existed outside the scheme of things. Thoughts became words, and words became actions that determined how we engaged with life. Normally we paid such little heed to the world, to the clouds overhead, to the feel of the cane chair supporting our backs or the morning sun flooding through the bedroom window, or that moment when we climbed out of bed to turn on the tap and make a cup of tea. In the end we all died. The unfolding of a particular life was, from the outside, unknowable. When we were gone, the hum of the world would continue without us. Hardly missing a beat. All we could do was paint, write, garden, love. Participate.

He felt a sudden surge of energy. Life was everywhere. Including in the midst of all this slaughter. His only task was not to lose courage, not to give in to despair. There was no grand design. No final answer written in the stars. The only moment he could live was now. The only journey he could take was inwards. The light was going and things becoming more chaotic. Soldiers unable to swim clung to inflated inner tubes and used their rifles to paddle in a last desperate attempt to reach any craft that would take them out to the waiting ships. All around him men were drowning. He watched, horrified, from the deck as they disappeared under the surface. Then he remembered Charon carrying souls across the Styx between the world of the living and the land of the dead and hoped that he'd be able to carry the near-dead back from those hellish beaches to their lives in the towns and villages of England. He remembered from reading Greek myths at school how a coin was placed in the mouth of the deceased in payment for their passage. How those who couldn't pay or were left unburied were destined to wander the shoreline for a hundred years, and suddenly he had a terrible vision of these French beaches, forever haunted by the wraith-like souls of young British soldiers.

He was very tired now, but had to avoid taking the high washes from the bigger boats broadside or he'd be turned over. Suddenly, a French ship up ahead struck a mine. Packed with troops, within seconds the deck was a firestorm and the ship began to go down. With all the force he could muster he swung the helm round and changed course, going flat out towards the desperate, flailing men. Frantically, he reached out to haul them on board but, covered in thick black oil, they slipped from his hands. He snatched a bargepole, straining to hold it over the side, but couldn't reach them. Slowly, one by one, they disappeared beneath the burning waves. And still the Stukas kept coming, the dead bodies washing backwards and forwards on the swell.

He couldn't wait any longer. He had to leave. Get what passengers he had on board out to the waiting boats. A pile of rifles lay on the foredeck where they'd been dropped. This lot were in a worse state than the previous lads, with burns and mortar wounds. Faces and stomachs half blown away. Legs hanging off. Young lives decimated. Many were screaming. The quiet ones slowly bleeding to death. He thrust back the throttle and headed full steam out to sea, zigzagging to avoid a hit by the prowling Stukas. Every now and again there was a near miss and the boat would lift, nearly capsizing with the force of the waves. He lit another cigarette and tried to look nonchalant, chatting with the squaddies about which pub they'd meet in for a celebratory pint when they got back in.

But the Luftwaffe was dive-bombing any target it could. He looked back over at the beach to see thousands of men still lying among the dunes, firing rifles at the overhead planes. The jam-packed ferry up ahead was waiting for them in the growing dusk.

Nearly there, he told himself. Nearly there.

As they approached the frigate, the men who could jumped up, waving and cheering loudly, making the boat rock dangerously.

Then there was a sudden blast, and everything shook like hell and burst into flames. Someone was yelling, 'Abandon ship! Abandon ship!' but he couldn't feel his left leg. Just something wet and sticky seeping into his groin. He tried to get up but didn't have the strength and lay back on the deck as burning men scrambled, screaming and shouting, over him, treading on his head and face, flinging themselves into the sea from the slowly sinking vessel.

A white haze came down and he began to slip in and out of consciousness. Everything seemed to be happening in slow motion. But he didn't want to go. Not yet. He wasn't ready. There was still so much he needed to say. To his mother. To Jess and Peter. Even Frith. Only now was it all beginning to make sense. He had to write everything down. He must find a pen and a scrap of paper before he forgot, let them know what it was that he had finally understood. He thought of that winter afternoon in Buckingham Place Road when he'd been small, looking at that fern in the conservatory. Now he realized what it was he'd been feeling. He could smell his mother's perfume filling his nursery and so badly wanted her to reach out her hand and brush his hair out of his eyes, to turn his warm pillow to the cool side, before kissing him on the nose and leaving to go out for the evening. He could hear Jess calling him her 'darling boy', and then he saw Frith with her bitten cuticles and fraying cardigan, and wanted to tell her not to be afraid, tell her that he'd help her, that she wasn't alone.

The pain was becoming unbearable, seeping through every pore of his body. It had all been so short and what had it been for? What difference had he made? But he'd remained true to himself. He could be proud of that at least. He hadn't lifted a gun, hadn't taken a life. He was leaving the world as he found it. His breathing was becoming shallower and he could feel it slipping from him. Amid the noise everything suddenly became very quiet. He turned his head towards the darkening sky and, for a second, thought he glimpsed what looked like a pair of white wings silhouetted against the rising moon. Then everything went black: blue-black-blood-black in the swirling water.

I HAD NO IDEA WHERE I WAS GOING. Even less idea how I was going to get there. But I knew that I couldn't stay in the lighthouse. You'd gone and now, so had Fritha. I was frightened Mr Willock would come searching for me. I took a last look around at the maps and drawings. At your books and the wind-up gramophone on which I'd first heard Chopin. I'd cleaned and tidied so everything would be shipshape if you did come back. Dust motes floated in the morning sun, yet still I was reluctant to leave. The place had changed me. I knew the person I'd become now would be different to the person I'd have been if we had never met. I'd understood that there were other worlds beyond hanging out the washing and collecting the eggs, doing errands and babysitting. Beyond the galvanized baths, the balls of string and sink plungers of our East End shop. Worlds full of paintings and books and music. That you'd opened doors I would never have been able to open for myself. I went to the bookshelf and glanced along it hoping to find one book that would contain everything I didn't know. But among those on navigation and Nordic sea birds, on palaeontology and ento-mology, I couldn't find what I was looking for so gathered up my rucksack and gas mask, picked up the painting and walked out of the lighthouse, closing the door behind me.

*

There was a clean-washed look to the day. Cotton-wool clouds floated across the clear wide blue. The May morning lay shiny and glinting over the marsh. Giant kingcups fringed the edge of the dyke and dragonflies darted in and out of the reeds. In the distance, I could see the Wash gleaming like polished tin. Above a skylark was singing and, in the distance, I could hear lambs bleating. On the far bank, a heron stood on one leg, watching for eels. When I'd first arrived the marsh had been a frightening, hostile wilderness. Now I'd come to love the big skies, to welcome the silence. You'd taught me how to look, how to identify and name things. To see what was unique and special. How could there be a war when the world was so beautiful?

I was anxious not to be spotted and gingerly made my way down the rutted lane, scared Mr Willock would come along the sea wall on his rusty bike and force me back. But there was no one about. I thought of what Mr Mackman had said about a boat and wondered what that could possibly have to do with you. Why would you have wanted a boat? I wished now that I'd opened the letter addressed to Jess. I had no idea who Jess was but thought you might have told her where you were going. I knew it was wrong to read other people's mail but, for some reason, I copied down the name and address on the front of the envelope.

As I walked, I passed a group of women in a field weeding rows of beet and celery. Others were cutting the last crop of red tulips. People, it seemed, still wanted flowers, even in a war. A plane droned overhead. I looked up to see the tail fin of a

Wellington bomber heading out across the North Sea from the nearby RAF aerodrome, perhaps where we'd had our Christmas party. When I got to the main road, I sat down on the verge by the finger signpost, uncertain what to do or where to go next. I had no money and no plan.

There were three of them in their grey-blue uniforms and distinctive cocked caps. They stopped their black car by the side of the road and the one in the front passenger seat, smoking a pipe, wound down the window and leant out.

Are you all right, young lady? Need a lift?

I knew by their uniforms they were RAF airmen. They looked smart and glamorous compared to the Tommies in their saggy khaki. In Sutton Bridge, the older girls gathered on the street corners, whispering and giggling behind their hands, when the airmen went past.

With no real idea where they were headed, I climbed in, but it seemed better than sitting by the road and I'd be further away from Mr Willock. The one driving said they were going into King's Lynn before heading back to their base. Could they drop me anywhere? They offered me boiled sweets and chewing gum, which they told me not to swallow.

The platform was empty. I sat for several hours on the station bench, watching the trains come and go. I had no money and no idea what to do. Eventually the stationmaster came and asked if I was waiting for someone.

There was a big round clock with a white face and Roman numerals on the wall of his office that had a loud tick, and timetables pinned all over the walls. Even though it was late May, a few embers were smouldering in the sooty grate. I was worried I might be in trouble when he told me to sit down in front of the big wooden desk. He kept asking what I was doing alone on the platform. Where was I going?

I explained that I was an evacuee. That I was trying to get home to my mum, and lied that the lady who'd been looking after me had fallen ill, so couldn't have me any more but that I didn't have any money. I hadn't planned to say any of this. It just came out, but he seemed to believe me. Then he went and poured me a cup of tea from the big brown pot on a little gas burner, dropped in two lumps of sugar and offered me a ginger biscuit from the packet on his desk.

Well, miss, it seems I'll have to give you a pass. Can't have you living here, can we? he said, rubber-stamping an official looking piece of paper, then signing it with a flourish.

I'd never travelled on my own before. When I'd left London, I'd been with my teachers and the other children from my school. I waited for half an hour before the ten minute past two train to Liverpool Street pulled in, and clambered on board, looking for the 'Ladies Only' carriage. It was empty so I parked myself in the corner by the window, cradling the painting on my lap. There was a shrill whistle, and a cloud of smoke drifted past the window. Then the carriage jolted forward and I began to feel the clickety-clack of the rails slipping beneath me. Leaning my forehead against the cold glass, I watched the flat black fields and villages give way to red-brick houses and tiny suburban gardens. To concrete cooling towers and crabbed, sooty terraces. It all looked so strange and unfamiliar.

Behind me lay the Fens. Another country. Dark, mysterious and unknowable. A place that, as I hurtled into London and an uncertain future, seemed now to be one of myths and dreams. When the train finally pulled into Liverpool Street, the doors were flung open and I could hear voices calling for porters and taxis. There were people everywhere. Soldiers with kit bags. Sailors in navy blue. Girls with bare legs and wedged sandals waiting at the barriers to welcome their sweethearts. A train whistled on the far platform. I picked up my rucksack and gas mask, stuck the painting under my arm and climbed out of the carriage, then pushed my way through the crowd and started walking.

Bernadette knocks on my door to tell me that everyone is gathered in the TV room, that the programme on Dunkirk is about to start.

We're all waiting for you, Freda. You wouldn't want to miss it now, would you? she calls out as she heads back down the corridor.

I thank her for letting me know and answer that I'll be along in just a minute. I realize my face is wet, that I must have been crying. It's a long time since I've shed tears. I close my notebook and put away my pen. Words have been the stuff of my life. They've helped me to discover who I am, make some sense of my story. I have no idea if anyone else will ever read what I've written. Why should they? Though some might be interested in a world that's gone. I close my eyes, trying to calm myself, but there's a sharp pain in my chest. And yet, a sort of bliss interwoven through all these old heartbreaks, an appetite for the texture of life that I learnt from you. For the clarity of a spring morning and the lonely honking of a skein of geese. For the shape and rhythm of a world that carries us forward as we stumble on, doubting, transforming, changing.

Jess died some fifteen years ago. It took me a long time to make up my mind to write to her. I held on to her address for many years before I plucked up the courage. I suppose I didn't feel I had the right. Didn't know how she would respond. But she wrote straight back and was very kind. We corresponded for a while. She'd become quite famous, a well-known writer who, after the war, went on book tours to America and appeared regularly on *The Brains Trust* with Jacob Bronowski and Bob Boothby. I have no idea whether she married or had children, but when she learnt that I was a librarian, she sent me some signed copies of her books. We talked of meeting but never did. Maybe it was for the best.

I know the others are waiting for me to begin tea, that they'll be settling down in front of the TV with David Dimbleby, and the Royal Marines Band playing 'Heart of Oak'. I get up and go to the mirror. Dab my face with a tissue, then powder my nose to cover the tear-stained blotches. Brush my hair and put on a bit of pink lipstick. I'm still here, and tomorrow is another day. Best foot forward, I tell myself as I straighten my new cardigan, pulling down the sleeve over the thin white scar on my left wrist that's still there, even after all these years. Then I open the door, turning left down the green-painted corridor.

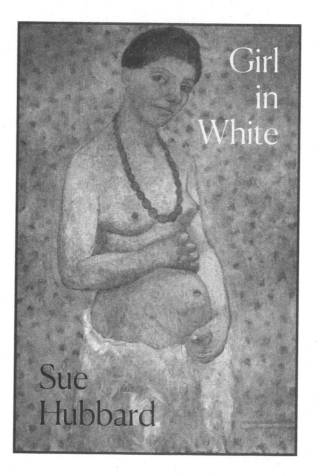

'A moving and rare, heart-warming take on
Paula Modersohn-Becker's life'

NICHOLAS SEROTA